Wild Lavender

An Emperors of London Novel

Lynne Connolly

LYRICAL PRESS
Kensington Publishing Corp.
www.kensingtonbooks.com

Lyrical Press books are published by
Kensington Publishing Corp. 119 West 40th Street New York, NY 10018

All Kensington titles, imprints, and distributed lines are available at special quantity discounts for bulk purchases for sales promotion, premiums, fund-raising, and educational or institutional use.

Special book excerpts or customized printings can also be created to fit specific needs. For details, write or phone the office of the Kensington Special Sales Manager:
Kensington Publishing Corp.
119 West 40th Street
New York, NY 10018
Attn. Special Sales Department. Phone: 1-800-221-2647.

First Electronic Edition: March 2017
eISBN-13: 978-1-61650-575-2
eISBN-10: 1-61650-575-3

First Print Edition: March 2017
ISBN-13: 978-1-60183-571-0
ISBN-10: 1-60183-571-X

Printed in the United States of America

A riotous passion and a forbidden love jeopardize the future of the Emperors of London . . .

Ravishingly beautiful and accomplished, Helena has her pick of suitable bachelors—and because she is the only daughter of a powerful duke, her mother is determined she makes a good marriage. But Helena won't marry any of them, because she is in love with the son of her family's most dangerous enemy. Though she has now been rebuffed by her beloved, she is resolved to win him back—no matter the cost.

Tom's forbidden love for Helena has only intensified over the years of their separation. But the discovery of his true roots has changed everything. His secret spells danger for his family and everyone he loves. Devoted to Helena, he will sacrifice anything—even his one great love—to keep her safe. And soon, caught between warring factions and hounded by a deadly assassin, the couple will be swept back together in a fight for their lives, and their destiny...

Books by Lynne Connolly

Emperors of London
Rogue In Red Velvet
Temptation Has Green Eyes
Danger Wears White
Reckless In Pink
Veiled In Blue
Wild Lavender

Published by Kensington Publishing Corporation

Chapter 1

April, 1750

The maid stood back to admire her handiwork. "There, my lady. You look perfect."

Helena stared doubtfully at the stranger in the mirror. "Thank you. You are dismissed. I wish for a few moments to compose myself."

The maid bobbed a curtsey and backed away. An angry yowl made her shriek, and then she bent to pick up the cat. "This creature should not be here. I'll take him back down to the kitchens."

Tabby had been sitting before the fire, minding his own business, before Sharman had tripped over him.

"No, leave him. I like him here."

The maid sniffed and dropped the animal like a hot coal. "Does her grace know you have a cat up here?"

Helena shrugged, trying not to show her fondness for the cat. If she did that, her mother would be sure to use him. She used everything to manipulate everyone around her. Nothing was safe, not even a scraggy cat. "He sleeps here sometimes. I don't mind. Yes, of course she knows."

The maid turned around and left the room, leaving Helena to face the horror she had wrought. She could not go out like this.

At least she'd had a say in the selection of her gown. The lavender-and-silver scheme pleased her, and the triple lace ruffles at her elbows were the finest she'd ever owned, but the jewelry was too heavy for a young woman and far too old-fashioned for her taste.

The rest was just...not her. Her mother had insisted Helena use her personal maid, and Sharman had turned her into someone different. Her

Lynne Connolly

face was painted white with a red dot on each cheek, and her lips tinted a bright scarlet. Her eyebrows had gone, covered with that white paint so she had a look of perpetual surprise. The stuff was smooth, not unlike plaster applied with a trowel. To protest to the maid would have sent the woman running back to her mother, who would have ordered the change, so she'd allowed it, praying for a moment when she could rectify the damage.

It had to go.

Crossing to the washstand, Helena draped a towel over her shoulders and tucked it into her bodice to protect her gown before she leaned over the bowl of tepid water. The can of fresh water by the stand was only half full, but it would have to suffice. She might be better scraping the muck off her face. It was so thick.

What the maid had done took Helena ten minutes to scrub off. Although she used fine white soap, her face was stinging when she finished the job. Then she could see herself again. Her face was rather pink, but that should wear off, and it was better than corpse white. Crossing to the dressing table, she picked up her usual pot of rouge and applied a small amount to her cheeks and lips. She could not appear at a ball without any paint. Even she knew that.

The jewelry went next. The heavy priceless sapphire necklace came first and then the matching bracelet and all but one of the brooches. They fell on her dressing table, dead weights that tumbled with a heavy clunk.

She replaced the necklace with her string of pearls, the ones inherited from her grandmother. They weren't family treasures, but they meant more to Helena. In a way, her beloved grandmother would be with her tonight.

Her nerves settled as she changed her clothes. While the maid had been arraying her in all her glory, Helena had watched the transformation in the mirror, her misgivings growing with every change and her stomach tightening with each stroke of the brush and each piece of extra jewelry. That piece was for the more mature woman, maybe even her brother Julius's wife, Caroline, whose flamboyant beauty could cope with such magnificence. But if Helena was beautiful, something she doubted every time she went out of doors, it was the quieter kind of beauty.

After her formal presentation, she'd fallen ill of a malady that had lingered long enough for her to miss her second season. That was last year, since she had been nearly eighteen on her first presentation. So this, her first London ball in two years, was little short of her debut into society. She had looked forward to it for a long time.

But she had never imagined doing it dressed like an actress and decked out in gaudy, outdated jewels.

She clasped a slim gold bracelet around her wrist. She was ready. She could do nothing about her hair, but at least the powdered style suited her pale skin. She'd seen creamy-skinned misses who looked positively ill. She would never criticize them again if they went through the same process she had just suffered.

She turned and faced the cat, who had gone back to snoozing in front of the fire. "Does that look better?"

The cat licked a paw and settled down again.

Helena grinned. "Oh, you're no use." Gazing at her newly recognizable features in the mirror, she made herself a promise. "I swear I will never allow my mother's maid to attend me again."

When she turned around, she nearly overbalanced herself with the unexpected width of her skirts. She strode from the room, picking up her fan on the way out.

Downstairs, her mother looked at her as if she were a specimen in a cabinet. "Did Sharman do that?"

So her mother had asked her maid to make Helena look like a Covent Garden doxy.

Helena swished her skirts, catching the hoops when they threatened to go too far. "Yes." She didn't even cross her fingers.

Julius stood with her father, smiling at her. "You look beautiful. Shall we go? Caro will meet us there."

Typical that Julius's wife was not here. Also typical that Julius outshone Helena in splendor, and would have done even with her previous appearance. Julius was not afraid of standing out in a crowd. He'd explained to her once, "As the heir to one of the greatest dukedoms in the country, people will stare at me. So why should I not give them something to stare at?"

He even smelled wonderful. He wore pink tonight, but never had a man appeared more utterly masculine than Julius, Lord Winterton. His stance, the hint of muscle under the satin sleeve, and the breadth of his shoulders all spoke to his gender. Perhaps that was why he flirted with the pretty and exquisite clothes he preferred. Or maybe it was because of the way their mother glared at him when he appeared.

They were here, in London, for the birth of Julius's child, the grandson of the Duke of Kirkburton and the heir to the estate, after Julius. A great event.

As they left the brightly lit hall and stepped into the soft September night, Julius drew her back and leaned closer. "Grandmother would be proud," he murmured. "You look lovely. I was so afraid mother would turn you into a doll."

"She tried. I scrubbed it off."

Their mother turned around at Julius's shout of laughter, but she said nothing, merely allowed the footman to help her into the vehicle.

The duchess did not declare herself satisfied until the ladies were settled, which took some time. The current fashion for wide skirts made arranging two ladies in a carriage more difficult than it should have been. Although she addressed her mother as "Mama," Helena never thought of her that way. In her mind, the diminutive but formidable woman sitting opposite her was always "the duchess." Her two older brothers always called her "madam" or "mother." Her younger sister, currently sulking in the country, recovering from a bout of influenza, was the only person to call the duchess "Mama" in any fond way.

While aware of her mother's voice, Helena did not listen to her mother's diatribe. Helena had become inured to her mother's lectures. Even as a child, she could enter her own world and shut off unpleasant things.

They passed a house with lights blazing outside and in, but it was not the one they were visiting tonight. London being thin of company meant only two or three dinners and gatherings every evening, not half a dozen or more. People waited to go in through the front door, and several beggars and other unsavory characters lurked in darker doorways or held out their hands for succor.

"Someone should do something about those poor people," she murmured, barely aware she spoke aloud.

"Some people are doing their best," Julius said.

That included him. If Helena had control of her own money, no doubt she would help, too, but she was a female, and although she was worth a great deal, she could touch none of her fortune. Julius had promised he would do what he could, but he had his hands full with Caroline. Pregnant, Caroline was even more volatile than usual.

The carriage jolted around a corner and entered Hanover Square, lined with the elegant houses that had sprung up over the last fifty years and made the West End fashionable. Although elegant, the houses were already marked by the ever-present smoke, the creamy stone stained and streaked with soot. Helena had not visited London often enough to become accustomed to the sight yet, but she knew from bitter experience that coming into contact with the smuts left stains almost impossible to get out. Powdery and hellishly greasy, they only got worse the more a person scrubbed at the stain.

She would take care not to brush against the wall when she left the carriage and went into the house.

The carriage drew up, the jolt enough to make Helena grab the strap. The leather pressed against her hand, and she gave it a final squeeze before she released it.

Julius helped her down himself instead of allowing a footman to perform the task and waited until the servant had assisted their parents to alight. The duchess gave a sharp nod and took her papa's arm.

He winked at Helena. "You look lovely," he said.

The duchess shot him a quelling glower, an expression she excelled at, but he took no notice. He intervened whenever necessary but for the most part preferred to ignore family disputes. He merely took himself to another place.

Helena took a deep breath.

"Ready?" Julius said.

When she nodded, they went in.

Inside, elegantly dressed people glanced at them. Some smiled, some bowed, but they were all intent on divesting their cloaks and hats.

Helena flicked her ruffles, but a glance in one of the mirrors in the hall told her the short journey had not caused any great depredations.

Her mother drew her aside to a space by the window by dint of grabbing Helena's elbow and pinching hard. "Tell me, Helena, why did Sharman deliberately disobey my orders? Where is the sapphire set?"

Helena avoided meeting her mother's glare by gazing at her ruffles. "They did not become the gown."

"And the face paint? You are positively naked, my girl." The duchess had not worn the white and red, but she was wearing more face paint than Helena.

"I disliked it."

"It is not your place to dislike." The duchess's voice chilled Helena's heart. Trouble would come from her small rebellion. Maybe the duchess would prevent her from attending London for the season next year. That would be too hard, and oh, Helena had been looking forward to the visit!

She would put up with any number of her mother's diatribes. And she would marry the first half-decent man who came her way and showed an interest in her. Plenty would appear because of who she was, but she still held the dream of finding a man who would want her. Or at least someone who would respect her, even like her.

People were listening, moving closer, but her mother did not seem to care.

"You are a disobedient girl, and I am tempted to turn around and take you home. The next time I send Sharman to you, pray do as you should and let her guide you."

Helena stuck to the promise she'd made to herself. "She made me look unnatural. People would have laughed at me."

"Do not cause a scene!"

If anyone was doing that, it was her mother. "Of course not, madam." From experience Helena knew that seeming obedience would calm her autocratic parent best. Then she would do as she chose anyway. Her mother liked to pick on something and make it symbolic of the conflict between them, causing trouble and giving herself another needle to taunt Helena with.

Although she tried not to let it concern her, of course the barbs stung. Helena received more opprobrium than her brothers and sister. For some reason, her mother had chosen her as the recipient of most of her attacks. Perhaps because Julius and Augustus had passed out of her reach, living their own lives in their own way. Gemina—or Lucinda, as she preferred to call herself—was their mother's pet.

Fire sparked and spread as anger flushed the unhappiness out of her. She needed to get away before she did something disastrous like rip out at her mother. The people watching her very public dressing down would no doubt be delighted with the fuss and would discuss her behavior with the glee reserved for someone enjoying someone else's discomfiture.

No. She would not allow her mother to ruin her evening.

Without listening to what her mother was saying, Helena spun around and strode away, her hooped skirt bouncing around her instead of gliding as it should. She did not care. She would not stay to make a fool of herself or appear as the subservient daughter who would not answer to a nagging parent.

Helena used the confusion engendered by the arrival of a bunch of people as cover for her flight. Keeping her head down, she ran up the stairs. She needed a place to cool down before she faced the people in the main rooms.

The guests headed to the set of double doors at the top of the landing, which were flung wide, lights blazing. Without hesitation, Helena headed the other way, narrowly missing cannoning into a man who uttered a curse rarely heard in a polite drawing room.

Helena did not give a toss of her head for that. Not pausing in her headlong flight, she continued until she reached the end of the corridor. Doors led to her right and her left. The right-hand doors would take her to the rooms open for tonight. She took the left and dragged the door closed behind her.

Before the door hit the frame, someone else caught it and came in.

Helena sighed and turned. "I would advise you to leave me alone—"

She stopped abruptly. Before her stood the man. Just The Man. Words failed her. He was tall, with liquid dark eyes. Not many had the felicity of seeing their dream standing before them, but Helena had that experience now.

All emotion leached away from her except one, and she didn't have a precise name for it or would not dare speak it.

"It's you," he said.

Helena licked her dry lips. "Yes, it's me."

* * * *

Tom walked into Lady Compton's house, determined to escape his family's problems for an hour or two.

At first his father had shown understandable reluctance to let him go, but as Tom pointed out, if he were seen in a place enjoying himself, suspicion would be so much the less. Since they had been engaged in less than legal activity, his words had done the trick. And the Emperors would be there.

Tom saw no harm in irritating them a little. After all, they had annoyed him more than somewhat ever since he could remember. An old personal grudge had turned into a political dispute and now had become a full-fledged feud, akin to the vendettas in Renaissance Italy. Probably not as deadly, though. Tom possessed no rings that contained secret compartments for poison. Tonight, especially, he needed to get away from the disaster that threatened his family. If they caught his father this time, that would be the end.

He took his time walking up the red-carpeted marble stairs, pausing to speak briefly to people he knew and receiving smiles and nods in return. The stairs were not the best place to kiss hands, but he managed it with a widow he'd had his eye on for some time. Going to a bedroom in another house would be a bonus tonight.

Then a lady in lavender piled into his side, almost knocking the wind out of him. Murmuring an apology to her, Tom quickened his pace, for something had appealed to him about the woman who had rushed past. All he'd seen of her was her white powdered hair and gown, but he caught the scent of violets and lavender, with a hint of something else he couldn't identify and he wanted to know what exactly it was. And what had caused such agitation in the woman.

At the top of the stairs, he caught sight of a flick of lavender silk as she turned into a room he was sure wasn't open for the ball. He followed her. The night had just become interesting.

Before she could close the door behind her, he caught the edge. Ignoring the sting of catching a door slammed with some force, he turned to face her.

Her shoulders lifted as she sighed. "I would advise you to leave me alone—"

His mind reeled. He knew her. How he did he had no idea, but here she was. "It's you," he said.

She licked her dry lips. "Yes, it's me."

She took the weight of the door from him. "Please," she said. "Go."

As if there were any chance of that happening.

He stepped into the room after her and closed the door softly. She stood with her back to him, facing the garden. Her knuckles were white where they gripped the back of the chair she was standing behind. Her shoulders were shaking, but as he waited, she lifted one hand and wiped it across her face, uttering a low curse.

"I should perhaps tell you that you're not alone," he murmured. He folded his arms across his chest and allowed himself a wry grin.

She gasped and whirled around to face him, her skirts rocking precariously. "I told you to leave. Who are you?"

"I could ask you the same thing. I'd certainly remember seeing you before."

She was ravishing. Her sweet face was saved from pure sugar by the firm chin and the sparkle in her blue eyes. What light there was in this room came from the bright moonlight outside and the barely there glow from the banked-down fire. Enough for him to make out her features.

She flicked her fan open and covered the lower half of her face, the spangles twinkling in the moonlight.

He kicked away from the door. "Do you want me to go? Truthfully?"

"I came in here because I was infuriated with someone and I did not wish to inflict my mood on anyone else."

The enticing sparkle in her eyes intrigued him. "But do not leave."

She shook her head, a curl bouncing on her shoulders. Finally, she took the fan away from her face.

His sharp intake of breath sounded loud in this room. He stared at her, just drank her in. She was enchanting, every part of her, from her powdered head to her dainty feet. He hadn't realized he was going to do it until he touched her cheek, ghosting the back of his forefinger along her silken skin.

Her eyes widened but she didn't move away, only lifted her chin and met his gaze with a direct one of her own. "Why did you do that?"

"To make sure you're real."

The pause was so complete a drop of water would have broken it. Her bosom lifted as she breathed. She pulsed with life, held it within her as a precious thing. The pearls around her neck glowed. He touched them lightly before he let his hand fall back against his side. "They say that pearls need wearing often, otherwise they'll die."

A slow smile curled her soft mouth. He longed to taste it, to feel that vitality against him. "I heard that pearls signified tears."

"It depends who wears them." He kept his voice low, not because he was afraid of someone coming in, but because he didn't wish to break the bubble enclosing them.

"That's pretty."

He grinned. "It is, isn't it? I'm not given to poetry. But looking at you, it comes to my lips effortlessly."

She flicked her gaze to his mouth and back to his eyes. "The pearls belonged to my grandmother. It seemed appropriate to wear them for my first ball."

"Your first?" He frowned. She did not look like girl fresh from the schoolroom.

"My first for years. I haven't visited London for a while." She shrugged, her gown slipping delightfully on her shoulders. He would love to help it the rest of the way.

She had none of the debilitating shyness of the very young, the bashfulness that would send him from the room. "I can only assume you were ill or abroad, because what other reason would a family have for keeping you away from me?" He'd meant to say "society."

"You're assuming rather a lot."

"I am, aren't I?" Unable to bear the distance between them any longer, he tilted her chin up with the tip of his finger and kissed her.

How had he lived without the touch of her lips, existed without the sweetness of her breath? She stunned him, this stranger, overwhelmed him. Before he'd arrived here, his mind had been in turmoil. She gave him a cool center with her living heat.

When he drew away, they were breathing heavier, despite keeping the kiss a mere brushing of mouths.

She did not turn her back on him, or move away. When she opened her eyes, they were considerably darker, the blue rimming a dark center, one he wanted to know far more intimately. Nothing existed outside her, nothing worth worrying about.

"What is this?"

"Could it be love?" The words escaped him before could stop them. Tom always thought about what he was saying long before he uttered it, except for just now.

The corner of her mouth quirked. "After a few sentences and a kiss? I hardly think so. Love at first sight is for the poets, not real life."

Could the tingles, the surge of pure need be lust? But that explanation did not ring true. Yes, he wanted her—who wouldn't? But he wanted more. To talk to her, to be seen with her—so much more. "That this could be the beginning of love. Shall we agree on that?"

"I could accept that." The quirk turned into a smile and the sparkle in her eyes turned to a glow. "And we have not even been introduced."

"I'm Tom."

He loved the smile that came to her face. "Good evening, Tom. Just Tom?"

He raised a shoulder in a half-shrug. "That is the part I prefer. It's my second name, but my first name is too common for general use."

"George?"

He repressed his shudder. "Charles."

"Ohhh." The long drawn out syllable pursed her lips into the most adorable pout, one he would not even try to resist.

This time he placed his hands on her waist. She wore the usual feminine armor of gown, stomacher, stays, and the rest, but under that, her body heat warmed him. He would love to peel those layers off her, piece by piece, like unpeeling the most delicious fruit. The underlying succulence would be well worth the effort.

She met his lips with uncertainty, her mouth giving the merest telltale tremble before she lifted herself and cupped his cheeks. She must have gone up on tiptoe. She was not a particularly small woman, indeed he considered her a little taller than average, but he was far too tall for comfort, towering above most crowds. The experience was not always a pleasant one, but right now he was glad he was big enough to enclose her, to fold her into his arms. Her overlarge hooped skirt pressed against him uncomfortably, but it was the collapsible kind, so he did not discommode her too much.

He finished the kiss, glanced down at her sweet face, and then kissed her again. This time she curled her hand around his neck. Tom loved it. She stroked his nape gently, her nails grazing his skin, the difference in texture sending sharp tingles through him.

When he licked her lips, she opened her mouth hesitantly, and he dived in, lost in her. The taste was almost more than he could bear. He cinched her closer, ignoring the uncomfortable cane hoop of her skirts pressing against his gut that barely skimmed the head of his erection. When he touched her tongue with his, gratitude shivered through him when she responded with one shy touch. She undid him completely with her response, untutored but eager.

Nothing mattered now except this. Her taste, her scent, and the feel of her intoxicated him more than a case of brandy. Although she might have doubts, Tom had none. He would set about a formal courtship as soon as he could. Wildness and abandon seized him by the throat. In the first impulsive decision of his life, Tom decided he would have this woman for his own.

Happiness raced along his veins along with the heady taste of arousal. He could kiss her all night, before he'd even think of getting her out of her clothes. Draw out the pleasure until neither of them could bear being dressed any longer. Kiss her and kiss her until she begged him for more. Or he begged her, it did not matter which.

But he needed to know just one thing first. Separating their lips hurt more than it should have, but he did it, only to lose himself staring down at her and smiling. Her kiss-flushed lips, her cheekbones delicately edged with pink, and those bewitching eyes almost drew him back to her before he asked his question.

"Tell me, sweet one. What is your name, so I may call on you tomorrow?"

"Helena!"

But the name did not come from her lips. It came from the direction of the door, uttered by a voice he knew well.

A voice that meant trouble.

Chapter 2

As close to Tom as she was, Helena could not miss the change in his expression. The melting softness of his brown eyes changed to shock. He mouthed "Sorry," against her lips and touched his forehead to hers.

His mouth, so warm against hers a mere moment ago, tightened, and his lids lowered over his eyes. His expression was akin to Julius's when he was displeased. Except that Julius's eyes hardened into sapphire intensity, and this man's eyes resembled mahogany that had been out in the rain for too long.

He turned around, standing directly in front of her, hiding her from Julius. That would do no good. Julius would have recognized her gown. She touched Tom's back, the soft velvet of his deep red coat silky-fine, nothing like the stubbled jaw she'd touched a moment before.

So she was caught kissing a man in a room. At least only Julius had caught them, and he would not tell anyone or cause a scandal. She'd heard the door close, so Julius was letting nobody else in. Tom would explain now and declare his intention of courting her. He'd said as much. She peeped out from behind Tom. She was wrong. Her other brother, Augustus, was here, too.

"Winterton." Tom bowed slightly, allowing Helena more time to compose herself. He had not disturbed her clothes, except for her hoops which had undergone extreme pressure, but they seemed to have survived. When she moved to the side, they sprang back.

She put up her chin, but before she could say anything, Tom continued.

"I take it I have the honor of sharing a room with your sister?"

Julius's face was white with fury.

"Do you intend to tell Mother?" She hadn't meant her words to come out with that high-pitched edge, making her anxiety obvious to everyone. The duchess would not hesitate to sweep Helena off to the country, and then she wouldn't see the outside of the estate until next Easter, and perhaps not even then.

Julius flicked a glance to her, concern edging his gaze before he returned it, hard once more, to Tom. "Is this what your attempted seduction of my sister is about? Will you tell everyone, Alconbury?"

Helena's heart doubled its rate, until she could barely breathe. Alconbury? That meant Tom was the oldest son of the Duke of Northwich, the avowed enemy of her family. He could have planned this, maybe to seduce her. Except—what he said, what he did, how he behaved and most of all, the shock in his eyes when Julius had spoken her name.

The Dankworths and the Vernons—indeed, all the family known as the Emperors of London because of the outlandish names bestowed on them by their parents—had been at loggerheads since the rising of 1715, the first time the Jacobites had made a bid for the throne. However, what had begun as a political dispute had turned personal. Why, she did not know, but the animosity simmering in this room was only partly to do with her.

Until that moment Helena had remained oblivious to the potential trouble she could be in. Tom had swept her off her feet, almost literally, her response to him overwhelming.

Tom glanced at her, his expression shuttered, and then away as if she were of no interest to him. "Why would I want to shackle myself to an Emperor? Or an Empress, in this case. You should take greater care of your womenfolk, Winterton. Who knows what I might have done?"

Julius glared. "Name your seconds—"

"Julius, no!" Augustus stepped between her brother and Tom, his powerful body forming an effective barrier. "Meeting him at dawn would ruin Helena's reputation."

Tom's mouth settled into a sneer. "You mean I have not done that already? How disappointing. If you gentlemen would care to leave, I can take care of that in a trice." Anyone would think he was trying to provoke Julius.

The animosity simmering in the room went way beyond personal dislike. What had she done? Blotting the memory of their kisses from her mind, Helena tried again. "I tore a ruffle, and this gentleman helped me to pin it. That is all."

Julius's attention went from her to Tom and back. "Will you say that?"

Tom spread his hands wide. "How can I contradict a lady? Especially one as lovely as Lady Helena?" He kissed the tips of his fingers and opened his hand in her direction. Hardly a gesture intended to mollify her brother.

Disappointment arced through her, became a physical ache in her gut. So he knew her rank? Had he known who she was before he followed her into this room? Had he meant to trap her? Their families were at each other's heads most of the time, their hatred a constant source of amusement to society. Was that the only reason he'd kissed her?

"The lady tastes sweet. Another moment and I would have had her. Then what would you have done?" Tom sneered, his lip curling. "Made me marry her?"

Julius closed his eyes. Helena was sorry to bring him more trouble, but really, this was nothing. A man had made a fool of her. What of that?

So why didn't he want to make the incident public? Julius would never have made him marry her, considering he was a Dankworth, leaving Helena to bear the disgrace.

"I didn't know—" she began, but she was interrupted when Julius slashed his hand down.

"Do not speak," Julius said, his voice throbbing with fury. "Augustus will take you into the ball."

Augustus shook his head. "And leave you alone with Alconbury?" He jerked his head, indicating Tom.

She nearly missed Tom's movement. Nothing showed in his face, but his hand left his side for a bare instant, opening toward her before he clenched his fist and returned it to his side. He was concerned for her. Nothing else would have made him reach for her. For all his apparent disdain, he did care.

She had rarely seen her brother so furious, so close to losing control. Augustus was right; if they left him in here with Tom, they would kill each other. So she glided forward in her best grand lady manner and laid her fingers on the smooth sleeve of Julius's evening coat. "May a woman not have any amusement? Indeed, of course I knew him. I only intended to tease a little. After all, I must practice on someone, and who better than a nobody?"

The sharp breath told her she had hit her mark, and to her relief, Julius's expression eased a fraction. "Well said, my dear. Shall we leave the nobody to the gentle ministrations of our brother?"

Augustus was angry, but unlike to do anything too rash. He might plant a facer on Tom, but he wouldn't challenge him to meet at dawn.

Somehow, the sweetest minutes of her life had turned into disaster. That nobody had touched anyone in anger made it even worse, because the promise was there, hanging over everyone. Including her.

Julius pasted on his society smile as soon as he had her outside the room. "You will talk to nobody about this, but if anyone saw you, you may say we were with you all the time."

"I planned to do that."

Julius would never let her down by denying her. Truthfully she had not thought of anything beyond Tom and what they were doing. She would have continued doing it too, putting her reputation and her trust into his hands.

She still would. If he could make her feel as he had before, she would throw her reputation to the wind because it had done nothing for her so far. She was twenty and making her first appearance in London society. How ridiculously pathetic was that?

"He will not bother you again," Julius said as they approached the double doors leading into the main room. "If he comes within a yard of you, I'll kill him."

He'd done nothing she had not wanted him to. "Don't concern yourself. I can take care of myself." A notion occurred to her, one that her brother would understand. "I daresay he will try to come near me again, if only to provoke you. If he knows I am your weak spot, he will use it."

A pause, and then Julius said, "You are right. But tell me if he harasses you, and I will deal with him."

"Discreetly?"

"Yes."

Julius snapped the word, but he had given it, and Helena would hold him to it.

"I can manage him," she said. "Whatever else he might be, he was brought up a gentleman, and I know what to do with those."

Julius's huffed laugh relieved her mind considerably. Julius had a quick temper, but these days he rarely lost it, and when he did, he recovered quickly. He was, after all, a supreme manipulator of society.

The babble and heat of a hundred people crowded into a room meant for half that number met her in a suffocating wave. Their mingled perfumes hung over the whole, cloying and heavy. This was what she had longed for during her lonely hours in the last four years, ever since her mother had declared her intention of delaying her come-out until Lucinda was ready. Many people here knew her already, of course, but this ball marked her transition to full-fledged member of society. And of course that meant eligible for marriage, at last.

However, she no longer held the eager anticipation she had felt when she'd entered this house. Eligible men no longer appeared so attractive. Who among all the men she had met when she had been but Julius's sister had attracted her as much as the one she had encountered tonight?

One of the other men approached now, a pleasant smile on his genial face. "It's so good to see you here tonight, Lady Helena. Do you know how many years I have waited for you?"

Such banter she could cope with easily. "About as long as I have waited for you, Lord Elsbury."

Unabashed, he grinned. Helena had known Elsbury since childhood. He was of an age with Julius and visited their family home in Derbyshire. If she had to choose anyone for her first society dance, he would come high on the list, mainly because their relationship was easy rather than intense. If she'd danced with Tom, she wouldn't have kept her composure very easily.

When she was executing a turn in the stately minuet, she caught sight of him. Tom stood at the edge of the room, with a man who looked enough like him to be his brother. He was naturally taking no notice of her at all.

So why did his lack of concern strike her to the heart?

He had used her, if she was to believe him, used her to irritate her family and possibly create a scandal. If she believed him, of course, and didn't remember what had preceded his words. The way he had held her almost reverently did not tell her he was using her to provoke someone else, nor the way he'd stroked her cheek or smiled into her eyes. Or kissed her.

The memory of his kisses made her falter, but she recovered herself by the time she met Lord Everslade in the dance once more, and she could give him a careless smile. "You are my first cicisbeo," she told him.

"I am no such thing!" Revulsion filled his tones.

She ended the dance on a smile. Everslade was not the kind of man to attend a woman night and day with the devotion one could expect from a dog. Except for her mother. He was very much a sporting man, with heavy interests in the hunting field and fisticuffs, and only came to London when he had to, or so he claimed. His mother had urged him to visit, he told her, and he had business to conduct. A cicisbeo spent most of his days in ladies' salons, and if he was lucky, their boudoirs. Not a place one would look for the bluff Everslade.

Helena could not imagine herself entertaining a man in her boudoir. Except in the way most great ladies did, during the levee, when everyone was dressed and more than one person crowded in.

When Tom left, Helena knew it, even though she did not once look in his direction. She felt his absence deep inside, as if he had magically connected them with his kiss. Julius's inexpiable animosity troubled her. Of course he avoided and ignored the Dankworths whenever he could, as did the rest of the Emperors of London. But to show quite so much fury at a little flirtation? Julius dealt with adversity with chilling hauteur, a coldness that struck to the bone, not red hot anger.

After her second dance, she caught sight of the lovely face that haunted all their lives—Julius's wife, Caroline.

With a heavy sense of duty filling her heart, Helena approached Caroline and offered a pleasant smile. Before now, Caroline had turned a shoulder on her, but she would not do this in public. At least she had that much decorum. But Helena was the wrong sex to interest Caroline. The daughter of wealthy and high-born parents, she'd always known she would marry someone of the same rank, but her parents had not set a good example of constancy. She did not expect fidelity, and she did not give it. Marriage was not a personal contract but a public one that involved the occasional human contact. Caroline adored Julius and did not know how to manage her obsession. It made for a miserable marriage.

Which was why Caroline preferred to ignore Helena. Now she offered a slight smile in return. "My dear sister-in-law is experiencing her first taste of London society in two years," she said to the young men clustered around her. Several of those were definitely cicisbeos, Caroline's advanced stage of pregnancy not affecting them one whit. She wafted her fan. "Your evening is modestly successful."

Her barbs were sometimes wide of the mark, but this one hit. Helena had longed for this evening for years. Helena had never been comfortable in childhood, always longing for the more exciting world of the grown-up, and her mother had known that. She used it as a way of controlling her daughter. Knowing what her mother was doing did not make her existence easier. Caroline, tempestuous, restless, and beautiful, knew it too.

Smiling, she touched her belly in an apparently accidental way and lifted her glass of wine, moistening her lips and gazing over the rim of her glass at someone standing across the room.

The man Helena had recognized as the one talking to Tom lifted his glass in a toast, giving her a smile in return.

"Who is that?" Helena asked, not caring who heard. Surely this far along in her pregnancy Caroline would not be entertaining men intimately. Especially that one.

When the silence fell, Helena turned her head. "What is it? What did I say?"

"There is no reason you should know him," Augustus said. "He is Lord William Dankworth."

So he was related to Tom. His brother, in fact, as she had suspected. He appeared to know Caroline very well, from the way he smiled at her. That was no society smile.

As the true horror of the situation seeped into her, Helena shivered. For her to entertain a Dankworth was reprehensible. If Caroline was doing so, that had the makings of a major scandal. Caroline was wild and irresponsible, concerned only with satisfying her immediate desires. Her adventures had a "look at me" tone to them that made her look desperate rather than daring.

"Cold?"

She turned to Augustus, relieved to have a friend in this crowd. "A little. The night is chilly and they left the windows open."

"Come away. Let's find you some supper."

Helena was only too glad to do so. Behind her, Caroline and her friends began to laugh and chatter once more. "I don't want any supper," Helena said. "Take me home, Augustus."

Her brother did not argue and led her quietly from the room.

Helena's first London ball in years had not gone as she'd wished. An evening that had begun in excited anticipation had ended in this, whatever "this" signified.

Augustus did not speak to her in the carriage on the way home about anything significant, and he did not try to rally her with cheerful discussions about the evening. The experience was not one she would recall with any delight. Except, of course, for the first part, and those she would hug to herself and hold close until the memory faded.

Alconbury had not known her any more than she had known him. She was sure about that. So why had he turned on her once Julius had caught them?

"I enjoyed myself, yes," she said by rote when Augustus asked her. "But I would like one incident clarified." At her brother's frown, she said, "Not the one in the private room. The other. The way Caroline and Lord William Dankworth kept looking at each other."

Augustus let his head thud back against the cushions and stared at the ceiling, his blue eyes glinting in the light of the house they had passed earlier. The gathering there was still going on, as was the one they had just left. They would probably continue until the small hours, and Caroline would most likely be there when the company thinned. Caroline did not sleep much.

"You're growing up, aren't you?" he said.

"I did that several years ago," she replied. "I'm merely learning what I should have then."

"I would not wish that on you," Augustus said quietly. "I wouldn't wish it on anyone."

When the carriage came to a halt, Augustus helped her down and ushered her into the house, where the blessed quiet surrounded her like an intimation of peace. Ignoring her urge to go to her room, strip out of her finery, and go to bed, she took Augustus's hand and led him upstairs to the small parlor next to the drawing room. With a sigh, she dropped her fan on the nearest table and sank into the chair. Although the fire had been banked down for the night, a comforting glow of warmth still bathed the room.

Her hairpins dug into her scalp and her stays were too tight. "So tell me," she said as Augustus resignedly took the chair opposite her. "Does Caroline entertain Lord William Dankworth?"

Augustus stared at her tight-lipped. In a sudden movement he got to his feet, went to the sideboard, and returned in a moment with a large helping of brandy, which he swallowed in a couple of gulps. The sound of the glass meeting the table by his side sounded far too loud in the quiet room. A carriage rattled by in the street outside.

"Caroline entertains Lord William, or she has in the past."

"So that was why Julius was so upset when he discovered me with Lord William's brother." Understanding swept through her in a great wave. Then another horrifying thought clutched her throat. "The baby—is it his?"

Immediately Augustus shook his head. "No." He paused, looking longingly at his empty glass. "At least, I don't think so. If Julius suspects that, he's keeping the information close to his chest."

An Emperor sired by a Dankworth? It didn't bear thinking about.

Sighing, Augustus returned his attention to her. "You cannot be unaware that Caroline enjoys male company."

She snorted. "She isn't exactly discreet."

"I think she is." Augustus got to his feet and took his glass back to the sideboard.

"You can pour me one of those," she said. "I didn't even get my supper."

"You could have stayed." He brought her a drink, not as full as his, but generous enough.

She sipped the fiery drink. Heat coursed back into her veins. "After I'd disgraced myself, the mood left me. I wanted my home and my bed. I only stayed as long as I did because people might talk." She lifted the glass and swirled the amber liquid around it. "They'll talk anyway, will they not? Except that it won't be about me. Not about the beauty who amazed London by her dazzling appearance." Next to her family, Helena paled into insignificance. She should have known Tom meant nothing from his extravagant compliments. Beauty was not her forte.

"You are lovely," Augustus said firmly. "But next to Julius's magnificence and Caroline's beauty, we're sometimes overlooked."

She laughed. Augustus was bigger than Julius and very difficult to overlook, being tall and strongly built. "Perhaps it's just as well."

"You have a quiet beauty," her brother told her. "The kind that lasts."

"Well, thank you, kind sir." She took another sip, the alcohol giving her a lift she would not have achieved on her own. The brandy was a good idea. "But I don't want to talk about my evening tonight. How could you have allowed me to walk into that place so unprepared?"

He blinked and shook his head. "I know. I spoke to mother, and she assured me she would tell you what you needed to know."

"She did not." Helena was still finding it difficult to understand what she had unwittingly walked into. "So Caroline is Lord William's lover, and you caught me in a room with his brother?"

"That puts the business in a nutshell." Augustus paused. "Sometimes I forget you are twenty. You should know about them. God knows the rest of London does."

"What more can there be?"

He sighed. "Julius blames himself for Caroline's behavior. When they were first married, they enjoyed their lives together. Julius revelled in his freedom after our mother's efforts to control him, and they both took a variety of lovers."

Shocked, she didn't try to hold back her gasp. "I thought they loved each other, at first at any rate."

"They did, but I think they loved what they represented to each other as much as anything else." He waved a hand vaguely. "Julius tired of it early, but Caroline is still engaged in it."

"Why didn't I know?"

"Because their behavior was a secret. At least, they kept it that way at first. Julius was wild, certainly, but not much more than any man thrown on the town can be. Caroline grew worse when Julius tired of it. In him, the madness was only temporary. Sometimes I think Caroline is truly mad. She had never stopped, but her family is prestigious enough to hide most of her foolishness."

"And because his wife is having an affair with Alconbury's brother, Julius believed the worst when he discovered us in a room together." Tom was nothing like his brother. She had no concrete proof. She just knew.

She was still trying to absorb the information as Augustus knocked back the last of his drink and got to his feet. "I'm not surprised you didn't know the identity of the man in the room, but if anyone but us had walked in, we could have found ourselves in a deeply difficult situation."

"You mean a forced engagement?"

Augustus gave a rough laugh. "Hardly. Can you imagine our two families not at odds with each other? The world would think we'd gone mad. But a duel, or a public airing of bad blood. The papers would have been full of it in the morning, and they would not hesitate to drag your name through the mud. They would relish it. They love to bring great families down."

Helena knew she could not object to that. The family meant more than its members, after all, but sometimes she longed to be just Miss Vernon of Anywhere, to be welcomed and appreciated for herself. That longing had fed into her interlude tonight, the one that had ended so badly but started so well. "You don't like it any more than I do."

"I don't. In fact, I'm leaving for the continent as soon as I can manage."

Helena blinked. "You are?" Along with Julius, Augustus had gone on the Grand Tour. He had returned enthused with classical literature and art, but Helena had not expected him to quit England completely. "Because of this?"

Augustus waved around expansively. "All this. The feud, the ceremony, the scandals, the bowing and scraping, all that too. I hate it, Helena. I'm going to Rome as plain Augustus Vernon."

"Plenty of people visit the city. I've heard it said that Rome is as full of English aristocrats as London. They'll know who you are."

"I can avoid them better there. I don't have to attend gatherings and balls that bore me rigid, or talk about things that don't interest me. If I were as fascinated by politics as our brother, or able to shut myself off as you do, I could perhaps bear it, but I cannot."

"Will you return?" Was she about to lose her brother?

"Of course. I know this isn't a permanent solution, but I can have a few years for myself."

"Can I come with you?" The life he described sounded wonderful.

"No." He spoke shortly, but he smiled. "I did not choose Rome arbitrarily. I'll be researching a few small matters while I'm there. You can't be any part of that. You must stay and do your duty."

"Which is?"

"To find happiness." His voice lowered and softened. Few people saw Augustus's gentler side, but she saw it now. "Don't let them marry you to someone you don't care for. Don't let your fear of becoming mother's unpaid servant hold you back. It will not come to that, Helena. We are determined on it."

"Oh." Stunned, she sat back. "I am determined to marry the first man who asked."

"Don't. You deserve more than that. You will have it." Augustus sounded so firm she didn't have the heart to contradict him, even though matters were nowhere near as clear as he tried to make them.

"Thank you." She put her empty glass down and got to her feet. "And thank you for telling me about Caroline." Arrested by a sudden thought, she stopped. "Why would she do such a thing?"

"Because she's Caroline," Augustus said. "Because she will do anything for attention, any kind of attention. Because she knows Julius is slipping away."

"Ah." Now she understood. "Caroline still loves Julius."

"She does." Augustus passed his hand over his forehead. "She adores him. It's too late, Helena. He won't go back to her, not after what she has done."

"But one of you needs to produce an heir." She could not do it, and neither could her sister. Her father was the only male in a family of six. That meant a distant cousin would inherit if neither Julius nor Augustus provided an heir. How her mother would dislike that!

"I know," Augustus said. "One of us will. Plenty of marriages exist merely to make an heir, and if Julius fails in his mission, I'll make the ultimate sacrifice."

Why such a sad remark should make her laugh Helena wasn't sure, but she felt easier in her mind as she made her way upstairs to bed.

Chapter 3

After a convivial and profitable morning at Jonathan's coffeehouse in the City, Tom made his way back to his family house situated at the edge of the fashionable part of London. He nodded to the liveried footman standing to attention in the hall. The green and gold livery made quite a show, even gaudy, but livery was like that.

He took the stairs two at a time, with the aim of reaching his rooms without interruption, but his father interrupted him. He popped out of the smaller salon with a promptness that indicated he had seen Tom's arrival. "Ah, Alconbury, a word, if you please."

All Tom had wanted was a few moments on his own, perhaps a nap to rid himself of the copious bottles of wine the man he'd just done business with had pressed on him. As if that would have made any difference to Tom's business. "The house is purchased," he said softly, so that nobody else should hear.

"I'm glad to hear it. Please." His father opened the door wider and waved Tom in.

One glance at the other occupant of the room drove Tom to execute a low bow, one suited to royalty. "Your royal highness."

"Rise." The faintly Italian-accented voice sent shivers through him. What in the devil was his father thinking, to bring this man here? Speculation raced through his mind, superseding the freezing horror he had experienced when he'd recognized their visitor.

He straightened slowly, meeting the prince's eyes, although the man preferred people did not do that. He had not met Prince Charles more than three times in his life. Three times too many, in Tom's opinion. No, to do him justice, two times too many. The first time he'd been dazzled by royalty. The stars had long since fallen from his eyes.

The Stuarts did have a considerable presence, though whether that was from their birth or their expectations Tom had no idea. Charles could behave like a haughty aristocrat, if the need took him. The brown pop-eyes gazed up into his.

Tom had last seen Prince Charles five years ago. They were of an age, born in the same year, but where Tom considered himself in his prime, the prince appeared to have passed his. His jaw was softer than Tom remembered, and although he still had the long face and high cheekbones typical of the Stuarts, his cheeks were rounded, an effect of high living, particularly drink. His mouth, described as full by some and feminine by others, was looser, too. An aroma of sour wine hung around him. He wore relatively ordinary clothes, a russet coat and plain white silk waistcoat, and his wig was not out of the ordinary. At least the man had more sense than to prance around London dressed to the nines. He should not be here. His very presence spelled treason for anyone harboring him.

"I am surprised to find you here, sir." Not to mention shocked. Was his father insane to let this man in here? Sometimes his father's idealism drove Tom to despair, and this was most definitely one of those times. "This house is honored by your presence." Tom was surprised to discover how hollow that sentiment sounded, even to his own ears.

The prince acknowledged the compliment with a small regal nod. Arrogance was bred into Prince Charles's bones. The Stuarts had no conception of humility, other than using it for their own ends and citing it in their correspondence. "We will visit often, once matters have fallen to our satisfaction. Our last setback was unfortunate, but we shall rally once more, thanks to the help of loyal subjects like you and your father."

The Dankworths had always been allied with the Stuarts. Five years ago, when Culloden had signaled the end of their hopes, only the payment of considerable bribes and some legal maneuvering had helped them escape, and that was on condition they did not become entangled in Stuart fortunes again.

Now here they were, back again. Tom's mood plummeted, and anger sparkled in his veins. Had he worked so hard only for the Dankworths to end here? He'd be damned if they did. His family had suffered too much and wandered too far to let themselves fall again. No more exile, no more waste.

He had to get the prince out of here. "I have obtained a house for your use while you are here, sir. It is yours, should you deign to accept it." Needless to say, the house was not in Tom's name. Nobody would trace the ownership to him, because it would be his word against the man who sold it to him. From there, Tom could work to distance the family from this renewed threat.

The prince waved his offer away. "I have no need of it. I am lodging at the house on Theobalds Street. This coming Sunday I will receive the communion of the Church of England. I have sent a message to all the nonjuring chapels left, for their members to come and witness my conversion. A relative of mine, Henry the Fourth of France, God rest his soul, declared that Paris was worth a Mass. I am merely moving in the other direction."

Too little, too late. He should have converted in the Cathedral in Edinburgh five years ago, in front of hundreds of witnesses. Not here, hugger-mugger, in a small chapel in London. A few nonjuring chapels remained, whose incumbents refused to take the Oath of Loyalty to King George. They were the only places that would accept the Stuart, or not report him to the authorities.

"Do you plan to stay in London long, sir?"

The prince took a seat in the chair Tom's father was fond of using, but he did not bid them sit, and being royalty, they had to wait until he gave them permission. He stretched out one leg before the fire. "I will stay as long as necessary. I have viewed several of the establishments I always wanted to see. I have a few more on my list."

Perhaps he should employ a tour guide. As long as it wasn't Tom.

As if reading his mind, the prince said, "I understand you are busy about my business? I would ask you to introduce me to White's, otherwise."

That Whig stronghold? Did he want to find himself in the Tower before the week was out? He was deluded.

"Does your highness wish to search for a bride while you are here?" Because truly, that would be the best way to spend his time. To ally himself to one of the great families of would prove more than helpful at this stage. Prince Charles had no campaign, no set path. His father had appointed him Regent. Of what, Tom wasn't sure, but he would have no part in it.

The prince's mouth formed what looked suspiciously like a pout. "I have no mind to saddle myself with a wife. My father is constantly harping on the subject." He glared at Tom's father. "What does a man have to do to get a drink around here?"

An empty wine bottle stood on the table, and another two unopened waited by its side. Rather than open another topic of conversation Tom went to open it. His mind clicked into action. He needed to get the prince out of this house, but without upsetting his father. He would not do that.

His father never thought in a straight line when he could take the scenic route. As usual, Tom would be sweeping up the pieces.

He felt much older than his thirty years. His father did not have madcap schemes. He had dangerous stratagems and risky ventures. But Tom loved him.

He sniffed the bottle. "I fear this wine is off. If you will excuse me, I will fetch another."

After bowing to the prince, he left the room and summoned a footman. Lowering his voice, he said, "Bring another bottle of this, please." He turned away as if to go back to the parlor, and then turned. "Does not my father's visitor, Sir Humphrey, look like the exiled Stuart prince? Anyone looking at him could make a foolish mistake."

The footman nodded. "I was only talking to Robinson about it a moment ago, sir. He does indeed, but what would the prince be doing in this country?"

"Exactly." Fortunately Tom had five guineas in his pocket which he had no hesitation in handing over.

The footman winked. "Sir Humphrey Smith, my lord?"

"Just so," said Tom, relieved to have dealt with the matter. The last thing he needed was to have this visit reported all over London. If he had not nipped potential gossip in the bud, that was exactly what would have happened.

Reality was pushing idealism aside, and they must move with it or perish.

He would not deny that his first sight of Prince Charles in five years had been a shock. The man was heading for perdition faster than anyone could have imagined when he'd been the handsome young hero of legend. His reputation already damaged by the failure of the '45 campaign, he seemed determined to drive it the rest of the way down on his own.

Disillusioned, depressed, and dejected, Tom went back to his father and his prince.

* * * *

Helena had accompanied her mother on a visit to Leicester House to visit the Prince and Princess of Wales. Most of fashionable London was there, the house being thrown open for one of the lavish entertainments the prince occasionally held.

Julius was there, and this time Helena watched them closely, observing Caroline's frantic flirting and sideways glances to her husband when she thought nobody was looking. Julius conversed, admired the Prince's new acquisitions and behaved like a sensible man. Only his extravagant costume drew comment.

Back home, they dressed and sat down to dinner. Despite there being only four of them, their mother had ordered two courses served, with a dozen dishes on each. They sat to eat at the fashionably late hour at four and did not finish until half past six. Two and a half interminable hours of lectures and cold silences. Augustus bore the brunt of their mother's opprobrium, having announced his intention of leaving for the continent as soon as Caroline had given birth safely. "I have some work to do," he said, but would add nothing more, except the enigmatic, "Ask Julius."

Their mother railed at him, but he would say nothing.

Helena had had enough. Getting to her feet, she bowed to her parents. "I have a headache. Please excuse me."

Her mother would call it bad manners, but surely arguing with her son at the dining table was worse. Gathering her skirts, Helena left the room.

Night had not yet completely fallen, so she went downstairs and outside. Pausing on the terrace, she took a few deep breaths until her tension eased.

If her luck held, nobody would notice her coming out here. All she wanted was peace and quiet for a while and a chance to think.

Helena had a special place in the London garden. Right at the bottom, past the ornamental terrace, the green lawns, and the showy grottoes stood a small pavilion. Nobody used it except the gardeners if it was raining. A sprawling elm spread its branches over the structure, hiding it from both the sun and any onlookers from this house or any other. Privacy was hard to come by in London, and here she could find it.

The trouble with being a valuable commodity was that she was rarely left alone, and her presence was usually marked and noted. Not because she was Helena, but because she was Lady Helena Vernon. While she did not underestimate the privileges of her position, sometimes she longed to be ordinary.

The wooden benches in the building were dry, if not particularly clean. Whisking her handkerchief from her pocket, she spread it over her chosen spot and settled with a grateful sigh, stretching her legs out before her.

So many problems were piling up that she did not know where to start. She adored her brothers, Julius probably more than Augustus if she were to confess the absolute truth, but they could not help her now, not after her encounter with Tom Alconbury. What was she to do? She could not dismiss him from her mind, as she knew she should. Before their idyll had shattered, he'd shown her a world she'd never imagined. The more she thought, the more she persuaded herself that he'd been sheltering her when he'd turned against her, protecting her from her family's opprobrium.

She started when a shuffle came from the other side of the old wall at the end of the garden, the wall the pavilion was built on to. Before she could stop herself, she gave a "Who's that?" of alarm.

As shock chilled her, she held herself completely still, only now aware of how close she was to the outside world, and how much peril she was in. If someone got over that wall, high though it was, she could be in deep trouble. Heiresses were abducted all the time. All the journals said so. Lifting her skirts would cause a rustle of sound. Best to stay still until danger had passed.

Silence met her ears, and then a muffled curse. "I beg your pardon. I didn't mean to disturb you."

The voice came from above. She looked up, startled. "It's you!"

Even in an ordinary coat with a cocked hat pulled low over his forehead, she recognized Tom.

He grinned. "It is, yes. You're perfectly right. I'll go now." The gate rocked. He flattened himself on the top of it. The padlock fastening it to the stay was rusted shut. The gate was a foot or so lower than the wall—the perfect place for a man to hide, if he wanted to risk life and limb.

"No!" She swallowed. "That is, yes. You should go. You're my family's greatest enemy. What are you doing here?" Try as she might, she could not be afraid of him. Not this man, this ordinary man with his cheeky grin and the twinkle in his eyes.

"I came to see you. Like any lover, I wanted a glance." He leaned his cheek on his hand, gazing at her soulfully. "I've had a trying day."

When he gazed at her, she felt stripped down to nothing but Helena. She liked it.

"You mean you did not reject me at the ball?"

"Had I not, it would have meant scandal and disgrace for you. I could not have that, so a little private scene was in order." He sighed. "You probably don't believe me, but it's the truth. What we shared was magical. I did not know who you were when I followed you."

"I know. I saw the expression on your face before you turned around. You were as shocked as I was."

"Yes, I was. Where were you that I didn't see you before?"

"I was ill just before my second season, so I stayed at home instead. The next year…" She shrugged. "I stayed at home, too."

He watched her, his eyes far too perceptive for her liking. "Your parents don't want you married?"

"Something like that. My portion is large enough that I could marry at fifty if I chose." The way her mother was acting, that could well happen. The duchess seemed determined to keep Helena at home, although she had no idea why.

The gate rocked alarmingly when he moved.

"Get down here before that thing collapses under you. There's a much safer way of leaving."

"The front door would be the most perilous way for me to come and go," he said, his grin broadening.

"No, I did not mean that. There's another gate, a safer one. Come down before you kill yourself!" He must be seven feet up. A person could break something.

He lay on his side on the rickety gate as if it was a sultan's couch, resting his cheek on his open hand. "I should not. If the ball was compromising you, think what this would do."

"Are you afraid of my brothers?"

"No." He swung over the rail and dropped down, dusting off his gloved hands, and then turned to face her, spreading his arms wide. "Take me to them now. I'd rather face them and get it over with. I'll sacrifice myself for your honor."

She made a sound of exasperation. "Tcha! Men and their honor!"

"It's more than honor." He glanced around at the weathered walls, the chipped and stained mortar barely holding the soot-marked red bricks together. "Is this place safe?"

"It's stood for a hundred years," she said. "It was here before the house, or so my father told me once."

"Very interesting." He did not take his attention from her face, studying it as if to memorize it. "I prefer you like this."

"In my house clothes, with not a stroke of paint on my cheeks?" She could not believe that.

"I can see you properly. You, not the duke's daughter." He lifted his hand and then shook his head. "I want to touch you. May I?"

"You didn't ask before." Her heart beat madly, not from the shock she had received but from the nearness of him. Oh, yes, she wanted him to touch her.

He stripped off his gloves and shoved them in the pocket of his brown coat. Then he grazed the backs of his fingers over her cheek. His touch, so gentle, awakened parts of her. "You're so soft and warm. Are you not afraid of me?"

"You won't hurt me." She knew that for a fact, as certain as the sun coming up every morning.

"You're right. I could no more hurt you than I could my favorite horse."

She pokered up. "Oh, so I'm a horse now?"

A smile lit his features. In repose, he seemed standoffish and haughty, but that smile lit him from within and brought a glow to his dark eyes. "I would have you know that I've had my gelding Mist nearly all my life. I won't let them get rid of him, even though he is over twenty and well past his active days. But I did not mean that."

He had not referenced his parents or his siblings, but an animal. Knowing the tensions that racked families such as theirs made Helena understand. "I have a cat. Officially he's a kitchen cat, but he lives in my room most of the time."

"I would be that cat. I've never longed for anything more." His voice deepened and he took a half-step, bringing them so close their bodies were nearly touching. He glanced down. "You're not wearing a hoop."

"I am, but it's a small one." So small it might not be there, and it only held out her gown decently at the sides. Her mother would have sent her back to her room if she'd turned up for dinner in a quilted petticoat or a morning gown.

"I could capture you and hold you to ransom."

She refused to take his threats seriously. "I might welcome it. We could at least find time to talk that way."

He held up his hand, palm out, fingers straight up. "I swear I will never hurt you."

She already knew that, but like her brothers, he appeared very protective, as well as anxious that she should believe the best in him. "I learned something at the ball."

"So did I," he said. "What did you learn?"

"About my brother's wife and your brother William."

A spasm of pain crossed his face, but he didn't look away. "I know. My brother is a fool, but he goes his own way. He is much indulged, but that is no excuse. What he did was reprehensible."

It was at least as much Caroline's fault. "So two people of the same mind met…" She could not say they fell in love. They could not feel like this, the way she wanted to be with him, in his presence.

Her world ground to a halt. Wait, had she just thought of love? That could not be so. They hardly knew each other.

"Yes, that's it, isn't it?" He was not talking about Caroline.

"Yes." Neither was she. "I'm confused. We can't—I mean, I've read the stories, but such things don't happen in real life."

"They seem to." He took her hands gently, and she let them lie in his, his warmth soothing and exciting at the same time. "This is beyond reason. I want you, but not in the way my brother took your sister-in-law. I will not have you traduced or harmed. That is why we must not meet again."

"No!" Her reaction was without thought. It came from a much deeper part of her. "I know you won't hurt me or do anything to dishonor me."

He nodded. "I will never do that. I swear it."

"You don't have to."

"Then let us seal our pact another way." Leaning forward, he pressed a gentle kiss to her mouth.

Her mouth trembled and then firmed. Stretching up, she reciprocated, pressing against him. His response came in the form of a groan, and he flicked his tongue out to moisten her lips. She responded, opening her mouth for him, letting him take her where he would. Releasing her hands, he gathered her into his arms, holding her firmly.

Helena pushed her hand under the tail of his wig, sliding her fingers against his nape. She shoved his hat off with her other hand and then held on to his shoulder while they kissed as if their lives depended upon it.

Perhaps they did. Who knew when they would meet again, or how?

Tom plunged into her mouth, his tongue gliding against hers, licking into her in unimaginable intimacy. Her breasts pressed against his chest, the soft fabric of his waistcoat stroking above her neckerchief. She wasn't close enough. She never would be close enough.

Half lifting her so their mouths could come into closer contact, Tom tilted her chin and kissed her again. Only her toes made contact with the rough boards beneath their feet. With one hand lashed around her waist, he stroked up and down her back until he reached the top edge, and pulled at her fichu, pulling the cloth away. "I need to touch you," he muttered before he kissed her again.

She wanted to touch him, too, but she had a long way to go. He was covered from wrist to throat, in several layers. But she tried, dragging his neckcloth until he pulled away.

"I'm sorry, sweetheart."

He didn't sound sorry. Her fichu was half off now and considerably loosened. He glanced down at her cleavage and groaned. "We cannot do this. Must not do it. What if you were found?"

"They'd take me back to the country, which they will do anyway once Caroline has given birth. I've ordered the clothes I will need for next year, so there is only that to keep us. And Caroline is due any day."

He buried his head in her shoulder and licked the bare flesh. "You taste so good. I want more. I want everything."

"Why should we not have it?"

When he tried to pull away, she tugged him back.

"You know why we can't do this, why we can't even contemplate having each other." He drew back enough to gaze down at her face. "You have silver hair," he said wonderingly.

She huffed. "Actually it's a very pale blond. I have a few years yet before I turn silver."

He rubbed a curl between his thumb and finger and let it fall back to her cheek. "It's moonlight fallen to earth." Then he laughed again. "I've never been given to extravagant compliments. You bring them out of me."

"You should use them on suitable women, not on me." She was trying so hard to remind both of them why they couldn't be together, but the more she thought of that melancholy prospect, the worse she felt.

"You are suitable in every way but one."

"Would you want me to go into exile with you?"

"It might come to that," he said ruefully and then met her sparkling gaze. "It's a possibility. William is my father's favorite, so he would hardly miss me."

"But you have done the most to bring your family's fortunes back around." Everyone knew that, from the reports in the papers, and she was not too proud to confess that she had perused them obsessively since she'd met Tom. She frowned. "That hardly seems fair."

"Nothing is fair. Otherwise you would bear another name, or I would, and I would come a-courting. But if I turn up at your door I'd be lucky if all they did was slam it in my face." He kissed her forehead. "Of course, if you want me to do that, I will." He wrinkled his nose. "I could do with a snippet taken off the end."

Tom had a fine nose, a patrician one. She would not see it hurt. "If you came calling even Julius would insist on sending me away." She shuddered at the notion of the uproar that would ensue. The Vernons were not a quiet family. "I'd never get back to town."

"Then we will bide our time. But I want to court you." A faraway look crossed his eyes until he snapped back to her, alert once more. "There might be a way, but we must be careful. Can you ever get away from the house on your own? Or do you have a servant you can trust?"

She frowned. He kissed it away, and they lost a few moments, until she broke away, her mind sparkling with an idea. "I know! Madame Crisset."

"I don't think I know the lady."

"Of course you do not, unless you are in the habit of visiting ladies' dressmakers. She has a shop at the end of Oxford Street, and I have ordered quite a few gowns from her. She owes me a favor." Yes, she could do it. Eagerly, Helena nodded. "I can go for another fitting, order another gown, and make it clear to Madame that it's contingent on her not noticing when I leave the shop the back way. If I leave my maid in the main part of the shop, I can do it. My maid steals my clothes. I know she does, and she is a spy for my mother. There's another shop in 'Change, too, where I get my fans and trinkets."

"I see." He grinned down at her. "How long do you generally take at these establishments?"

"An hour or even two. I might stop for refreshments, if they ask me."

He loosened his hold on her and tucked a hand into his coat pocket. He came out with a key, an old one, big and black and slightly corroded. "This is one of the two keys to a house I have just bought."

Before he could change his mind, she took it, snatched it off him and shoved it deep in her own pocket. "Where?"

"Folgate Street in the City. It's where a lot of silk workers and owners live. It's perfectly respectable, but not a place one expects to run into anyone."

"We will not be recognized, you mean."

He touched her hair once more. "Except for this. It's distinctive and particularly lovely."

She gurgled with laughter. "I can wear a hat."

"Hmm." He drew her closer, and she laid her cheek on his chest. Perfect contentment flowed through her. Already she knew how rare that moment was, how few of them a person could expect. She relished this one. They would not share many more, unless they could find a way.

"Monday," she said. "At noon."

He touched her chin, and she lifted her face. Already she knew his touch, the little signals that meant he wanted her kiss.

He'd replaced the despair in her heart with something else. Excitement, anticipation and perhaps a way to find a happy ending.

Danger? She was at the point where she did not care. Constantly harried and criticized, Helena was coming to the end of her rope. If disgraced meant she'd be sent to an outlying house on a little-visited estate, as her mother kept threatening, she'd welcome the peace and quiet.

Chapter 4

Tom and his father had watched the conversion of Prince Charles from the back of the small chapel, although Tom had considered the act unwise. If the prince thought he was eluding the government, he was sadly mistaken. His father was too old a hand to believe that, so he and Tom had arrived separately, dressed plainly. He'd worn the brown coat he'd last used when he scrambled over the garden gate of the Kirkburton property.

He must have been mad. On both occasions, come to that. To risk his life at the Kirkburtons and the reputation he was carefully constructing this morning at the chapel. But his father was set on attending, and someone had to take care of him.

As the prince had promised, several men of the cloth were in attendance. The service was discreet, but definitive. Tom took communion after the Prince, as did his father.

As they left the chapel, a group of men came forward. Tensing, Tom found the hilt of his sword and took his stance before his father. The prince had left first, through a discreet door at the side of the place. Had they taken him? Was this when the Dankworth family lost everything they had fought for? For this time they would be branded traitor and they would not escape. They had slipped through authority's hands far too often to escape now.

But the men did not give Tom or the duke a second glance. Marching past, they took the arm of a man in company with the other clergymen, his white collar and lappets proclaiming him a member of their number.

"W-Where are you taking me?" the man faltered.

"The Fleet, for debt," one said.

Only then did Tom relax. These people were debt collectors, and the unfortunate man would remain in prison until he paid his debt. Or died, whichever came first. Perhaps he could earn enough from conducting the clandestine marriages the Fleet was famous for to pay his way out.

Tom took his father to the end of the street and hired a hackney for him, following on foot. Hackneys were not supposed to ply their trade on Sundays, but the authorities did very little to stop them.

They had done little to stop the prince. "We will all be watched until the man leaves London," he said. "They will not take him now. That small disturbance after was most likely a warning."

They went home to breakfast.

"It is a great pity we cannot entertain the prince here," the Duke of Northwich murmured over the meal. "It would be so much more convenient for him. And we could treat him the way he deserves."

Tom shuddered at the notion. "We'd be in the Tower by nightfall."

"More's the pity." Even talking about such things was risky, but the duke loved tempting fate. He liked to say that all his servants were loyal to the Crown, without mentioning which crown.

At least they were alone, and a trusted man stood outside, ensuring they were not disturbed. But there was still the jib door, the hidden servants' door, where they would lurk. Tom took care of the safety of his family, otherwise they would be in much more trouble.

"Papa, we cannot continue like this. The authorities watch us. You know that."

The duke shook out his napkin and placed it over his lap. "Of course I know. I have been eluding the authorities for longer than you've been alive."

"Times change, Papa. Much though we may deplore it, we have to deal with reality, not dreams. As the King has done." In this house the King referred to James III, not anyone called George.

The sun streamed through the windows, striping the snowy tablecloth. "At least the prince had a fair day for his conversion," William said. "He may see that as a good omen." He picked up his coffee cup and raised his dark brows as he gazed at his oldest brother.

"Indeed," the dowager agreed, glancing between her oldest grandchild and her son. As usual, Tom's grandmother was the peacemaker. The family disputes had increased recently—at least inside the privacy of their home. Outside they showed a united front, as always. "It is a great pity we could not all attend the momentous event."

Tom eyed the plateful of food he had optimistically gathered for himself. He could perhaps manage the chop. Picking up his knife and fork, he set to eating, although his appetite had long gone.

"If they catch him, they will," the duke said. "They could finish the problem there and then. We must do everything we can to make sure that tragedy does not happen."

Tom was far from convinced. "If they take him, they make a martyr of him. Do they execute him, as the law demands? Can you imagine what that would do?"

The Stuarts still had friends abroad. The recent treaty between Britain and France had effectively ended French support for the Stuarts, but Rome could not turn its back on them. They supported the Roman Catholic cause.

That had been one of Tom's victories, to persuade his father to convert from the old religion. His father had never been a religious man, and Tom agreed with him that it did not matter which church one used, as long as the prayers were sincere. But he still hankered after the old ways and frequently complained of the lack of incense and the Mass. As long as he only complained, Tom didn't mind.

Converting to Anglicanism had opened a lot of doors for the family. Tom was still building on that. It opened Parliament to them, too, and he had hopes of sending his younger brother Edward there one day. Edward was clever and level-headed and would prove a great asset once he'd come down from Oxford. Edward had spent most of his life in the shadow of his older brothers, being blamed for the death of Tom's mother, his father's beloved wife. Although everyone knew that was hardly fair, since he had nearly died along with her, the family's grief had been such that somebody had to take the blame. And God was out of the picture.

Edward would help Tom mark a new chapter for the Dankworths. But not yet.

His father glared at him. "Perhaps so, but the Hanovers would recover. The Stuarts would not."

"So if this is the end of the Cause, perhaps we should let it go." He hated to remind his father of that eventuality. "Even if the prince gets out of London, he shows no inclination to marry, and his brother is hardly likely to do so."

"Prince Henry will do as his father wishes," the duke said firmly.

"As he did when he turned Cardinal?" Tom shook his head. "And his father favors him, too. Only because he wishes to spite his oldest son. I pray we never become so conflicted."

The duke sighed and dropped his fork on his plate. It landed with a clatter. The dowager winced, but said nothing. "The Stuarts were always that way. They aired their dirty linen in the public eye for all to see and comment on. We, their supporters, must endeavor to reconcile them. And find the prince a bride."

Tom could at least agree to the reconciliation part, but he disliked the spark in his father's eyes. "The family is a political force." He saw a future for the Stuarts if they agreed to work with the British government instead of against it. But he knew that would never happen. A more pragmatic family would have agreed to work for the country it professed to love, but this one would not.

"Indeed, the prince has expressed his interest in meeting Chloe or Emilia."

Tom froze. Over his dead body would his sisters sacrifice their future. They would not have a comfortable life, and by God, that would bring the family into the heart of the conflict.

But if he said anything, his father would determine to go ahead with his wild plan. King James would agree. To wed the daughter of a British duke would give him a foothold he'd longed for.

Tom kept his face smooth and clear, only showing mild interest. "I am sure either of my sisters would be honored." Not from the expressions on their faces. They were not as practiced as he was at hiding his true feelings. But he had determined one thing. The prince would be leaving London tonight. That would ease Tom's avoidance of any further negotiations. "However I have heard a few unsavory comments about the prince, as you must have."

Women complained about the prince, the rumors starting in the last two or three years, since he had begun drinking heavily. Tom had seen the black bruises he'd left on someone's body, a woman who had followed him to the Continent and offered herself to him. That had been her reward. His sisters would not suffer that fate.

The duke shrugged. "I have only heard malicious gossip. In any case, they could have a clandestine marriage, one conducted in private. That way we may deny it if need be."

Always thinking from both ends of the argument. The duke's heart was with the Cause, but he was wavering. If the prince abused one of his daughters, that would deter him for good, but Tom wasn't willing to risk that.

He had a busy day ahead.

* * * *

Later that day, Tom paid a visit on a new acquaintance. General Court was a loyalist to the bone, but he also had a pragmatic streak. Tom met him by a coffeehouse close to Covent Garden, which was rather irritatingly called Tom's. It specialized in ladies of the night, driving the authorities mad. No girls ever conducted their business on the premises. The owners made good and sure of that, but they made appointments and met there.

This afternoon Tom King's had a quiet hour or two, enough time for a man with his hat pulled low to meet with an equally nondescript person. For a powerful, well-built individual, the general could merge into the background with impressive effectiveness.

"Sir." He gave Tom a nod.

Tom granted him the same response. "You have no doubt heard of the presence of a certain party in London."

The general snorted. "I couldn't miss it. He has not been particularly discreet. Are you turning your coat then, sir?"

Now it was Tom's turn to snort. "Hardly. Do you really think you could accomplish the task so easily? I only speak to you when the topic is in both our interests. If you had wanted him, you could have picked him off the street."

"Or off the ship," General Court said. "I would prefer to be back on the battlefield than attending to all this clandestine business. I do not appreciate the underhand affairs I am expected to accomplish. So let us speak straightforwardly, sir. No, the government is not interested in capturing the Stuart prince. Nevertheless the ports are being watched."

Tom winced. Such straight talking pained him. His upbringing had not encouraged it. No doubt he would get used to speaking plainly in time. It certainly led to a faster result. "We, too, want him out of London. Would you prefer the matter fulfilled sooner rather than later?"

"Yes."

The general was certainly good at keeping his business to himself. "Then if you may contrive to leave a particular ship unattended at, say, midnight, I can achieve that for you."

"Why would you do this?" The general stamped his feet, even though the evening was not particularly chilly.

Tom just stared at him.

The military man shrugged. "Very well. Yes, if you tell me the name of the vessel."

Tom waited until two gaudily dressed ladies had walked past. The task took them some time, because they paused to ensure the gentlemen were not interested—absolutely, positively not interested. Until the general swore at them and threatened to escort them personally to Bow Street, which was not far away at all they showed every inclination to linger.

"The ship is the *Timor*. One of mine." Tom had a few other errands he could accomplish at the same time. He would hardly get paid for transporting the prince, so he needed to make the journey pay. A few barrels of brandy would do the trick. If the ship was impounded, Tom would know not to trust the general again. In the usual way of things, Tom did not allow his ships to engage in smuggling contraband. Considering who he was, the risk was too great. But not tonight. He had tacit permission to go ahead.

He walked away without thanking the man. He would thank him in good French spirits and ensure a cask of brandy found its way to his door.

Chapter 5

Tom was waiting for her when she came to the house. She was on time, which surprised and delighted him. He let her open the door and come in before he snatched her close. After an initial gasp, she chuckled into his chest.

Drawing away enough to see her face, he raised a brow. "And what, madam, is so amusing?"

"You are. You did what I wanted to, but I would never have done it if you hadn't led the way." She glanced around. "This is a small house."

"It is. And a family of six plus servants all led a comfortable existence here before they left for pastures new." He followed her gaze to a row of prints depicting the king and his ministers. He grimaced. "I had no time to redecorate."

"They left everything?"

"Not quite everything. They took their personal belongings. I gave them a good price for the rest." They had taken rather more than they were entitled to, but they'd left most of the furniture. The house was stripped of ornaments, paintings, rugs, and all but the most basic china and kitchen utensils. Not that Tom cared. The prince had disdained to stay here, but Tom had a use for it. "This is our house now."

The notion thrilled him. On a day when all he wanted to do was hold her and soothe his exhausted spirit, he was surprised at how easily his body responded to her. "Should we retire to the parlor and discuss politics over tea, like civilized people?"

"No." She bit her lip, so he kissed it, persuading her not to abuse that lovely morsel. "I want—"

"What do you want, sweetheart?"

"Madness. I want madness." She lowered her face, and he let her, knowing shyness swamped her. "I want to touch you. I wanted it before, in the pavilion, and at the ball. We have only met twice. I should not want this."

"Plenty of time for lust to take hold." He'd had women within an hour of meeting them, and he rarely had to pay. "But I will not dishonor you. Don't ask it of me." He knew how far he would take her. His Helena was all fire and spirit, and he would have a hard time keeping to his resolve.

"It depends what you call dishonor. Is there a bed in this house?"

Holding her so tightly, he could not miss the increased beat of her heart. It pounded in her chest like a bird fighting to leave a cage. "Sweetheart, you cannot mean it." He had anticipated private conversation and kisses, no more.

"I do. Who knows how long we'll have? Today, I have two hours. Madame is at this moment discussing the possibility of altering some of my existing gowns with me. Madame plied my maid with so much good wine she has fallen asleep. She snores, my maid. I want this, Tom. So much I can hardly think for it."

She had described his situation exactly, although half an hour ago he was prepared to kiss her and then call a hackney to take her back to the mantua-makers'. "You should not tease me so. A man can take only so much."

"I want to feel your skin against mine." Roughly, she pulled at her delicate kid gloves. She'd tear them into shreds if she carried on that way.

He stilled her hands by clamping them together and then enclosing them with his. She looked up.

"I want the same. But I meant what I said. I will not dishonor you, or take what is not mine." He would keep to that resolve if it killed him.

The trusting expression in her eyes killed him already. He would not let her down, he would not take her honor, even if she offered it. The exhaustion of staying up all night melted away as if it had never existed.

Taking her hand, he led her up the first flight of narrow stairs, the worn wooden treads creaking under their feet, to the floor that held the main receptions rooms, and stopped. He turned to her and took her hands. "Are you sure?"

She nodded, her cheeks flushed, her mouth full.

Tom groaned. "You'll be the death of me." They ascended another flight of stairs to the next floor. Opening the nearest door, he led her into the bedroom.

Gauzy drapes at the window shielded them from view but gave enough light. Heavy velvet curtains were held back by faded worn cords. The bed was modest by their standards, but it filled most of the room, an old-fashioned four-poster with green silk hangings shredding with age and use. But the sheets were new, crisp and clean, and the bed cover was new too, a dark green that he considered, when he'd bought it, would be adequate for royalty.

It would never see royalty. "Let's pretend we've just come from church," he said. "We married at nine, and we have come back from a modest celebration at a nearby inn with our closest friends and colleagues. We're Mr. and Mrs. Fisher, moderately well-off silk merchants, and we are in love."

Her expression relaxed. "Yes. I'd love to be Mrs. Fisher."

They could say no more, but he wanted to tell her so much. Three days? Three years, thirty years, it didn't matter. He would not change his mind. Every time he met her the certainty hammered itself home. And now they were here at last, in the bedroom they would share as Mr. and Mrs. Fisher.

There might be a way they could do this.

His heart in his throat, he turned to her and curved his hands around her upper arms. She was so delicate, and yet great strength lived in her. She would not bow to pressure. "Are you sure? We could wait."

"What for?"

Not yet. He couldn't tell her yet. She might bolt. He longed for this taste of her, to make her his as much as possible. No, that was wrong. His mind churned with possibilities and the one clear fact that would not move. Nor did he want it to. "Do you know how lovely you are?"

Lifting his hand, he gently loosed the first of her hairpins. She'd worn her glorious hair in a light style today, topped by a pretty confection of lace which the fashionable laughingly called a cap. She might have dressed plainly, but she had not dressed cheaply.

"What are you smiling at?"

"You're going to cost me a fortune in lace, Mrs. Fisher."

"I will do my best to economize, sir," she replied in the prim tone of a good wife.

He laughed, surprising himself. He'd been deeply unhappy when he arrived here, but she had changed all that. He continued to work on her hair, carefully laying the lace and pins on the small dressing table that stood by the window. "You probably have a much larger one in your room at home. But this will suffice, will it not?"

She gave the piece of furniture a glance before she turned her smiling face back to his. "Indeed. And I have a great deal more pots and powders, which I rarely use and my mother frequently replenishes. The night of the ball, her maid tricked me out like a doll, but I scrubbed it off."

"I'm glad you did, but if you think that would have deterred me, you are mightily mistaken, madam."

Her laugh enchanted him, but then everything about her did that. He shrugged off his coat and tossed it over the chair by the narrow window. Outside, carts and carriages rattled past, and a church bell rang, a reminder of life going on, but here, the sound was hushed.

When she put her hands to her bodice, he moved them away and laid them on his waistcoat. "I need your hands on me. Touch me, Helena."

He shuddered when she unfastened the first of the buttons, but roused enough to unhook her bodice. Six hooks and eyes led him to paradise. The gown fell apart, revealing her pretty stays, thin red-striped silk sewn into the myriad tucks and bones that a woman had to endure. Not for much longer, if he had anything to do with it.

While he undressed her, he kept careful watch on her face. When she was down to stays and shift, he stopped. He had shed everything but his shirt and underwear, so that would suffice him. Disappointment edged his joy in having her to himself for two whole hours. "We don't need to go any further, if you wish. Lie with me."

Her answer was to turn around. "I can't lie down comfortably in my stays."

More practiced than he cared to admit at the moment, he unlaced the garment and eased it off her. She slipped the straps down and let it fall away. Her knee-length fine lawn shift hid little, and he took a moment to admire the sweet curve of her bottom and the glorious dip above. "You're divine," he murmured. "Come, sweetheart."

He guided her to the bed and turned the covers down for her. The view as she climbed in nearly undid him, as her flesh glowed through the fine white of her shift. Her garters peeked cheerfully at him as he joined her. When he held out his arms, she snuggled into them, and he could kiss her. Deeply and sweetly, reminding them both of the pleasure they found together.

"You taste like no one else," he murmured as he gently lifted his head away from her. He rose on one elbow, the better to look at her. The darker pink of her nipples marked the fine cloth, their peaks creating puckers of fabric.

"I wouldn't know," she said, mouth pursed. "I don't want you kissing anybody else."

"I will not. I swear." That would not be difficult to fulfill.

"Do you have a mistress?" Her look of anxiety nearly killed him.

He kissed the fine lines between her brows. "No."

"Do I count?"

"No. You are not my mistress, nor will you ever be. I shall never have another while I am with you."

"You promise?"

She must be mad if she thought he'd want anyone else. Seeing her here, lying next to him, her shining hair spread over the pillow, he could not imagine anything more perfect.

Well, perhaps one thing. She should have his ring on her finger.

He pushed the thought away. Bending, he kissed her, keeping the caress gentle, loving the sensation of his body against hers. He leaned back and took her free hand, pressing their palms together and keeping his fingers straight. He kept her gaze while he spoke. "I swear that I will never use what we have here for any other purpose. I will tell nobody and I will not embarrass or constrain you outside these walls."

She gave a slight nod, but didn't look away. "I swear to do the same." Her mouth relaxed into a smile. "I don't want to tell anyone. It might break the spell."

"I fear it's a spell akin to madness," he said, "but it's our madness. There are any number of reasons why we should not be here, should not even consider what we do, and only one good reason for doing it."

"That overpowers everything else." Her voice shivered in the quiet space. "Because we cannot stop. If we did, we would be committing the greatest of sins."

He folded his fingers, threading them between hers. "That is the reason." He bent, but before he kissed her again, he murmured the word against her mouth. "Love."

This time he deepened the kiss. Tutored by him, she opened her mouth slowly and accepted his tongue, sucking on it slightly. Freeing his hand from hers, he slid it around her waist. A rush of sensation forced his shaft into hard, aching need. He'd considered it primed and ready before, but now he was on the edge of pain. Her skin was soft, and as he slowly slid his hand up to her breasts, the heat of her body increased.

She arched into his hand when he covered her breast, her nipple pressing into his palm, a sublime invitation to carry on. She curled her hand around his neck and tickled his nape in the way he had come to love, and he groaned into her mouth.

The sheets rustled as he moved, rolling over her, careful not to give her his full weight, holding himself steady on knees and elbows.

Helena shoved his shoulders. Immediately he broke the kiss and moved away, but she grasped his waist, holding him in place.

When he quirked a brow, she said, "Naked. We should be naked."

"My dearest one, are you sure?" The suggestion sent him into a fever of imagining, but the control he would have to use—it would be worth it.

She nodded.

He rolled off her enough so they could he could tug the linen up her body. She sat up and held up her arms so he could draw it off and away. He let it fall where it would, never taking his eyes off the bounty before him.

Her breasts were soft cushions of elegance tipped with deliciously uptilted rose-pink nipples. Her neat waist framed a gently rounded belly and hips designed for his hands, her thighs luscious invitations to sin. The hair covering her most intimate parts was silvery, with a little more gold in it than the hair on her head. Unusual and utterly enchanting. He covered it with his hand. "Mine," he said, because he had to.

She gasped. "Yours," she agreed. Her glance clearly told him that it was his turn to disrobe.

She pulled the knot of her garters undone while he unfastened the buttons at his cuff and the one at his neck so he could pull his shirt over his head and toss it aside. Then he rid himself of his drawers. Sitting back on his haunches, he let her look.

Her lovely blue eyes went wide and she swallowed.

"It's still me," he said helpfully.

"It's more of you, though," she answered, her gaze roaming over him from his neck to his knees and everything in between. "All of you."

"All of me," he agreed, smiling. "And I see all of you."

She nodded and reached for him but then snatched her hands back.

He caught them and drew her closer, pressing her hands on his chest. "Touch me," he said. "Please." He would die if she didn't.

Her smile returned. "Warm and hard and strong." She ran her hands down his chest, as far as his navel, and stopped.

"It's all me. All yours."

"While we're here."

"Forever," he said, and meant it.

But she only smiled, and continued her tactile exploration. To his disappointment she reversed direction, smoothing her hands up to his chest again and touching his nipples. "Why do men have nipples? They can't feed babies."

Gasping, he managed, "So that women can touch them."

"It's hard." She wasn't referring to his nipples. Her gaze was elsewhere.

His shaft was straining to get to work, the end shiny, the tiny opening emitting a bead of clear liquid.

"It is. It wants you."

"Then it must have what it wants." Drawing closer, she made to straddle his thighs, but he stopped her, his hands on her waist.

"No, not yet." Not yet meant no, although she could not know that. If she did, she would make him do it. He knew her that well, at least. "Come here. I want your skin against mine. I've dreamed of this. The first time I saw you, I wanted to touch you, to have you touch me."

"Yes."

The need in her eyes was echoed in his body. He urged her back down against the sheets so she was lying on her back. He could control their lovemaking that way, make sure they didn't pass what he'd deemed acceptable. But this he could take. He climbed over her, tucking his erection against her stomach, pressing into her soft flesh. He moved from side to side, groaning when her heat made his shaft as close to unbearable as he could ever remember. But the torture was so sweet. He never wanted it to end.

He claimed a kiss. It felt like their first, but better, because he knew her taste and what she liked. Dotting small kisses around her lips, and then to her ear, he savored the different tastes and textures. Her skin was warm silk, her arms welcome bonds he never wanted release from.

She watched as he kissed her throat, and then down to her breasts. He knew because he checked often, needing to be sure she was enjoying this—enjoying him.

She wound her hands into his hair, what there was of it, for he kept it cropped short. "It's almost black," she said, "but there are glints of red in it."

"So there are." That was right; she'd never seen him without the trappings of his rank, the wig, the fine clothes, the arrogant manner. He was naked, completely stripped, exposing himself to her. He would allow nothing to come between them. Nothing, he thought savagely as the memory of all that did lie between them hit him again. He shoved it aside. It didn't matter here. Nothing but Helena and Tom and lovemaking.

He was dark, his hair, the hair on his chest and at his groin. She was fair, an angel to his devil. But he would have her and he would keep her.

She shivered when he kissed her nipple. "You taste wonderful," he told her, and sucked. She cried out, but not in pain, even though he gave her a playful nip before he moved to the other peak of perfection. "I have never known anything so soft." He had not imagined living tissue could be so silky, but with a firmness that invited him to taste even more.

Farther down he encountered her navel. "I want to taste every part of you, learn how different you are."

"What do I taste like?"

He growled against her belly. "Woman."

She laughed, her skin vibrating against his mouth.

He'd never had a virgin in his bed before. He had to take extra care, not just for her but for himself, to guarantee her pleasure, to learn what she liked along with her.

Helena was no passive participant. She stroked him, curved her hands around his shoulders, ran them over his muscles and back to his throat. The touches sent shudders of delighted awareness all the way through him.

He reached the hair curling between her thighs and nuzzled it. The scent of her arousal wove around him, as intoxicating as the best French brandy but far more heady and unique. Thirst dried his throat. If he didn't taste her now, he'd die.

"Open your legs," he murmured against her thigh. After a short pause, she did so, lifting her knees and setting her feet on the sheet. Groaning, he took his first lick.

"I didn't know you could—oh!"

He loved her little gasps and sighs. Carefully, he worked her up toward her arousal, licking, sucking, and kissing, absorbing her into him. He lifted his head and met her gaze, impossibly intimate. "Don't hold back. I want it all."

Her eyes were round with wonder, but they sparkled, and her skin was flushed adorably. "Yes." She moistened her lips.

He went back to his delicious task. He caressed her inner thighs, keeping his touch light, and then moved to her stomach and her breasts, rubbing his thumbs over her nipples, urging her to let go, but not using words.

A sharp jerk indicated the beginning of her peak. He concentrated on enhancing her first orgasm, pushing her as far as he could. Tucking his hands under her buttocks he raised her, drinking from her like the finest cup of wine, giving no quarter until she screamed.

The sound was better than any music he'd ever heard. The dying notes rang around the small chamber. He didn't stop until they had subsided into sobs and then ebbed away to small whimpers, but by then he was past thinking, because he'd experienced something he had not gone through since he was an untried boy.

He had no thought for himself, but scooted back up the bed to hold her and share the last tremors. She made sound that was distinctly like a purr and curled into him, nestling against him. Drowsiness suffused him, but he could not sleep. That would be far too dangerous. But if she slept, he'd hold her and keep her safe.

"I didn't know that was what all the fuss was about," she murmured, but he heard her clearly enough.

"Neither did I."

The drowsy, sleepy kittenish expression on her face when she raised her chin nearly undid him. She clearly expected his kiss, and he obliged, sealing their mouths together in their first kiss after making love. She tasted him this time, licking into his mouth with a delicate stroke of her tongue.

She pulled away, smiling. "Is that what I taste like? My oath, it's not too bad, is it?"

"It's wonderful." He kissed her again. "Utterly perfect."

"You've tasted women before, of course."

"You're not supposed to ask that." He shook his head slightly. She was quite something, his Helena. Not the sweet virgin she was supposed to be, but something far more exciting and precious. She'd eagerly accepted and encouraged him in all he did. Had he not come, he might have transgressed, crossed the line he'd promised himself he would not take.

She laughed, totally carefree. He'd give anything to keep her that way, but he feared it was beyond his powers.

"I love you, Helena."

She stilled, the smile gone, her eyes pure. "I love you too."

He replaced her smile with his own. "After three days?"

"The time doesn't matter."

He pressed her closer, giving her a tight hug. "We can say that here. We can say anything we want to, but we don't have to mean it once we've returned to the world outside."

She shook her head. "I won't change my mind. I won't tell anyone, but only because they would hurt you if I did." She glanced down at their bodies. "I would like to sleep with you. To sleep with you and wake up with you."

Rolling on his back, he groaned and pressed a thumb and finger either side of the bridge of his nose, pressing in, as his nurse used to when he'd suffered nosebleeds as a child. He'd grown out of the bleeds, but not the gesture. "I'd like that too, but we cannot."

"Perhaps in time we can. Tom, I want you." She lifted up, her breasts touching his chest. Her nipples were still hard. "Nothing matters more than this."

"We should give ourselves more time."

"What time do we have?"

He tried to remonstrate with her. "You're twenty, love. We have plenty of time."

She snorted. "Lives pass while people think that. No, I won't have it."

"Another month, dearest one." He pressed a kiss to her lips. "Give us that. When is your sister-in-law due to give birth?"

"A week, perhaps two. She says any day, but Julius says maybe not."

"He would know," he said dryly. He tucked his arm behind his head and kept a firm hold on her. This part, the after part, had never appealed to him before, but with Helena he could stay here all day. "So we have some time." He smiled. He had the feeling he would always smile when he saw her, although he might not always show it. "This house is ours, Helena. To use as we see fit. I'll never sell it. Whenever you need sanctuary, whether I'm in town or not, come here."

"I'd like that." She smoothed her hand down his chest, pausing at his waist. "A place that is totally our own. But won't we need maids?"

"Mr. and Mrs. Fisher live in a cozy villa by the Thames." He stared at the bed canopy. He could see the place. "When they began to prosper, they moved out of town, as people do. But sometimes they have to stay in London, so Mr. Fisher bought this house. They don't have live-in maids, but someone comes in once a week to clean when they're not in residence."

She wriggled against him, lifted her leg, and draped it over his. "Mrs. Fisher likes to be with her husband. She loves it, in fact. They have been married for two years. He saw her across the room at a Guildhall dinner."

"And fell instantly in love," he said, because that was what he'd done. What he felt for Helena was more than lust. He'd seen her and wanted her, but more than that. He'd wanted women before, but he'd never wanted to care for them so strongly. Never wanted to claim them. But instinctively he'd known that Helena was his.

Helena was ethereally lovely, as well as lively and intelligent, but although he enumerated all her assets, something else lay there, just out of his reach. Perhaps he would never find out what it was. He wasn't sure he wanted to.

"We need time, sweetheart. If we take steps to be together, we will hurt the people we love. We can't do that."

"We might have to."

From the gravity of her tone, he could tell she understood what he was saying. They must be completely sure. In the meantime, they would manage.

"I can ask for more fittings at Madame's. Men are lucky," she continued in a disgusted tone. "They may go wherever they wish. I will dismiss my maid and ask for another. That will give us more time, too. My mother will complain."

"Does she complain much?"

She paused. "Yes."

Turning his head, he kissed her. "I'm sorry, sweetheart. I should not pry. Here's another rule, if you wish to accept it. Anything we say here goes no further." Because he longed to tell her what he'd done. As if reminded of his long night, he stifled a yawn.

"I thought you looked tired," she said.

"Nothing would have kept me away from you."

"She traced an imaginary pattern on his chest. "Have you been carousing?"

He laughed. "No. Far from it. I was at the docks in the early hours of the morning. They delayed the departure of the ship with the prince, and I had to wait to make certain he left—" Startled that he found confessing his secrets so easily, he opened his eyes wide and stared at her.

"We said nothing leaves these walls," she said softly, and kissed him. "We knew the Pretender was here. That is, Julius knew, and he told me."

"He trusts you." Tom was not surprised. Helena possessed gravity far beyond her years. "So do I. But you know he hates me."

"He hates your family."

"And my brother." He grimaced. "William is fully convinced that the prince will return. I am not. The world is moving along, and it rarely goes back. But that doesn't mean I'll turn my back on my family."

"Of course not," she said quietly. "And I will not betray mine."

"This is neutral territory."

"Yes." She lowered her head, but when she lifted it again, her eyes were sparkling. "So what is he like?"

He stroked her back, the supple skin smooth under his palm. "The prince? Charles is not as handsome as he once was. Culloden destroyed him. He should never have turned back at Coventry. I have no idea why he did that. If he'd taken London, the impetus might have taken him through. He will not have that chance again. The defeat broke something in him, and he is chasing the path to perdition. Women and drink mainly. I'm not telling you anything you don't know, am I?"

She shook her head, her curls tickling his chest. "My brother keeps an eye on him. As do others in the family. Last night Julius confessed the Pretender was in the country."

It did not surprise Tom to know that the perspicacious Earl of Winterton had discovered as much. "He is no longer here."

"You sent him away."

"I put him on a ship from the docks in the early hours of the morning. He did all he came to do. There was no reason for him to stay." To say any more might put others in peril. Certainly he didn't want to compromise General Court. Having someone he could talk to in government saved a great deal of time and expense. The prince had not wanted to leave, but his propensity for strong drink had eased the way for Tom to get him on the ship and away.

"So you've been up all night," she said.

He nodded.

"I'll go and leave you here."

His chivalry would not allow that. "Who will lace your stays?"

She laughed. "You can lace stays?"

"I wasted much of my youth." He drew her closer for a kiss, and she came to him willingly. With her body wrapped around his, Tom was in danger of forgetting everything except her. Helena surrounded him, her taste, her delectable body, and he could wish for nothing more.

But he must not take her, could not make her irrevocably his. He had to keep his head enough to do that. She was not his to claim, however much he might wish it.

* * * *

Tom returned home to find his father demanding his attention.

The Duke of Northwich spun around to face his son, the skirts of his dark green coat whirling, gold braid catching the sun. "The prince has left the country."

"I know. I helped him."

"You did what?" his brother Will thundered.

"The prince wanted to leave the country. I merely helped him." Suppressing his grin of triumph, Tom faced his brother and let his eyelids droop, as if the matter was of supreme indifference to him.

"Without referring the matter to me?" his father demanded.

Tom folded his arms, tucking his hands into the warmth of his coat. "The prince was ready to leave. I had a ship in port, so the matter was done."

His father growled and then uttered a curse so inventive Tom memorized it for future use. But his father never knew when to stop, and he proceeded to more earthy but less inventive phrases. Tom waited. His father had a fierce temper, but it never lasted for long.

"You should have consulted with me."

Will's face turned red. "Why did you not try to stop him?"

Tom ignored him and addressed their father. "Would you have wanted me to?" Tom shrugged. "What more good could he have done? The authorities could have taken him."

The duke paused near the window, the thin autumn sun streaking his snowy wig. It must be well fixed on his head to cope with the duke's sudden movements. Anything unlike a stately and dignified ducal presence was hard to imagine. He made a sound at the back of his throat, something that would be better suited to a wild animal than a duke, and then he turned and paced.

Good. Soon he'd see reason. Tom only had to wait him out. Too wise to interrupt his father mid-flow, Tom settled into a waiting pose. He'd have leaned against the wall, but he was not close to it.

Tom tried not to care that his younger brother was his father's favorite, but he could understand the preference. William shared his father's idealistic views, even appeared more nearly like him than Tom did. Will was of a height with his father, while Tom towered over them, and he had the distinctive broad-browed, narrow-chinned face shape, where Tom's face was longer. He took after his mother's side of the family, or so his grandmother claimed. His mother had died in childbirth, leaving five children and deep grief.

Tom saw nobody but himself when he shaved every morning and stared into the mirror. No family echoes lay in his face. His brother had the deep blue-gray eyes of his father, too.

No matter. Tom would start a new tradition of brown eyes and unconscionable height. He had long since ceased trying to make himself unobtrusive, trying to stoop to conceal his height. Now he stood tall. "Father, do not distress yourself."

"He did not want to leave." Will glared at Tom. "The night before his departure, he spoke of storming Parliament."

Tom's blood ran cold. "He did? How could he do that?"

"He had supporters. We were arranging a council meeting."

The duke whirled around and seized a piece of paper from the stack on the side table. He shoved the paper under Tom's nose, though how he expected Tom to read when the hand holding the paper was quivering with rage he was not entirely sure. "Look at this!"

Tom took the paper. It was a letter sealed with red wax but with no significant seal impression. He read. It was not from the prince but from one of his advisors in Lunéville, where the prince currently resided with his mistress, the Princesse de Talmond. "His highness is not pleased. The Princesse displays the bruises of his displeasure every day. He accuses her of not loving him enough and then sends her to her room, where she writes him impassioned letters pleading for mercy. The woman loves him, or so she claims."

The report disgusted Tom. Charles had taken out his bad mood on a woman, one he should be cherishing, not abusing. Tom could not imagine doing that to any woman.

A memory flashed into his mind, of Helena as he'd last seen her. Tom much preferred to see her laughing. Or crying out in delight, as he loved her.

He wanted her badly. Even more so now he knew what lay under the silks and laces she wore. Something far more costly, and far more precious. He was in a fever for her.

They had not fully consummated their relationship, although he had touched her everywhere and brought as much joy to her as he could without compromising her. He feared he had done too much already. Any man taking her to bed would know she was not completely innocent.

But he could no more stop than he could stop breathing. He had soared past want, straight into need.

The words on the page danced before his eyes, and he was glad to have something to look at until he reined in his self-control. "Does it matter that the prince is a woman-beating drunk?" He asked the words mildly, and it was a genuine question.

"If he were on the throne, then no," his father replied.

At the same time Will cried, "How can you talk of our rightful monarch that way?"

"He's the Regent." Tom was too used to his brother to allow any irritation from that direction. "Not the crowned monarch."

Will waved a beringed hand. "You have the right of it. But we cannot speak of him in those terms."

"We have to," Tom said. "For God's sake, Will, can you not admit that the Stuarts will not win the throne by conquest?" Frustration seized him by the throat. He had not meant to lose his temper, but it was done. At least he was still capable of rational thought, although his blood was up. "They will not gain it by inheritance, either, if the Hanovers continue to breed the way they do."

He faced two men, one white-faced, the other with a ruddy tinge to his handsome features. He had said too much. They would not agree with him.

His father spoke first, interrupting Will, who had begun to shout invective. "Quiet, Will! I had not thought you had so much sense, Tom."

Tom stopped, his mouth open in shock. He'd thought his father's anger was directed at him, for not informing him about the prince's departure. But perhaps meeting the man again and realizing what he was had brought the duke to a sense of reality.

The duke continued, "We cannot expect conquest to win the day, not any longer. With the Peace of Aix, Europe shifted its allegiances. Unless the Prince breeds and soon, the Stuarts are lost. The Prince of Wales has bred a nest full of children, and he is well thought of."

Tom tried to recover from his father referring to the Hanoverian Frederick as "The Prince of Wales."

His father caught his son's startled gaze and grimaced. "I have to accustom myself to using the words. You think I have not been thinking about our situation? This visit from the Prince brought matters to a head, and I have spent some time doing what I should have done long ago. I have brought myself to see reason. We cannot lurk in the shadows any longer. We've done all we can to rebuild our title and the land, but now we have to move further into the light."

"So we are turning coat?" Will said bitterly. He flung himself across the room, his coat flying behind him. "How can you think so?"

"We have to." His father turned to Tom, effectively dismissing Will. "You two can marry into the old families and the new. Develop our connections. We may continue to work for the restoration of the rightful monarchs, but we have to do it in a different way. Become as powerful and successful as any other family of our rank and prepare to welcome the king when he returns. We should think of building a strong foundation for them, somewhere they may return to. The king will not win by conquest, but if the will of the people have it, he may be asked back. Why should they not realize their mistake?" The duke glanced at his desk. The big old-fashioned piece of furniture had papers scattered over its worn surface. He selected one and handed it to his oldest son. "I've drawn up a list. Next season, you two will go a-courting."

They would what? "So our new ambitions include wives?"

"They have to," the duke said.

"What about you?"

"I have done my duty. If I marry again, it will be for entirely personal reasons. But believe me, I will not marry to disadvantage. I would rather not."

"You married for love the first time." Tom remembered his father in gentler times, when the duke had smiled more and laughed often.

"I did. I was fortunate." He reeled off a few names. "They are comely lasses and ripe for the picking. They have fortunes and useful alliances." He glared at Tom, his eyes sharp. "For your latest trick, you owe me."

The names omitted the one he was most interested in. "What about the Emperors?" he asked mildly.

His father burst into gales of shocked laughter. "The Emperors of London? You are jesting, are you not?"

"There are not many more influential families in the country. Together they encompass all the seats of power."

The duke shook his head sadly. "The optimism of youth sometimes astounds me. They are and always will be our enemies. Too much bad blood lies between us for us to reconcile. One marriage will not accomplish that. They hate us, and the sentiment is heartily reciprocated."

"But you were just saying we should let our history go."

The duke's mouth tightened. "Not that history. That remains an open book. Do not even consider it."

Will stepped forward, waving his hand, his abundant ruffles punctuating the conversation. "We could discommode them. We could court them and then not come up to scratch."

"No!" The emphasis was more than Tom would have expected from political rivals. "You will not go near them. The Duke of Kirkburton, his sisters, their husbands, and their families. I will not have that poison infecting my family. Do you hear me?"

Tom's dreams of courting Helena openly faded into nothing. He rarely heard his father give edicts, but this was most definitely one. Something other than allegiances had fired that denial. His father was nothing if not devious, and he rarely laid down the law, preferring to make the choice obvious or denying all other choices so that the object of his attention had no other way to move forward.

His father was perfectly capable of arranging matters so that Tom and Helena would never be together.

He could not tell the duke. He would have to find another way.

"Why are you so against the Emperors, when you do not mind us marrying a Cavendish or a Holles?" Both names were on his father's list of potential brides, and both families were as against the Stuart cause as the Emperors were.

His father shot him a calculating look. "The Duke of Kirkburton cut me to the bone once, but I will not tell you why."

Despite all Tom's protests, he refused to say a word. Tom would have to do some investigating of his own.

Chapter 6

Helena sat at the breakfast table and beamed at her family. The last two weeks had been the most glorious of her life. She'd met her lover several times more in the house, and she'd seen him once in the theater and been forced to take no notice of him. Her cheeks had burned the whole time. Her mother had commented that perhaps London was too much for her, and she was going down with a cold. She had replied that Sharman had tightened her stays far too much, and that had given her the excuse to dispose of her mother's spy and ask Julius to find her a replacement.

That was until today. She found her appetite healthy, made even more so because she had an appointment at the mantua-makers in Change later today. She would have two hours to love and talk with Tom. Although Tom still refused to take their intimacy any further, buoyancy still filled Helena.

Her mother jarred her out of her daydream. "Helena, pay attention!"

Not willing to admit she had not heard a word her mother had said, Helena lowered the strength of her smile and did as she was bid. "Of course, ma'am."

"Then you agree?"

Cautiously, she said, "Could we go over the details again, please, Mother?"

The duchess's already thin lips tightened, making a harsh slit in her face. "Why do you never listen? I was talking of Sir George Seward, who is finally out of mourning. If you marry him before April, you would not even have to go through another season."

It took Helena a moment to process her mother's calm statement. Sir George Seward was their neighbor in Derbyshire, a middle-aged man who'd lost his wife to smallpox a year ago. He'd come to town a few days ago and paid them a duty visit, but Helena had done no more than greet him and smile. He was built on comfortable lines, had a fondness for sweet things, which meant he had few of his own teeth, and assumed women only had two functions in life—to bear children and to make him happy.

He spoke to her parents but not to her? For Sir George had never said a peep to Helena about his ambitions.

A marriage between them could not happen. Must not. "I do not agree, Mother."

Her mother shrugged, her lace shawl dropping off her shoulders. "We will discuss the settlement before we go home. That should not be too long."

"I do not agree." That was all she could say. Sir George was not love's young dream.

Horror built quietly but surely in Helena's breast. Her mother was a woman of determination and guile. She would make Helena's life miserable if she set her heart on her daughter marrying Sir George. She could accomplish it in myriad ways, from removing the books Helena preferred to read to refusing to allow her out of the house.

Helena could oppose her all she wanted to, but her mother held most of the cards in this hand. And if Helena refused outright, the duchess would take it in her head to compel her, so that Helena's life would be not worth living. Her new maid would be dismissed and another spy put in her place, one that would turn Helena into a marionette for every ball, would do her best to ensure Helena never appeared to advantage.

Rather than suffer that fate, Helena would seek employment as a governess or a kitchen maid. A romantical notion, to be sure, and one that was unlikely to come to fruition. What did she know about service, and how could she possibly expect to remain hidden? In her world, everybody knew everybody else or was related to them. Networks fed in to other networks, a room full of spiders' webs that nobody could negotiate without making a disturbance.

But what else could she do?

Julius. He had enough power to stand up to their mother, and while Helena could be as stubborn as the next person, she needed more armor to effectively fight back.

Except—was it fair to expect Julius to help her? He was busy with his wife, and soon he'd be busy with his heir. Caroline had become more volatile than ever with her advancing pregnancy, and Julius was forced to dance attendance on her to assure she did not do anything reprehensible. She had tried to take his phaeton out last week, and Julius's house was still reverberating from his furious displeasure.

She would do as much as possible to dodge her fate until she could obtain Julius's help. With Augustus planning to leave soon, she could only count on his help for a few weeks. He was not here this morning, but she'd tell him as soon as she had the opportunity. Together they might contrive a scheme to keep their mother busy until Julius could attend to the matter.

She picked up her spoon and stirred her tea. Round and round, turning the tan-colored liquid into a small maelstrom. Her mind raced, while she forced her face to calm tranquility.

"Helena, I do wish you would pay attention!" Her mother's voice rang around her head.

Helena jerked up her head. "Of course, Mother." Her face was as perfect as she could make it, smooth and calm. "I beg your pardon."

She listened as closely as she could, because she might need the details. "You may tell Sir George that you accept his kind proposal on certain conditions. I want you in our house, of course. His is too small to contain a duke's daughter—"

Would her life always be one of service and obedience? She firmed her resolve. It would not.

The door opened to admit a footman with a silver salver. On it rested a letter which, whatever it was, bore Helena's salvation.

The duchess snatched up the note. It bore no seal, so must be hand delivered.

"My goodness," the duchess said, groping for her magnifying glass. "This writing is almost incomprehensible. Dear me, what does it say?" Knowing she had everyone's attention, she trained her glass on the note and peered again, taking her time adjusting it.

"Oh, I see." She glanced around the table. "Caroline is currently giving birth."

The metaphorical stone dropped into the imaginary pool, but the effect was far more dynamic. The duke leaped to his feet. "Good God, I will call the carriage immediately!"

The duchess gave him an indulgent smile, or as much as her face-paint would allow without cracking. She wore a skim of the stuff today, but Helena could not remember a time when she had faced London bare. "My dear, it could take Caroline days to deliver. Truly, there is no hurry."

"Nevertheless," the duke said. "I will pay a visit to Brook Street." He glanced at Helena. "You will come too, my dear."

With relief surging through her, Helena recognized her father's tactic to get her out of the firing line and rose from her chair to curtsey to her mother. "Indeed, sir."

* * * *

The baby was born within four hours, a shockingly fast time for a first child. As Caroline strained and swore, Julius paced downstairs, and Helena had little time to think of anything except making sure Julius had company and Caroline did not work too hard trying to get the baby out.

As soon as he was allowed into the bedchamber Julius strode in, only to reappear an hour later, beaming. "Caro is asleep," he said to his family. "Exhausted. The baby is beautiful, everything I could wish for."

"Except it's a girl," their mother pointed out.

Julius waved her concerns away. Helena thought she saw relief on his features and understood. If the baby was Lord William's child, Julius might have been forced to reject it if it was a boy. But a girl couldn't inherit the dukedom. "Caroline and daughter are well and recovering. We will have others, no doubt." He paused. "Caroline wants the baby named for her. I have no objection."

Typical of Caroline to insist on that, however much confusion it would cause everyone else.

Her mother got to her feet and dusted crumbs of cake from her lap. "We will leave you now."

Helena wanted to see the baby, but how could she ask that?

Julius must have seen her disappointment and caught her hand in his. "Come and see," he said softly.

The baby was in the powder room next to her mother's. "Her ladyship complained that the child cried too much," the nurse said. "I would like to take her to the nursery."

Julius glanced at the closed door. "I thought Caroline was feeding the baby herself."

"She's changed her mind." The nurse's mouth tightened and she smoothed her neat skirts, although they did not need it. "We have a wet nurse, my lord, and with your permission, I'll put her to work when the baby wakes."

"Do that." Julius did not seem surprised. Carefully, he lifted the baby and put her in Helena's arms.

Such a tiny weight! The sweet creature's lips pursed, as if seeking the nipple, but she would find nothing with Helena. Her breath caught. This child was so beautiful, so precious.

"I love her," Julius said softly, his voice packed with emotion.

"Of course you do." How could anyone not love her?

* * * *

Unfortunately, someone failed to love the baby. Her mother. Since she had given birth, Caroline had refused to see her daughter. Complaining that her figure was ruined and her love life nonexistent, Caroline had concentrated on her own recovery. Julius bore his wife's temperament patiently, but unlike her, he visited his daughter every day. As did Helena, when she could, except for tonight, when her mother had commanded her presence at the theatre.

The play wasn't holding Helena's attention. Not surprising, really, because sitting next to her was Sir George Seward. He was firmly attached to her and driving her mad. He opened every door for her, seated her carefully, and behaved as if she were already his. Not as in "his wife" but "his possession." And his constant toadying to the duchess put Helena's teeth on edge. He'd try to kiss Helena soon, and that would be the end.

But her mother was determined she should have him. George was young enough, handsome enough, well born enough, but nowhere near enough for Helena. She knew what she wanted. If anything was needed to compel her further toward the unthinkable, Sir George Seward was it.

Currently, he was sitting so close to her that his breath gusted against her cheek, and the odor of a man who loved sweets and cleaned his teeth infrequently made her long to turn her head away. If she had, her mother would have accused her of being rude, and indeed she would have been. So she kept her face clear and her posture rigid, and mildly complained of a headache, preparing for her speedy exit once they went home. She could excuse herself after the play. Accordingly, she spread her fan and closed her eyes, as if in pain. When she opened them, her attention landed on Tom. He was sitting in his family's box, opposite her family's. Her mother always claimed they'd hired that box deliberately, and considering the nature of the Duke of Kirkburton, they may well have, but the box only held one occupant now.

The contrast between his lean, handsome features and Sir George's softer ones was cruel and pointed up the difference between them. Why would she want one and not the other?

One answer came to her. Tom's eyes gleamed with intelligence. By contrast, Sir George was a dull dog. He knew little about current affairs, only what interested him in his little part of Derbyshire, and then with a particular emphasis on land and rights.

"Antony was a fool," he murmured, reminding her they were watching a version of *Antony and Cleopatra*. Not an enormously popular play, but this was far from the height of the season. "He should have kept Cleopatra as a lover. What man in his right mind gives up his possessions for a woman?"

"Who indeed?" she murmured, glancing over the top of her fan at her lover. Even though they had not shared the ultimate intimacy, he was still her lover and, she feared, the only one she would ever want. Their clandestine meetings had done nothing to ease the tension and excitement every time they met, the sheer hunger for him that invaded her every moment. If she had decided on the risky affair to get rid of the emotions, she was failing significantly.

She yearned to reach out to him, to call him.

Sir George was still talking, but she had lost the train of what he was saying. That was unforgivably rude, but she could get by with a few gentle agreements.

"So you would agree to a wedding in November, then, ma'am?"

That brought her back to earth. She opened her eyes wide, alarmed at what she had so nearly agreed to. "No indeed, sir!" Forgetting all attempts to mollify her mother or the man next to her, she got to her feet. "If you will excuse me, I will be but a moment."

Gathering her skirts, ignoring her mother's fierce glare, she left the box. The footman guarding the door, ostensibly there to see to their needs, stood before it, but she glared at him, and he gave in. At least she still had that power, even if the footman was a favorite of her mother's. All the footmen were, and the maids.

She swept past him, head high, tears misting her vision. No doubt her mother would send someone after her, so to go into one of the retirement rooms set to one side would be to imprison herself. Even without Tom she could not marry Sir George. He had driven her demented over the last day. A lifetime of the droning sycophant would send her to an early grave.

Outside, the hallway was deserted. They were on the level where only the moneyed sectors of society had sway. Since this was not a popular time for visitors to London, very few of her sort had attended the play tonight. Perhaps she should risk ducking into one of the unoccupied boxes. But she could hardly climb over them to the others. No, she needed to get away.

Footsteps sounded behind her. "My lady!"

The footman's voice was sharp, commanding. Helena took no notice, except to quicken her step. She would not stay, could not listen to any more. Whatever it cost her, she would leave now, even if she had to walk the streets on her own.

That prospect made her pause. Her heart beat hard, but she refused to go back.

"Helena!"

"No!" Wildly she glanced behind her. The footman was some way back, but gaining ground fast. She could not see Tom, but that was his voice.

"Turn left."

She did so, and someone dragged her into a dark place.

A door closed quietly behind her and she was in his arms. He released her quickly. "Come."

"What is this?" They were in a narrow corridor, with only a few oil lamps to guide their way.

"Theaters have servants' quarters, too," he said briefly and caught her hand. He pulled her along the passage and then turned into another. From the direction, she guessed they were moving to his side of the theater.

"Do you want me to go into your box?"

He gave a sharp, hard laugh. "No. Not yet. I want you to tell me what distressed you so much."

She wanted that too. Concentrating on hurrying and listening for the sounds of pursuit, she went with him. They passed a startled manservant, who flattened himself against the wall.

Tom dropped a crown into his hand. "You saw nobody."

"Yes, sir," the man replied, but they were well advanced by then.

He brought her out into a better lit corridor, the twin of the one they had left, but in reverse. Without pause, he led her into one of the rest rooms on this side of the theater. He closed the door and locked it before he turned and pulled her into his arms. "First," he muttered, before he kissed her.

She leaned against his shoulder and relaxed into his arms. He didn't linger over the kiss, although he separated their lips with lingering reluctance. "Now tell me why you ran out that way. What did that man say to you?"

"I thought you were watching the play."

He shook his head. "Strategically placed mirrors. I never took my attention away from you. I know it's wrong to watch someone so obsessively, but I can't help it. When you're near, you are all I think about."

Typical of the Dankworths to have a theater box that was more about watching people than watching the entertainment. "He's a neighbor from Derbyshire, Sir George Seward. My mother wants me to marry him."

He didn't let her go. "Do you want to marry him?"

"No!" She spoke the word with such vehemence she startled herself.

"Would you have considered it before you met me?"

That was unkind of him, because it was so perspicacious. "I can't bear the thought of anyone close to me except you. But it's not just that." Tears came to her eyes unbidden, but she would not give into them. "He worships my mother. If I marry him, I will be expected to remain at home with my mother for the rest of my life. Sir George will move into the Abbey and we will dance attendance on her until she dies." She closed her eyes. "And his breath smells." A petulant addition, but if she had to spend a lifetime with a man, she would rather not spend it with a man who had rotting teeth.

Tom's teeth were as sharp and white as a wolf's.

He placed a kiss on each of her closed eyelids, soft as an angel's wing brushing against her heart. "Then don't marry him."

"Easy for you to say." She opened her eyes and met his, so understanding, but not in this case. "I can refuse, but Mother will go on and on. Then she will banish me and refuse to allow me my season next spring. I will never find anyone. I'm worth a fortune, but I can touch none of it. It's for the aggrandizement of my future husband or my family."

"I don't care about your inheritance. I am not on speaking terms with your mother. Marry me, Helena."

She blinked. "How can we?"

"Easily. We may do it tonight."

Her mouth dropped open in shock. He could only mean one thing. "A Fleet wedding?"

"Why not?"

For any number of reasons. A Fleet wedding was legal but illicit, used often by the unscrupulous adventurers who seduced or abducted valuable heiresses. Public uproar, especially from the families of the heiresses who found themselves saddled with unsuitable sons-in-law, was rising, but for now such marriages were legal.

"We cannot."

"It's a matter of finding a cleric and paying him. Even at this time of night that won't take much effort."

He cupped her cheek, and she nestled into it. She loved the way his hand encompassed the side of her face.

"I love you, Helena. I will protect you in any way I can, however I can."

"But what about after? What then?" They would hardly be welcome in either family. She couldn't imagine taking Tom home and introducing him as her new husband. Julius and Augustus would fight for the right to kill him.

He frowned, but only for a moment. "I have money of my own. We may buy a house wherever we wish, call ourselves whatever we like. We can make Mr. and Mrs. Fisher come to life."

Awed, she stared at him. "How do we do that?"

"We could go abroad and live there, or go into a remote part of the country."

She choked a cynical laugh. "My family is everywhere. All my relatives are wealthy, and they all own numerous establishments. Besides, what happens when your father dies? You must inherit."

"We don't have to live in exile forever. We would write to our loved ones and tell them we are well and married. When they forgive us or allow us to be together, we may emerge once more."

"It's a fairy tale." Dare she believe it? "I cannot touch any of my money, and I assume yours is tied up in your estate."

He shook his head and moved around, cupped her face in both his hands and kissed her fiercely. "I have helped my father rebuild the estate, but I did not give him everything. I have a competence of my own. It's nothing like the fortunes your family commands, nor the Northwich title, for that matter, but it is enough to ensure that we and our children may live in comfortable obscurity."

She sighed. "That sounds blissful."

Could they really do it? But no. "Our families will come in pursuit of us."

"If they can find us. They will not do so, my love." Snatching her close, he gripped her in an embrace that knocked the breath out of her, but for all that she would have stayed there forever. He groaned, the sound rumbling through his chest. "I cannot let you go. All my life I have done what is right, what is expected of me. Only recently have I tried to break free. I want this for myself, the first time in my life I have been utterly selfish. I cannot see you married, not to a lout like Sir George or even to an exquisite who would know how to treat you. You are mine."

"Yes." In her heart she knew that was the absolute truth. Nothing else mattered but that they claimed each other. "Yes, I'm yours. Yes, I'll marry you."

Whatever happened after that, she was his.

"Then come."

Trusting him completely, she let him lead her from the room. Together they went downstairs, where, hatless and without her cloak, she let him help her into a common hackney cab. They rattled down the narrow street, down another and yet another until they reached Fleet Street.

Ladies of the evening and their clients jostled and laughed while respectable citizens looked on. Even they had more freedom than she did, but in this, she was finally herself. Braziers next to the boxes occupied by the night watchmen glowed, with urchins gathered around them. Inn doors lay open invitingly, light pouring out and people shouting and laughing, the sound passing like a wave as the carriage rocked past them.

Upper windows beamed light on to the street below, glimpses of people passing before them, or leaning out, elbows on the sill, to watch life teeming below them. All these people had their own lives, their own worries, but Helena felt none of them. Could she truly be doing this? After instructing the driver, Tom held her hand tightly but said nothing, staring out of the window for the short journey to the Fleet prison.

The Fleet took up a plot of land close to Ludgate Hill, adjacent to Doctor's Commons, where marriage licenses could be had in the general way. The regular way. She was not fated to have one of those marriages.

They climbed out of the vehicle, and Tom threw the man double his fare and added a guinea for good measure. "You never saw us," he said.

The driver touched his whip to the brim of his hat in salute. "Want me to wait, sir?"

"Yes." Tom paused and glanced up at where the man perched nimbly on his precarious seat and then at the door of the prison. "I will get them up even if I have to knock the doors down."

The Fleet was a debtor's prison, notorious for the high charges it levied on its inmates. They owed when they went in and owed even more when they had been there a while. Some prisoners lived outside the jurisdiction of the building, and with the place locked up for the night, this was obviously the better course.

The huge doors under the arch were closed, but as they approached, a small door to the side opened.

A man stepped into the light, rubbing his nose and sniffing wetly. "'Ave you got business 'ere?"

"We have." Tom handed over coins.

The man clutched them, rubbed them together but forbore to test them with his teeth. If he had any. "Who with?"

"A clergyman. The lady and I wish to be married."

The man sniffed again. "At this hour?"

That was a cue for more money, which Tom handed over. "I'll wager we're not the first."

"Nor you might be. Mr. Clegg is still up—I swear he barely sleeps two hours a night. Worries, you see, about his wife and fam'ly."

He wore a strange collection of clothes. His coat appeared dirty and worn, its original color hard to determine, but underneath his stained waistcoat was silk, and embroidered, a costly item, or it would have been in its day. The fine buttons were gone, probably sold separately, the cheap horn ones incongruous against the once-fine background.

The man turned around and shuffled through the door. Tom guided Helena through, his hand around her waist.

Although Helena was not dressed for a ball, she appeared far too fine for this place. Her red-and-white striped gown was clean and crisp, her lace good, and her shoes fine brocade ones, not meant for the street. But they were all she had, and she would not be ashamed or afraid. Not on her wedding day.

The stink of overcooked cabbage, stale urine, and sour milk mingled with the yeasty aroma of beer wafted around her, but Helena had known worse, or so she told herself as she boldly stepped forward into the gloomy yard that lay beyond the lodge at the gates. A number of shadowy alcoves signified where doors to the lodgings were.

The man took them to the second on the left and rapped hard. "Mr. Clegg! Customers!"

Helena swallowed as the door opened.

A man in shabby clothing, but a decent appearance stood up. "I appreciate it, Mr. Jones." A single candle glimmered inside, together with a bed covered with a rough blanket, a chair, and a rickety table.

The clergyman asked no questions, but took the money and opened the book they would sign when they had done.

They stood before him, and in a low voice, he began the ceremony.

In that room, Helena Vernon became Lady Alconbury, or more importantly, the wife of Tom Dankworth, the man she loved. She learned that his full name was Charles Thomas Maria Dankworth, which forced a smile to her face. She put her hand in his.

For a ring, she received his signet ring. Not the one with his family coat of arms on it, but a more personal one with an ancient carved ruby on the bezel. She had to crook her finger to keep it on.

The vows were as sacred here as they would have been in the family chapel at home or in a fashionable London church. They meant the same, and she meant every word. He repeated them in his turn, and to her shock added "obey" to his vows, too, giving her the crooked smile she loved as he did so.

The whole thing took less than ten minutes, start to finish. The warden and another man acted as witnesses, and they signed the book afterward. So many names lay before and after theirs she felt safe from discovery adding hers to the list.

"I will not go home tonight," she told him. She could not bear to be separated from him on this, their wedding night.

She bought a piece of paper from the clergyman and wrote a quick note to her father, telling him that Julius had requested that she attend him and she would be home in the morning. It was a risk, but one she would willingly take.

They went outside, her hand resting on her husband's arm.

"You're mine now," he said in a low, intimate voice that thrilled her to the core. "Nobody will take you away from me."

The cab was still waiting. They stepped inside, Tom threw the man a coin, and they went to the house in Folgate Street. The house belonged to them, nobody else, and this was the only place they could be themselves.

The strangeness of entering a house that was not lit or with servants to greet them overwhelmed her for the second it took Tom to turn and take her into his arms. He buried his face in her hair, breathing deeply, as if to take in her very essence. "My wife. My love. Nobody else can have you now."

"No. And nobody can have you."

They belonged to each other.

When he would have kissed her, she held him off. "No, wait. If you do that I will lose every sense I have left." She glanced down at her gown, which had now collected some of the dirt of the prison on its hem. Her shoes would be ruined. "We cannot run off tomorrow morning, can we? You will need to make preparations."

"You may stay here if you wish," he said. "I will find everything we need."

She shook her head. "I'm leaving people I love. I won't do it hugger-mugger. My brother would never stop until he found us. He deserves an explanation."

His mouth firmed, and two lines creased the space between his dark brows. "What would you do? Confess all to your parents?"

"No," she said, although she would prefer to do that. "I have a friend, Mary Steed, in the country. She lives in Devonshire now. I can forge her handwriting well enough. I will have her send me a letter inviting me to stay with her. Then I may pack and bring my belongings with me."

"Will it work?"

"If it does not, I will come anyway. I want to try."

His mouth tightened, and he paused before he spoke. "Your mother will let you go?"

"She liked Mary and she was sorry when she moved away. Mary married a wealthy gentleman who owns a fleet of ships, so my father will be glad if I visit. He has urged me to do so. I will tell my mother I wish to speak to Mary before I agree to marry anyone, or I will beg her for this one last indulgence. At any rate, she will let me go."

"I can hardly believe that sweet Lady Helena Vernon could be so devious." Smiling, he touched her chin, grazing his fingers along her cheek. They were trembling. So he was not unaffected by this evening's activities. After he'd taken her from the theater, Helena had wondered at his calm, but now she realized it was his way of coping with strong emotion. She had her serene face, the one she'd practiced in the mirror until she had it right. He decided on a course of action and then went ahead and did it.

Were they truly married? The possibility hardly seemed likely, but here they were. "I've not finished yet. I'll send a note to my father's house, telling him that Julius wished me to come and help with Caroline."

"You're taking too much of a chance," he said. "Let me take you back home. You may say you were taken ill at the theater."

That was not the way she intended this evening to end. "And miss my wedding night? No, indeed, I will not do it." She shot him a laughing grin. "This isn't the first time I've played my mother off against my brother. They rarely see eye to eye on anything, and they often quarrel."

"Ah. I do not have that problem."

"No, you do not." His mother had died too long ago. Going up on her toes, she kissed his cheek. "But I will do everything I can to make it up to you. Will we have children?"

"Undoubtedly." He smiled down at her, all the warmth in his eyes for her alone. "We should perhaps make a start." He pressed his hand to the small of her back, urging her toward the stairs. "Up with you, my lady."

Laughing, she ran up to their room.

Tom had arranged for a maid to come in to clean. The bed was made up with fresh sheets, and the sparse furniture gleamed with polish. Struck by a thought, she turned impulsively to him. He wrapped his arms around her, holding her close.

"It feels as if I'm coming home," she said softly.

"Yes it does." He kissed her, as if in welcome. It started as a gentle kiss, but soon progressed once she parted her lips and let him in.

Without hesitation he took what she offered and dived in. They devoured each other, touching and fumbling for fasteners, hooks, and buttons, going as fast as they could manage, undressing themselves and each other with a speed that defied the skills of even the most skilful body servant.

He had her down to her shift before he stepped back and looked at her. His eyes glowed. "Remember our pact? In here we are nobody. We mean nothing to anyone else except each other." He caught her hands, pressing them against his bare chest. "My love, I want to take you tonight. I want this to be a true wedding night, but I don't want you to give me anything you might come to regret."

"I won't." Her conviction shook her. They were ending this life and starting a new one, so a child would only be welcome. But if she denied him, she would regret it forever. Never to have him inside her, loving her, was too painful to think about right now. "I want everything, Tom. Please."

"Then you shall have it." His heart thudded against their clasped hands. "Everything I have is yours, my love. I swear you will never lack for anything, as long as we are man and wife. Which will be forever." Drawing closer, he kissed her again.

Her fever to have him rose, so she could no longer bear to be apart from him. When she tore frantically at the fall of his breeches, he clasped her hands and drew them away.

"Not like that. Get into bed, my sweet love."

Swallowing, Helena drew her last remaining garment over her head and tossed it aside to join the rest of her finery on the floor. Watching her closely, Tom unfastened his breeches and drew them and his underwear away. Then he joined her. His cock was boldly erect, standing proudly against his belly, and as he slid his arms around her and drew her close, it burned against her flesh. He slid his hands into hers, came over her, and pressed their joined hands against the pillow on either side of her head. "Mine," he said, with all the confidence of a man who knew he loved and was loved in return.

"Always," she replied. She longed to have him, but she must allow him to do this his way, because she knew it would hurt. When he had touched her most intimate places, he'd been careful not to push her there, to disturb her virginity in any way. She'd respected his choice, but it had been his choice, not hers. She had given him everything else and been well rewarded for it in terms of sweet pleasure, so why not that, too?

Tonight they had taken a step they could not pull back, and they were headed for somewhere new. How appropriate, then, was this final act of possession?

In law it would be Tom possessing her. He could claim her fortune and stir up so much trouble that their families would be even more at odds than they were before. But she trusted him not to shake the beehive and force the families to take the action that could destroy them both.

But no. Here they were a reasonably prosperous merchant and his wife. Nothing more.

"Will we always be Mr. and Mrs. Fisher?"

Poised over her, he stopped and smiled. "Yes. Always. Nothing can take this away from us. I will always keep this house for us, and we may always retire to it when we feel the need."

She had the key. She could come here whenever she wished. That knowledge had made her life more bearable and infinitely sweeter.

"Open your legs, my love. Let me in."

With a laugh of sheer pleasure, she did as he bade her, raised her knees and slid her feet up the sheets until he was nestled inside her thighs, his cock grazing her cleft. He rubbed against her, nuzzling his member into her, collecting the wetness her body had made for him.

"You feel too good to be real," he said.

She grinned. "I know what you mean. So make it real, Tom."

He kissed her. "Your wish, as always, is my privilege to obey."

He slid against her again. "You're ready. There's nothing I want more than to plunge in deep, but I don't want to hurt you."

She braced herself, pressing her feet down. She would not move, because the reward for a little pain would more than compensate. "Do it."

With a grunt, he freed his right hand and brought it down between their bodies. When he touched her, she jerked up and turned her head, to be confronted by his sinewy bare arm. She swallowed and turned her face back to his. "What are you doing?"

"Easing my way." He sounded breathless. "You feel wonderful, Helena, as wet as I've ever known you." He slid a finger into her, right inside, and moved it. She forced a smile, but she'd lost her society face. She couldn't have pasted on her quiet serenity if her life depended on it. Nor did he want it, she knew. She would not insult him by trying. The lack of any useful mask made her feel painfully vulnerable, but this was the man she had fallen deeply in love with. She needed to show him that, if only for her own sake.

"I can't do any more." He withdrew his finger and rested his hand next to hers on the pillow. Unhesitatingly she threaded her fingers between his. His forefinger was wet with her essence. "I'm as untried as you in this instance, Helena."

She loved that this powerful man confessed he was in new country, that he opened himself enough to say that.

Their eyes met, and they watched each other as he made her his.

Helena couldn't suppress her swallow when he eased in, stretching her in a way that alarmed her and then brought her pain. But she trusted this man, and she pressed closer to him, silently urging him to continue.

Tom set his jaw. "I've never known anything like this," he said through his teeth.

He pushed until he was fully embedded, their bodies pressed together in unimaginable intimacy. Only then did he kiss her, and he kept the caress brief. "How do you feel?"

"Odd. Invaded—wonderful."

He quirked a smile and his eyes danced. "Wonderful? Truly?"

She nodded. "Absolutely. Is this the right time to tell you that I love you?"

"Any time is. I love you too, my darling."

Helena had never felt so cherished and cared for. Tom had eyes for her alone. Until that moment she hadn't been aware how much she'd needed that—for someone to concentrate on her only. Her world shifted a little. This whole mad plan could work.

"You're my world." She loosened her hand from his and curled it around his neck, tickling just below his hairline in the way he liked.

He purred. "Ready?"

He'd remained still inside her, allowing her body to accept him. On her nod, he slowly drew out, nearly to the tip, and then pushed back in again, keeping his movement firm and steady. He gave her the time to assimilate what he was doing.

She felt every inch as he slid deep inside, her body stretching to admit him and then clasping him as if it would never let him go.

She grazed his flanks with the sides of her feet, and he groaned. "Around my waist," he murmured. "Please."

She wrapped her legs around his waist, resting her heels on his buttocks.

He moved again, and she gasped. The movement had opened her to him more fully, so when he drove in this time, the effect was deeper, and—

"Oh!"

He chuckled, a rumble low in his throat as he saw and felt her reaction. As he moved again, he dropped a kiss on her lips. With every stroke, his movements became easier, and deeper.

She had not been aware that she'd arched her back until he touched somewhere new, a place inside her she hadn't known about before. "Tom!"

"There we are," he said in a voice of deep satisfaction. "Don't hold back, my love. Let me take you there."

"Where?"

A few moments later she knew. He stroked in and out of her, his thrusts deepening, opening her up to take everything and welcome it. At first she tried to mark the sensations rioting through her, but with her whole body involved in learning and marveling, she could no longer use her mind.

"Your body knows what to do," he murmured. Sweat gathered on his brow, and he levered his upper body up, placing his hands either side of her, leaving her free to touch him, to run her hands over the bunched muscles at his shoulders and arms, feeling the strain when he powered into her. Each of his breaths ended in a sharp grunt, and she watched him, pushed her body up to meet every thrust. She fell so deeply in love with him she would never get out.

Nor did she want to. She cried out, his name the only word she was capable of uttering as the ripples of sensation rioting through her coalesced and joined in one surge, washing over her, drowning her in pure emotion.

She opened her eyes, staring at him in wonder. He was waiting for her, a wicked grin curling his mouth, his gaze sparkling. Then he closed them, and his whole body shuddered. He released into her, jetting his seed deep inside her body, groaning as he came.

With a cry of triumph he rolled away, taking her with him. He helped her uncurl her legs, restoring one to drape over his thigh as they lay on their sides facing each other, entwined in each other.

Chapter 7

Tom could not sleep, but he didn't care. Watching his wife—his wife!—sleep in his arms was all the succor he needed. She was truly lovely. Her bright hair shadowed at the candles in the sconces guttered down to nothing. The smell of molten wax mingled with the heady aromas of their lovemaking, and the moon rose high outside, finding its way between the heavy curtains in a fine ribbon of silver.

He was watching when she opened her eyes. She moved closer, snuggling into him. "Have you slept?" she asked.

He shook his head. "I have no need. My love, you're even more beautiful when you sleep." She had conquered him completely. The glory of their lovemaking was followed by her utter surrender to sleep.

"What time is it?"

"About an hour before dawn." Cupping his hand around her neck, he brought her closer for a kiss of welcome. "You're mine now," he said when their lips parted. Possession roared through him.

"I always was. That was why we were attracted from the moment we met. We were waiting for each other."

"I won't argue with that." He returned for another kiss. "I've never felt so at ease, and so happy. I've been planning, sweetheart."

"You do that a lot." She treated him to a mock pout. He rewarded her with another kiss.

"I do. It's part of my heritage. It's who I am. I don't seem to be able to control it. But this time it's for us." Smiling, he stroked her shoulder, then draped his arm over her waist, the tips of his fingers just reaching her buttocks. The intimacy felt thrillingly natural and right. "Your plan is a good one. Go home, arrange to stay with your friend, and send me word."

"My father will wish to send me in the family coach."

"Let him. While I'd love to escort you, traveling in the coach will give us time."

"I hate the subterfuge."

There was just enough light for him to see her eyelids droop very slightly. "So do I, love, but it's the only way. One day we may be able to return. We will write to them. I'll make sure they don't know where the letters originate, and they may reply the same way. I won't use any of my usual channels, so my father cannot find us."

"Yes." She lifted her gaze and as she gazed at him, her eyes sparkled once more. "They will forgive us. We may live quietly somewhere."

"I'm glad to be out of it, to tell you the truth."

"Out of what?"

"The Cause, the mess the Stuarts have dragged our family into and the way they turn their backs on us the minute we displease them." He twined a lock of her hair around his finger, the words flooding out of him. "I have worked for years to rebuild the family. That is why I kept some of it back and built an income of my own. I cannot bear for my father to throw it at the prince yet again. But I think he may be coming around."

"I always thought that you were convinced the Stuarts should return."

"I did, but then I was young and I had ideals." He gave a self-deprecating laugh. "I sound ancient. I am older than you, love, but still in the same decade."

"You're as old as Julius, are you not?"

"While I'm not used to being compared to your brother, in this case you have the right of it. We're of an age."

"Nearly thirty."

"Indeed. Does that make me old to you?"

"Not when we're like this." She wriggled in a way that made his cock come instantly to life.

"Don't do that. I'm determined not to overtax you tonight. This is your first time. I can't take you twice."

With a delighted laugh, she rolled him onto his back and straddled him, her legs on either side of his. "Is that all that concerns you? Don't let it. I want to practice my skills."

"Nothing would give me greater pleasure." He could deny her nothing, especially this. "Since you're there. But tell me my love, honestly. How do you feel?"

"Deliciously used."

She sat up, making him groan at the sight of her. "I wish the candles hadn't gone out. I can barely see you in the dim light."

While they'd been speaking, dawn must have broken because the light from the window had increased. It poured over her lovingly, and he could hardly blame it. But it cast her into shadow, and he could barely make out her pretty breasts and the delicious indentation of her navel. Her shape, though, was thrown into sharp outline, and he revelled in the beauty of her curves and the way her moonlight hair spilled over her shoulders, nearly to her nipples.

He looked down to the apex of her thighs, where the silvery curls covered a world he was only just beginning to explore. He would see her every day like this. He couldn't wait. He touched her, stroking her, sensing rather than seeing her smile. "Your skin is magical. It draws me in." The silky smoothness was unlike anything he'd ever touched before.

She caught his hand and brought it to her breast. Her nipple hardened and peaked under his fingers, and she moaned softly. "I like you touching me."

"That's just as well because I plan on continuing for some considerable time."

She flattened her palm on his chest, and he drew in his breath through his teeth in a hiss. "I like touching you, too."

"I love you touching me."

Laughing in delight, she explored him with her hands, moving so her breasts swayed. He cupped her breasts, wondering idly if he could make her come that way. One day he would try. But not today.

Today he had a burning ambition to see her ride him.

He gripped her hips and lifted her. A fresh thread of her scent came to him, and his cock hardened even more. When she glanced down, her eyes went wide.

"Gratifying," he murmured. "Consider, do you truly want me to put that inside you?"

Her voice shook as she laughed again. "And I thought passion was deadly serious."

"Never." Not with Helena.

He brought her down, holding her above him. His cock reared up without any extra help from him, but he feared any more bravado might tax his prowess. "Take hold of it, love. Put it where it can do the most good."

She flicked a glance up at him, but didn't comment. Instead, she did as he bade her. The feel of her cool fingers wrapped around his shaft nearly undid him. Then the heat of her seared him. Her hand trembled but she positioned him in the right place.

He thrust and his head went back against the pillow. Every time he entered her she overwhelmed him. Rational thought scattered to the four winds, and one resolve filled him. To take her, to make their joining as good as possible and then find heaven inside her.

Sitting up, he banded his arms around her and thrust up inside her, exploring her with an avidity he could never remember feeling before. Oh, he had enjoyed sharing a bed with a woman, but not this enveloping feeling of rightness. Joining with her was meeting his match in every sense, in a way he had not believed existed.

When she bent her head to claim a kiss, he gave it to her gladly, but he worked his hands on her hips, showing her how to move.

She was a fast learner, his wife. She rose and fell without him guiding her more. All he could do was respond, and kiss her.

The feel of her breasts against his body enticed him, aroused him more. He punched up into her, no longer entirely in control of himself.

She murmured against his mouth, "You told me to do it. Now you do it. Let go."

He needed no more urging. Holding her down, he thrust up into her, piercing her, claiming her. She cried out, but not in pain. As long as she stayed with him, he would continue. He drove up hard, again, but this time she ground down, meeting him in a duel of desire.

They kissed again, sloppy and uncontrolled. He drove his tongue into her mouth, desperate to take everything, to claim her for good. A ceremony meant nothing. This was their true blending of bodies and souls. It would only get better.

This time they exploded at the same time. He held her while she shuddered and cried his name, but he was no mere participant. He was part of the shattering orgasm that wiped away everything that had gone before and left them together, facing a new world.

* * * *

After letting her sleep another hour, Tom slid out of bed and went down to the kitchen. He brought her hot water and tea, and roused her gently. When she wound her arms around him he wished for time to stay exactly where it was, but in his experience, wishing never made it so. Washing her was a delight in itself—urging her to stand on a towel while he took the sponge and passed it over every inch of her, adding the occasional kiss for variety, and because he could do nothing else.

She stood in the beam of sunshine that had replaced the moon, laughing. She washed him in return, teasing him, stroking his cock into full, painful rigidity, forcing him to grit his teeth and remind himself that they could not make love again. She had to get home, to pave the way for them to leave.

"I will have you to myself. I'll keep you in bed for a month for this."

"Good," she said, her eyes gleaming. "I can't wait."

She straightened, thank God, because he couldn't have lasted much longer. He'd have taken her against the wall because he wouldn't have managed to make the bed, even though it was but a few steps away.

He retrieved her clothes while she drank her tea. "Did you make this?"

"I am capable of a few basic tasks," he said with a grin.

"I know." She gave his body a smoldering stare before taking her shift from him. "I sometimes think my oldest brother would just lie in bed until he died if he didn't have servants. He tells me he can shave himself, but I have no idea if he was telling the truth."

The notion of the exquisite Lord Winterton undertaking mundane tasks gave him a moment of amusement. But the man had a fine mind, and he refused to underestimate him, as Northwich tended to do.

All too soon she was dressed, and so was he. He gave her the plain straw hat and the cloak he'd collected from downstairs. They probably belonged to the maid, but he'd left more than enough recompense on the kitchen table.

He had made his plans, and when he arrived back at the house, he would have to make haste putting them into action. He dared another kiss now they were both dressed. "If when you arrive home you discover your subterfuge has not worked, come to me. Do not let them take you from London."

She nodded.

"We'll bring our plans forward. Do not send messages here, but to an address I will give you. It's an office where my man of business resides, but there are many businesses in the building. I can trust him. He will send the note immediately to me by messenger."

"Tell me. Don't write it down. My brother is bound to know your handwriting."

He hadn't thought of that. He gave her the address and made her repeat it. "Send messages back the same way. But it will not be for long, my love, I intend to claim you by the end of the week."

"What?"

He caught her in his arms, gazing down at her lovely face. "I don't intend to wait longer than that."

She nodded. "Yes. We will do that. I'll write to Mary in Devonshire and warn her she might have visitors. Because my father is sure to send someone down after a time. She may say she knew nothing of my plans, because I will not tell her what we plan to do."

"Be ready, my love, because we are committed now." He glanced back at the bed. "We may not see this place again for some time."

"But we will keep it?"

He kissed her. "Forever. This is where everything started."

Chapter 8

Helena's heart beat uncomfortably as she gained access to her parents' house, but nobody took much notice of her entrance. They had accepted her story, it seemed. That story was her greatest risk and would continue so until the end of the week.

Up in her room, she ordered a change of clothes and then set to composing the letter from Mary. Pleased to note her old skill came back to her, she penned a letter pleading for Helena's attendance in Devonshire. She added a caveat, saying the local aristocrat was holding a ball and asking her to request her mother's attendance.

To her shock, her mother agreed with little demur. "Sir George will be here when you return," she said. "A little waiting will do him good."

Did Sir George need to be brought up to the mark? But Helena felt safe from him now. They could never marry, because she was already married.

How long before she could call herself Lady Alconbury? Would she ever use that name?

Not that she cared overmuch, because she had the man inside the grand titles and fine clothes. Tom—she had him. She had never asked him why he didn't use his first name, Charles. She liked that he had two names. Tom seemed a much more private individual, the man deep inside all the wrappings, and only she had him.

She could not even begin to imagine her father's reaction if she told him she'd married the son of his bitterest enemy. Julius she could never tell. His personal animosity to the Dankworths exceeded even his father's.

Events spun out of control after that. Sharman commenced packing. Helena did not intend to keep her long. Certainly not to accompany her far on her journey.

Her parents were complacent and her brother far too busy coping with his own problems to concern himself too much with Helena's sudden journey. He only commented that the notion was a good one, and he would try to stop their mother continuing with her matrimonial plans, since Sir George was obviously not the man for her.

Standing in the hall of the house she might not see for a long time, facing her beloved brother, Helena was overcome with emotion. She flung her arms around his neck and hugged him close, ignoring his protests about his lace and his new waistcoat.

Laughing, he gave in and hugged her back. "You're a goose, but I love you."

She loved him too, but the words reminded her of the last time she said them, and how soon it would be before she said them again.

Tom would meet her on the road and take her to his yacht on the coast. Then they would become Mr. and Mrs. Fisher, a gentleman and his wife, spending time abroad to develop his business. The stories they had concocted lying in bed came to life, and what had begun with laughter and lovemaking was becoming all too real.

Julius helped her into the crested coach that was to take her to Devonshire. She had two footmen, two drivers, a maid, and an older lady who was to ensure Helena did not speak to anyone she did not want to, and that the unworthy didn't approach her. She had been terrified that Augustus would offer to escort her, but that fear passed and she was embarking on what her mother regarded as a perilous adventure. "We should add more outriders." There were already two.

Helena assured her she would be completely safe. She had begun to wonder how she could get her luggage away, but if she did not, so be it. She would order one of the footmen Tom brought with him to do it.

She set off, listening to the chatter of her maid, nodding at regular intervals, but letting her mind drift elsewhere. They changed horses, and then they stopped to eat, and then set off again.

Eventually night fell and they stopped for the night. Tom would collect her here. Excitement built inside her.

* * * *

Tom tore through the preparations for his elopement. He longed to claim Helena, to take her to the snug little property in the Languedoc, which he had bought on impulse three years ago and neglected to inform his family about. How fortunate that was, almost as if he were planning for a future he had not envisioned then. He adored Helena. No matter who her family was. He was not marrying them, he was marrying her. No, he had married her.

He could not feel anything but pure delight that he'd claimed her, although occasionally he wondered what devil had entered him that he had suggested the scheme to her. In the privacy of his chambers he admitted to himself that panic had pushed him forward. That, and a powerful need to possess her, to prevent anyone else from taking her from him. Her parents could have her married in a trice, but not if she was married already.

He told his father that now the prince had gone, he would leave for the country. "I will visit an old friend and then come up to the house in time to meet our guests." As usual, his father had arranged a large house party to fill their sprawling country house for Christmas and the new year. His grandmother was engaged in the arrangements, leaving Tom free to make his own more secretive plans. He wanted nothing to trouble her, once he had his wife in his keeping.

The day before his departure his father demanded his presence in the study.

His father was pacing the floor, never a good sign. He tossed a note at Tom. "What is the meaning of this?" His voice rose to a bellow.

Tom did not flinch. He had put up with his father's ill moods too many times to allow the bluster to concern him now. Probably a bill or some scheme of his brothers.

He opened the paper and froze. The handwriting was Helena's.

"I hear and obey," she said, in unmistakable reference to the marriage ceremony. "I will hold my breath until we meet again."

She had not signed it, of course. He could pass it off as a note from a mistress. His father would know no better.

"Well, boy?"

His father never called him "boy" these days, ever since Tom had proved to him that he was a man. The first time he had beaten his father in a sword fight, just after Culloden, his father had given in. In those days they had practiced regularly, in preparation for the Stuarts' arrival.

Something had passed from father to son with that event, and ever since, the duke had not called him a child. What had happened to make him use the name now? Tom detested it, and his father knew as much.

"I fail to see what has disturbed you in this note." He managed a sneer. "A letter from a mistress should not disturb you so much, Papa."

"A mistress? Is that what she is?" The duke's face tensed, his already spare features gaining the aspect of a corpse. "Tell me you have not taken that step!"

"Why?"

The duke's eyes narrowed. "Do you know who she is?"

What was he supposed to say to that? Tom tried a shrug.

His father gave a "Pah!" Of exasperation. He strode to his desk, the fashionably full skirts of his coat whirling. "I had thought you less foolish. Look at this!"

Seizing another piece of paper, he gave it to Tom. "Compare them."

Tom held a letter, a chatty missive, one woman to another. He recognized the writing immediately. "Where did you get this from?"

"Does it matter? I have a collection of them. Know thine enemy is a good legend to live by. You know I do my best to comply with that. Would it be so strange that I would recognize the writing?"

Unfortunately, in neither letter had Helena used the schoolroom formal copperplate everyone was taught. The handwriting she used in her more informal moments was far more distinctive, backward-slanting, with circles over the I's instead of dots. She had not needed to sign the note she'd sent to Tom, the note he had not seen until this moment. The writing proclaimed the writer.

"You opened my private correspondence?" Tom demanded. "You dared to do that?"

His father shrugged. "It arrived with a number of other things. I opened it because I thought it was for me. But I have not had a mistress for some time, and if I did, I would not look in that direction." He passed his hand over his forehead and pinched the bridge of his nose, as if a headache was forming there. "What are you thinking of, to imagine that Helena Vernon would want you?"

"She does," he said without thinking, desperate to deny their attraction to each other.

"It is not possible."

"Why?" Tom demanded. "What is this rivalry? We no longer expect the Stuarts to accede, do we? He was courting us this time. That was what the prince's visit meant. He will do what we command, as long as we continue to support him. So what quarrel do we have left with the Emperors?"

"The Vernons," his father corrected him. "The rest of the clan can go hang as far as I'm concerned. The Vernons are different. But first, tell me, please. Is this a plan of some kind? Do you think to embarrass them in some way?" Eagerness sharpened his features.

Tom shook his head. "I would rather reconcile with them. We need to progress, Father, and for that, we need neutrality. If we cannot reconcile, toleration would work better. We have more in common with the Vernons than we have differences."

In business and in the management of the country they had much in common. They were loyal to Britain, but in different ways. Could he make his father understand? Guilt bore down hard on him when he realized how much he would hurt his father. But what else could he do?

His father paced again, passing before the window and back twice before he spoke again. "You cannot become involved with her under any circumstances. Even if we reconcile, if we eat at the same table, we cannot grow any closer."

He favored his son with a sharp stare. "It is time you knew. I had hoped to spare you this, but there is no hiding the truth now."

He waited until his father spoke again.

"Do you remember what your mother and I did after our wedding?"

Tom nodded. "You went to visit King James in Rome and pledge your allegiance."

"Do you know why we stayed so long?"

The answer to that seemed self-evident. Tom shrugged.

"Because the child your mother was expecting was not mine."

Shock rocked Tom. He'd been born in Rome, his parents' first child. He spread his legs, making his stance firmer, in case he staggered. Light-headedness threatened to fell him, but he refused to give into it.

Flinging his hand out, he found purchase on the sideboard that stood by the window. That was the only sign of weakness he would allow. His vision cleared and he met his father's gaze. "Explain."

The duke nodded. "Your mother had an affair, and her family were keen to hush the matter up. The father of the child refused to acknowledge it. We were not in a position to argue. In 1720 we were barely holding on to the dukedom."

Tom was not surprised at that. It had been that way for most of the century.

His father paced and then turned to face Tom. Tom studied him with new eyes. If his father was telling the truth, he could see cracks of light in the problem. Surely if his father could prove his allegations, he could disinherit him? Or could he? His grasp of the finer legal matters was not strong in this case, but why should it be? He had never had cause to question it before.

Tom had assumed the family resemblance, but they did have differences. He was dark, like his father—his father?—with the same olive-toned complexion, but that covered differences in eye color, shape, and the shape of the face and mouth.

He was already assuming the duke was telling the truth. He jerked his chin. "Carry on."

The duke crossed to the massive desk and unlocked a drawer, pulling out a few papers. He lifted his gaze. All Tom saw in his father's expression was unutterable sadness. "I wanted the consummation to be special and precious, so I elected to wait until Rome, until after we had the Pope's blessing, and then the King's. Once she had recovered from her travel sickness, I planned—" He waved in dismissal. "It matters little now. We were in Rome for a month before we saw the Pope, but that night, I went to her. I was young, in love, and I could not wait any longer to claim my bride. It was then that she told me she was expecting."

Tom's shock was reflected in Northwich's eyes as he shared his misery. But he remained on his guard. He would not allow anything until he knew more. Had his mother lied? A child could be a month early, or even late, and still be accepted.

"I had to think of the title and the future," he said. "I left Rome. I ordered it given out that I was on a mission for the King, and it is true. He found work for me so I did not have to face my bride, her body swelling with a child that was not mine."

"Without…?"

The duke nodded. "Without consummation." So coldly put, but what a terrible decision to make!

With his newfound love came new understanding. He could accept that his father took his mother back, even after her betrayal. Perhaps he was not the child. Some alteration of dates? "But you loved my mother."

"I could do nothing else but love her. The original plan was for her to bear the child, and then we would find someone to foster it. I could not accept a child not of my get for my heir."

"Did the child die? Did you father another?" He was grasping at straws now.

His father met his gaze head on. He shook his head and that small gesture made all Tom's wild suppositions die. "The King persuaded me to change my mind." He was not speaking of the King at St. James's Palace. He meant James III, who was then, as now, in residence in Rome. "After the child was born, he called me to his presence. He begged me to take the baby and acknowledge it as my own. Society in Rome knew your mother was pregnant, and so if we returned without a child, gossip would ensue. Rome was as full of Englishmen on the Grand Tour as it is now, and although we did our best to conceal her condition, we were unsuccessful. Moreover, your mother was heartbroken at the notion of leaving the child behind."

He paused and pushed two pieces of paper across the desk. "And he paid me."

Those words dropped like poison into Tom's heart. He stepped forward and read the first paper. It was a receipt for the payment of a staggering sum of money into the Northwich account. Although the donor was unnamed, the dates were exactly right. They coincided with a week after his birth date.

The second paper was in his mother's hand, likewise signed and dated.

"I hereby declare that the baby I bore a week ago was not fathered by my husband, the third Duke of Northwich, but by James, the fifth Duke of Kirkburton. The child is his get. I swear I will discuss the matter with no one, not even the boy I bore."

Tom read the short statement over again.

"I have several copies," his father said. "They are all accounted for. You may take that one, if you wish. The Kirkburtons were in Rome at the time on their own bride-trip. I did not see them, but plenty did. Including your mother."

"Why would you do this?" Tom said. He crumpled the paper in his fist, the implications pounding in the beat of his heart and the throb of the pulse in his temples. Forcing himself to retain his senses was the worst thing he had ever done.

"Because I loved your mother, and she loved you. And because I had an heir. You." He glanced away. "Before you were born, I had not fathered any other child. I was an enthusiastic lover to the mistresses I'd had, and I had begun to believe I was incapable."

"You were but twenty!"

"I had my first mistress at fourteen." His father bit out the words. "However, your mother proved me wrong. William, Edward, Chloe, and Emilia are undoubtedly mine. But by then the damage was done. You were my acknowledged son, and the Earl of Alconbury. All I could do was bring you up as mine and teach you well."

He could take no more. His face twisting in agony, Tom strode from the room.

In his chamber, he gave up the contents of his stomach.

Nothing mattered any more. He could not think or move without hurting. He refused to believe the calumny. How could what his mother had written be true? He could believe that his grandfather would snatch a woman from under the nose of his greatest rival and political enemy, but marry her off to his son?

His grandfather had died while his parents were still abroad. His death and the duties of the title had brought his father—the new Duke of Northwich—home with his bride. And the baby they claimed was their son.

He was the biological son of the Duke of Kirkburton.

He had made love with his sister.

The knowledge pounded through him, forcing him to face the horror of what they had done. If—if his father was telling the truth. He could not, surely. But that letter was undoubtedly from his mother. He'd know her writing anywhere. She taught him to read.

He could not tell Helena. The knowledge would destroy her. Rather than that, he'd let her believe she was the victim of a cruel trick. That would keep her away. He spent an hour composing the shortest, most terse message he had ever sent, ripping his heart out in the process.

He could not stay here, not with this hanging around his neck.

The notion of escaping seized him by the bollocks. Within ten minutes he'd shoved enough items into a bag to cope for a while. He paused in the middle of his room.

And his mother. His mother had confessed to his parentage. He stuffed the crumpled ball that was her letter into the bag with the rest.

Tom left the house without looking back.

* * * *

The landlord of the inn handed Helena a note.

"Dear Helena," it read.

"I have a confession to make. Our elopement was a scheme concocted by my father and myself. We meant to shame you and bring your name into disgrace. However on consideration I no longer wish to continue with the plan. I will not mention our recent affair and I will say nothing to bring your name into disfavor. I advise you to continue your journey to your friend's house, as you planned. I will not mention the affair or the sham marriage, as long as you do not do so.

"I regret the damage to your good self. That is entirely the reason for my change of heart."

He had signed it with his initials.

Underneath, scrawled in the same hand, but much more untidily, there was a postscript.

"I will always stand your friend."

Her world fell apart.

* * * *

After a week Helena could manage a day without crying. By the time she reached Mary's, she could plead a nasty head cold. The duenna her mother had hired had not said a word about her condition, or the way she spent most of the journey to Devonshire sobbing into a handkerchief. Either she did not care or she assumed Helena was being sent away after a scandal. Helena didn't care which reason she believed as long as she was left alone.

Mary welcomed her, cosseted her, and teased her back to health. At the end of two weeks, Helena knew she had lost a part of herself, a part she would never get back.

And she was married. A clandestine marriage she could tell nobody about. He said it was a sham—she would ensure that for herself. Otherwise the Dankworths had a sword over her head that they could drop any time they chose. Interrupt any wedding she cared to engage in.

But that man, the man she'd shared a bed with, the man who had told her more about himself than he had anyone else. Or so he said. She was not such a fool—was she? Sitting in the pretty room overlooking the ocean, Helena dreamed about catching one and forgetting everything else. Taking a ship to the other side of the world, where nobody knew her and she could start again.

After another week, she stopped looking.

Mary invited Helena to join her at a nearby assembly. Helena laughed for the first time in weeks, surprising herself. She hadn't been aware one could laugh with a broken heart, but the feat was entirely possible.

She would never heal, but she had covered up her wound, scabbed it over. The scar would always remain, though.

At home the next day, Helena picked up a piece of embroidery that Mary had abandoned and found solace in it. She was creating once more. She made a bunch of violets in the corner of a runner and discovered a distraction from her pain.

Late autumn sunlight streaked over the oak table in the center of the room, making the old wood glow. The scent of furniture wax rose, and she went straight back to the morning after her marriage, when the sun warmed her back and the scent of spent candles wreathed around them.

She pushed the thought away, but the faint memories of the perfumes were harder to dismiss.

The doorbell clanged. Of course, this was early afternoon, the time for visiting, but she had no idea anyone was planning to arrive. Sounds in the hall heralded the visitors, but like the lady she was, she waited. When a masculine voice cut through the general chatter, she sprang to her feet, embroidery forgotten.

Julius entered the room in full command, as always, but he was on edge. She felt it rather than saw it, the nervous energy her brother always emitted when he was on high alert. Had he heard or discovered what she had done?

Her stomach tight, her heart beating hard, she forced herself to remain still. Her brother gave her a perfunctory bow. "I'm sorry to interrupt your visit, Helena, but I need you."

"What is it, Julius? What's happened?"

He surged forward and took her hands. "Caroline is dead. I have a fractious motherless baby at home. Please come back with me. I'm at my wit's end."

Part 2

Chapter 9

1755

"I cannot fathom why she isn't married yet."

"She's too proud for anyone. Too rich, as well."

Helena smiled as she passed the chattering group of ladies sitting by the dance floor, but her smile was tinged with bitterness. Even her family had taken to saying that, and at five-and-twenty she was nearly on the shelf. Her mother still wanted Helena to return home. Except that Julius's house was more home to her than the Abbey or the Vernon's London residence.

What would they say if they knew that today was the fifth anniversary of her wedding to Tom Dankworth, Lord Alconbury?

They'd probably call her mad. On her worst days she would agree with them, but she had cultivated her mask of quiet serenity so well that the "proud" epithet was often the one attached to her name.

A gentleman blocked her path—Lord Everslade, an earl from the north who had taken a particular interest in her. Not a passionate man, but he was friendly, handsome, and wealthy. Helena did not look for passion or love any more. She would happily settle for friendship. "Would you do me the honor of dancing the next set with me, my lady?" His smile revealed deep indents either side of his mouth.

Charmed, she laid her hand on his arm. "I would be delighted."

He led her on to the floor, where they joined the other couples preparing for the country dance. "London is growing more full every September," she remarked lightly. "I have no idea why."

"We live in interesting times," the earl said. "Also, many find the dearth of young, marriageable females a refreshing change."

She laughed. "They flood in every April, secure their prizes, and join the throng of matrons. But yes, I know what you mean. Their enthusiasm can sometimes be tiresome. I would have thought a gentleman like you would have enjoyed their presence. Fresh and nubile."

"And full of nonsense," he said, as the four-piece orchestra struck up for the dance. They played a country air Helena had heard many times over the last five years. "I prefer someone with a more mature attitude."

He gave her a meaningful look, and then, thank heaven, they parted in the dance and she moved on to her next partner. Lord Everslade was becoming far too blatant in his hints. He might be seeking an interview with her soon. The devil of it was that she was growing to like him. Most of her suitors did not interest her in the least. The love of her life had come and gone, but he'd left her with a legacy she could not overcome.

She was married to a man who all but ignored her in public and refused to meet her in private. They had to do something about their predicament. A divorce was impossible, since the procedure was so public, but if she was to give herself to another man, she needed proof of what Tom had told her that fateful day five years ago. That their marriage was invalid.

Thinking of her husband would not help. She had a copy of her marriage lines tucked away in a secret compartment in her jewelry chest, together with a key for a house in Folgate Street, which she had not visited in five years, and a signet ring with a carved ruby set in gold.

She needed to draw a line under her past, and for that, she needed to face the man she still called husband.

Helena moved by rote, every movement practiced and honed over the years. She'd moved to live with a newly widowed Julius, and except for a few times when her mother had tried to drag her back home, she continued to do so. On the whole, Julius preferred to live in London, but this last summer he'd gone to the country and had only returned this month to execute some business. Business that concerned her.

Julius was about to give Helena an annuity, enough to make her independent. Oh, she was worth a fortune, but she could not touch any of it. Her portion would not be available to her until she married. Five years ago, distress had scattered her mind and she could do nothing but force her mask into place and face the world with a smile.

Behind the mask she was numb and had remained so for at least a year.

By then Tom had reappeared in society, and she went into another spiral, until she pulled herself firmly out of it. Her mother unwittingly helped when she declared that as the unlovely daughter, Helena would become her support in her old age. Fighting that fate gave her a reason to continue, as did helping to care for baby Caro, Julius's acknowledged daughter.

As she turned in the dance, she caught a glimpse of a familiar dark head among the sea of powdered wigs. Tom had taken to wearing his own hair, in some kind of obscure defiance, to what, she did not know. Annoyingly, her heart quickened, until she took a few deep breaths to get it back under control.

The smile she cast on her partner when they came together again was probably brighter than it should have been. Lord Everslade's response was a smile as broad as hers.

After the dance, he offered her his arm. She laid her fingers on it, just so, and turned her full attention on to him, since Tom was glowering at her on the other side of the dance floor. "Could you take me to the supper room?"

His lordship moved closer, speaking quietly. "I have a better idea. You seem in need of a rest, my dear, and I wish to speak to you."

"Ah." Better get this over with. His green eyes twinkled with good humor. In other circumstances she would have been glad of his interest. "Very well."

They were in one of the few remaining mansions in London, which meant there was an abundance of small rooms where he could take her.

As they went outside, the realization struck Helena with the force of a hammer. They were in the same house where she'd first kissed Tom. And if she was not mistaken, Lord Everslade was taking her to the same room.

Perhaps finally she could kill all her hopes stone dead. Do what she should have done five years ago and refused a man's suit. It would serve as a reminder of what she should do, rather than what her impulses had led her to do.

Lord Everslade left the door slightly ajar, a gentlemanly thing to do. They could claim they were not alone, and in any case, she was old enough to claim a little leeway to society's strictures. She was hardly a newly brought out girl, fresh from the schoolroom.

His lordship led her to the sofa set in the center of the room and plucked her fan from her grasp. "Allow me," he said gently. "It is hot for September, is it not?"

"With the added heat of a hundred candles." She smiled as he wafted the fan in the perfect way, sending a cool breeze over her cheek and neck. "That feels so good."

"Then I dare not stop. Maybe I should apply for the position of your fan-holder."

What a lovely way to propose. "Perhaps you should." The least she could do was to hear him out and be as gracious as she could.

"Lady Helena, you cannot be unaware that I admire you enormously."

She turned to face him, pasting an expression of interest on her features. "I am aware of that, yes, but I'm not a coxcomb, my lord. I do not immediately assume that every man who speaks to me is interested in more."

"It is one of the things a man most admires in you." He continued to waft the fan, but lowered it and changed the angle somewhat. It meant he could gaze into her eyes without the sparkling edge of the fan interfering with their vision. "I have come to admire you more. My lady, this is not the place, but may I call on you in the morning for a private interview?"

His consideration charmed her. To reappear at a ball with a new fiancé at her side would be exceedingly gauche. To steal the attention of everyone present was not the behavior of someone well-versed in the way society conducted itself. Such a shame she would have to refuse him. "You will be wasting your time, my lord. I cannot say that you will achieve your aim."

"Then I will hope to persuade you." He moved closer, his lips parting.

Surely he did not mean to kiss her! If they were discovered thus, their engagement would be considered a reality. Perhaps he hoped for that. Helena prepared to move away. He could keep the fan and return it to her tomorrow.

"Am I intruding?" The dark, devilish voice breaking into her quandary held a note of sardonic amusement.

Helena snapped her head around to face her nemesis. "I fear you are, sir." She had not seen Tom so close for...years. A few lines were graven deeper into his face, but he had that same air of dark detachment that had drawn her five years before. He kept to his dark clothes, adding to the demonic air he cultivated so well these days.

Tom leaned against the wall next to the door and folded his arms. "I would have my turn speaking to the lady in private."

"I will not leave you," Lord Everslade assured her.

"Leave, or I'll throw you out," Tom said. "I wish for a few private words with my...friend."

The pause before the last word gave what he said connotations that made Helena even hotter than before. The threat was implicit. He would not call her "friend" next time.

Lord Everslade got to his feet and deliberately stood before her, blocking her view of him. "I think not, sir. I know the history of your family and hers."

"Who does not?"

She could still see him, if she leaned ever so slightly to one side.

Tom cocked a brow. "However, I don't mean any harm to the lady. I have a message for her, that is all."

"If this were tomorrow, I would have the right to knock you across the room."

Lord Everslade sounded thrillingly threatening. But Helena could not see trouble of that kind caused.

"And you wish me to be the talk of the ball now?" she said acidly. "I am perfectly safe with this man, my lord. For all his faults, he knows how to behave like a gentleman."

Reluctantly, and rather cravenly, his lordship returned her fan to her and left.

Tom closed the door.

"You shouldn't do that," she said.

"Maybe, but we need to talk." He kicked away from the wall, probably leaving a scuff on the silk wallpaper. He glanced around. "They've changed the decorations in this room since we were last here. Pity, I preferred it as it was." He strolled toward her but halted when she held up her hand. "You would not have done that once."

"I trusted you once," she said bitterly.

He sighed. "Yes, you did. I deserve that and every other calumny you choose to heap on my head."

"Was it you?" she said abruptly. If she had no other chance of speaking to him, there were a few things about him that puzzled her.

"Was what me?" He regarded her closely, hungrily.

"Have you been helping Julius recently?" In his fight against the Stuarts, her brother had found some help from an unusual source. Nobody knew why—except, perhaps, Helena. Was it for her he'd done this?

"Ah." His face cleared. "Perhaps. Your brother is probably aware of what small aid I can render him."

"Why would you do that?"

"If you think back, I told you once."

She never thought back. The memories hurt too much. "I daresay you did, but if you did so, I have forgotten. Besides, times have changed, have they not?" Since she had nobody to waft her fan for her, she did it herself. His lordship was right. The room was stiflingly hot, and the fire was not even lit.

"They have, in many ways." Pushing back the skirts of his heavy gold-laced dark blue evening coat, Tom stuck his hands in his breeches' pockets. "Not least of which is the revelation that King James was married to another woman before his official marriage that produced Princes Charles and Henry. That kind of secret?"

She had not been aware that he knew for sure. "You have proof?"

"My father does. But you are also aware that he wants to discover one of the children, especially a female, and marry her to either William or myself."

That was news to her. "He does?"

"Your brother knows." He shook his head. "I have no wish for it."

"Not to mention that you are already married." She had not meant her tone to be so acidic, but there it was. She felt that way, so why not articulate it?

His slumberous eyes opened wider. "That was a fraud." His voice gained a harsh edge.

"No it was not. I went to the Fleet and obtained a copy of the certificate. I have it still."

"So that's why you haven't married?" He laughed harshly and turned away, striding to the end of the room and back.

God help her, she still wanted him. She gazed over his legs and those broad shoulders, under which she had reason to know very little padding lay.

"We are not married, Helena. I told you in my note."

"You lied."

He shook his head and gazed up at the ceiling, as if to find the answer written there. "God, you're a stubborn woman! I say we are not. I can prove it, too." He paused and gazed at her.

She met his eyes steadily, but after a minute, she glanced away, tears choking her throat.

"Don't cry." His voice had softened.

"I have no intention of crying." She swallowed. "You used me badly. I will not forgive you for that."

"I had very good reasons."

"Then tell me what they were." Once the first numbness of her grief had passed, Helena had wondered why. The answer that he was the best actor in the world and set out to fool her did not ring true. When she could bear to do it, she thought back and recalled their times together. Not even Garrick was that good an actor.

Then when she heard rumors that he was helping her brothers and cousins discover the poor unfortunate but legitimate children of the Old Pretender, she had wondered even more. Was it for her, or for himself? Of course if his father wanted him to marry one of the children, that would explain much. The Emperors were hunting them down to keep them safe and prevent civil unrest. With the death of Prince Frederick, only the old King, who was getting frailer every day, and a young boy stood between the Stuarts and the throne. With the military option closed to them, they fell back on their first love—scheming. "Tell me!"

When she looked at him again, he appeared stricken. They stared at one another for a few seconds, or maybe it was minutes, before he said, "You deserve to know. You need to know if you are to move on. Come to the house tomorrow."

"I'm fully engaged tomorrow."

"Then the day after. At eleven in the morning."

A sob came unbidden to her when she recalled that was their time before. Too early for most of society to be about, but not unusually early. Just right. Those precious weeks when she'd thought he loved her and they would work out their problems, when she thought he wanted to be with her as much as she wanted to be with him.

"You still have the house?"

"I do. I didn't have the heart to sell it or rent it out. It's still there, the same as ever. Will you come? I will bring the proof you need. Then maybe I can convince you to move on with your life. I will not hurt you. I swear it."

Not in that house. That place was sacred to them. He would have met her somewhere else if he'd meant harm. How she knew that she could not tell, unless it was the stricken look she'd seen briefly on his face before he'd smoothly covered it up.

The thought of setting foot inside those doors terrified her, but she would not show it now. "So you think I'll come when you crook your finger?" She tossed her head. "You leave me alone for five years and then assume I'll come running? You should know me better than that."

His eyes gleamed. "We have so little to do with each other."

"Exactly." Why she kept the key to the house, together with a few other treasures she did not know. She would return them by messenger. If that was done, then she should cut all ties.

"Except you are not a stranger to me, are you, Helena?" He paced the room. She had a clear path to the door now, if she wanted it.

"I'm a society stalwart, a wealthy spinster," she said. "I am content."

He shook his head. "You are still a lovely young woman, eminently marriageable. And an heiress." His smile turned sardonic. "I do not intend to abduct you any more than I did five years ago. I hardly need the money."

"I know." He was richer than before, a mixture of wise investments and working to improve the estates having paid off tenfold. His very clothes tonight proclaimed his prosperous state. They might be plainer in style than those worn by many of the other gentlemen present, but they were very fine, and his buttons were diamonds set in gold.

"Except that I am not. I am wife to a man who refuses to come within three feet of me."

"I know that, too." His voice lowered, almost tender. He walked around the sofa to look at her. The arrogant sarcasm had gone, leaving utter sadness in its wake. "I told you. We are not married. You must move on, my l—lady."

For one heart-stopping moment she thought he was going to say "my love."

"The cleric was a real one, and the certificate is true. We entered our names in the correct book." Getting to her feet with a rustle of silk and a graceful movement she had taken hours to perfect, she tapped her closed fan in the palm of her other hand. "There is little you can say that will change those facts. And while I am bound to you, I cannot in all good conscience bind myself to another."

"There is a reason, Helena. A good one."

"Then tell me."

"Come to the house."

She laughed harshly, and raised her fan as if to strike him. She lowered it with great care and flicked it open, examining the spangles and lace confection as if for the first time. "No. I want at least one memory to remain intact."

"Where, then?"

"Here, now?" She stuck up her chin defiantly. "Just say it."

Impatiently he shook his head, his hair gleaming in the candlelight like a raven's wing on fire. "No time. What I have to tell you cannot be explained in a few minutes and brushed aside. But we are not married."

"I expect you will find poor Reverend Clegg and kill him and then destroy the book. You are aware that both acts are against the law?"

"I have done worse," he murmured, as if to himself. "I—" He turned away from her abruptly, his coat brushing the silk of her dress.

As if he had touched her, she flinched.

"This is not over. I will seek an interview with you any way I can." On reaching the door, he glanced back at her. "We are not married."

With that last rejoinder, he left.

Chapter 10

Perhaps she should not have been so hasty to reject his request for an interview. For days after their meeting at the ball Helena waited on tenterhooks, jumping at every clang of the doorbell, every knock at her bedroom door.

She went down to breakfast two days after the incident to find her brother and his wife at table. Julius did not release Eve's hand but brought it to his lips and kissed it before restoring it to her.

Her brother was in love. Deeply and sincerely. His feelings for Eve made his previous marriage appear an adolescent dream, the impulsive and wild connection of two adventurers. Only when she saw him with the lovely Eve did Helena realize how wrong Caroline had been for him.

Flushing, Eve applied herself to her breakfast while Julius stood and courteously held Helena's seat for her. She took her place awkwardly. Since Julius had returned from his country house with his bride she had felt more out of place than ever before. Sipping her tea, she watched them. They were perfect together. Although Eve was from relatively humble origins, scarcely a bride for a great lord, anyone seeing them together could not doubt the rightness of the match. Her heart ached, and almost without thinking she suppressed the reminder that she had nearly attained a love match of her own.

"I have been looking at properties by the Thames," she said brightly.

Julius smiled at her. "It is time, is it not? Helena, if you are determined to live your life single, you should have somewhere to call your own. We may employ a woman or find a relative for you to make you respectable."

Helena raised her gaze to the ceiling and sighed. "Ah, the necessity of a duenna! But nobody from the family, please. Just remember the problems you had finding a companion for me before! I will choose my own this time."

Julius chuckled. "Indeed you have a point. I do not have the knack, it seems, of finding nannies and duennas. Yet one more thing I have to thank my wife for." He said "wife" with such fondness, he might as well have said "love" and been done with it. "She has found a treasure of a nanny. The woman knows how to keep Caro in order without disruption and without upsetting my darling."

"You just have to ask the right questions," Eve said smoothly. She exchanged a laughing glance with Helena. "I can help you, if you wish."

"I'd appreciate that." Eve had a great deal of common sense. Helena would appreciate her aid, although the necessity struck her as sad. "Do you think Mother will accept my decision?"

"Not immediately," Julius said. "She will appeal to your conscience, to your sense of rightness and your position. She will say you will disgrace the family."

Those arguments sounded sadly familiar. "I will not give in. I cannot decline into a companion. She'll have me knitting shawls for the poor next. And she'll dress me in the drabbest, most unbecoming clothes possible. I still remember the night of one ball." She shuddered, recalling the doll-like makeup. "She sent a maid who made me look like a puppet. I scrubbed it off."

"Why would she do that?" Eve exclaimed.

"Because she always wanted Helena to be her personal slave," Julius said grimly. "I hadn't quite realized it then, but she always had that aim." He clasped Eve's hand once more, as if he couldn't bear not touching her. "Helena, I know this is your decision, but did you not feel the least amount of fondness for Everslade? Or for any of the men who have taken you in favor? I cannot help but think that you'd be better if you could find a man who would suit you."

He put that very delicately. As the heir to the dukedom, Julius could have compelled her marriage to a likely candidate. He had done the opposite, but Helena did not have to be a soothsayer to understand what he wanted now. To be alone with his family, so he could have intimate breakfasts with his wife and play with his daughter. "I daresay I will find someone. I'm not exactly in my dotage." Her laugh sounded artificial even to her own ears.

"You never know. It might come upon you all at once," Eve said, shooting her husband a glance. "As it did with me. In the course of one afternoon, my life changed. How much I didn't know until later."

"I did," Julius said quietly.

"You said you did." Eve picked up her china tea-dish and took a sip. "That tastes strange. Does your tea taste strange, Helena?"

Helena sipped her own brew. "Not at all. Perhaps you should change the dish. They might have left some cleaning salt in it."

"Yes, that will be the reason." But Helena pushed her dish and saucer away. "I've had sufficient for now. Will you be ready after breakfast?"

Helena racked her brain. Damnation, this was Thursday, which meant she'd promised to go shopping with Eve. "Give me fifteen minutes to find a hat and gloves, and I'll be with you."

Eve shot her husband a mischievous glance. "Helena has promised to show me her favorite milliner. She has an establishment at the far end of Bond Street."

"Not at all fashionable," Helena said. "But she has a startling gift for matching the woman to the hat. I've selfishly kept her secret until now, but I fear once she sees Eve, it will all be over. Everyone will be clamoring for one of her hats."

"So not expensive?" Eve had spent her early years as the daughter of a cleric's widow, scratching for every penny. She never made any secret of her humble origins, although Julius saw to it that few people asked her. She had come into a mysterious fortune, which made her eligible in the world's eyes. Helena suspected the mysterious fortune had come from her brother's coffers, but she never asked. It was not her concern. She had one of her wishes, in that her brother was blissfully happy with a woman he adored. Her other wishes would never come to fruition, but at least she had one happy outcome to show for her prayers.

Five years ago, she had sworn to herself that she would not repine, that she would make the most of what she had, which was a great deal when all was said and done. For the most part she'd stuck with her resolve. One day perhaps that pain deep inside her that leached her heart and her spirit would disappear.

Downstairs in the hall, she fussed with her broad-brimmed hat, tilting it this way and that, deciding which she preferred when she heard Eve's amused, "You cannot disguise your beauty, Helena, however hard you try."

She turned around, her skirts swishing around her. "Mother always says that Lucinda is the beautiful one."

Busy putting on her gloves, Eve said drily, "Your mother lies. I suspect she does not see her untruths as such though, merely ways of getting what she wants."

Helena found discussing her mother in such frank terms refreshing. "You married Julius so quickly, she did not have a moment to object. By the time she got wind of your union, the deed was done."

Eve gave a particularly warm smile. "Yes, he insisted on it. I thought his reasons quite spurious, but when I met your formidable parent, I began to understand. She would have delayed the wedding as long as possible and thrown every rock she could find on the path. If it is not as she wishes it, then it does not happen."

With a guilty pang, Helena agreed with Eve. Surely a mother should be more than that. Even in her own family, there were examples of loving parents. For the most part, her father kept away from family discussions, but he was capable of putting his foot down, should he wish it, and he had in Julius's case. The duchess was remarkably reticent about Eve's humble origins, and Helena suspected her father had dealt with her in no uncertain terms.

He had never intervened between Helena and her mother. Would he, if she asked him? As she followed Eve out of the house to the waiting carriage she wondered on that. She should certainly talk to her father, even if she wasn't sure what she would ask him. She could hardly tell him of her clandestine and utterly foolish marriage.

She gave the footman a word of thanks as he helped her up and then frowned. "Have I seen you before?"

"No, my lady. I'm new to his lordship's employ."

His accent was faintly foreign, French or Italian maybe. He was tall, and met her eyes boldly, something she was not accustomed to with Julius's well-trained servants. Not that she minded them looking at her, but society had its code, and that was part of it.

The contact was brief, before he bowed and closed the carriage door.

The journey to Bond Street took a little time, as the weather had broken last night, and rain teemed down. Carriages jostled each other, and drivers yelled curses, while people hurried past, the women's skirts hiked up as much as was decent, the men hunching their shoulders, and all rushing at a pace that threatened to cause an accident.

Of course the urchins and beggars took no notice of the rain. They still darted between people, confusing some enough to pick their pockets and begging from others. "I wonder if they are as indigent as they look," Eve said.

"No." Helena had her brother to thank for the information. "Many are ragamuffins who make a fortune from their begging." She didn't tell the softhearted Eve that some even deliberately mutilated themselves or their children to garner more sympathy. Others would just bind their eyes and pretend to be blind or make a false peg-leg to wear at the end of a perfectly well-attached knee, strapping the top part of their leg out of sight. It was a wonder some were not permanently crippled by using that tactic. Of course the regular beggars were there too, the ones truly in want, but Helena had learned to be selective with her bounty.

They were in no hurry and the carriage was comfortable enough inside, newly upholstered in a soft green leather that did wonders for Eve. Helena loved how avidly Eve watched their passage, laughing at the more colorful expressions of the coach drivers they passed and noting places she might want to visit in the future. "You have much to experience, Eve, and you should enjoy every moment."

"Have you been coming to London all your life?"

She nodded. "Until I met you, I had not realized how much I took my visits for granted. Even before I made my come-out I visited. Some families will leave their children in the country, but our mother preferred to have us where she could keep us correctly supervised, as she put it." Even that did not hurt anymore, although her mother had used her children's proximity to play one child off against another. That was why Helena had never grown close to Lucinda. Her younger sister was always held up as an example of the perfect daughter, until Helena dreaded the name. And she should have been Gemina, her first name, not Lucinda, her second.

Helena did not have a second name.

"We used to go to Vauxhall for the fireworks, and we thought ourselves very grown-up." She smiled recalling her wonder at the colored lights and the parade of women, not all of them of the respectable kind. "Julius could always be relied upon to relate the greatest gossip."

Helena gave a crack of laughter. "I can imagine. He has not stopped with that. I discovered this shop last year, with our cousin's new bride. Viola is married to Marcus, the Earl of Malton. Like you, she's from the country. You'd like her, I'm sure. Julius takes a lot of people under his wing," she added, anxious to assure Eve that there had never been any of the attraction between Viola and Julius as there was between him and Eve.

But Eve, secure in the knowledge of her husband's love, only smiled. Her fondness warmed Helena. Even if she could never experience it for herself, there was nobody she would have wished happiness more than her beloved brother. "It's part of who he is. Not just Julius, but Lord Winterton, too." She turned to face Eve, but caught her sister-in-law's shoulder. "I'm so sorry," she said when she spotted Eve's wince. "Does it still hurt?"

"Hardly at all," Eve said. She had sustained a wound a few months ago, and Julius had used it as a reason to transport her to his private home in the country. Tellingly, their mother had never visited it. Only the people Julius loved were invited to stay at the small Oxfordshire manor house. "I have a wicked scar, though. I'm rather proud of it. And of how Julius behaved."

Nodding, fixing her smile in place, Helena glanced away. She preferred not to recall how closely Tom had worked with Julius at that time. For two men who hated each other, they had a lot in common, in this case, an overblown sense of chivalry. Tom had no designs on Eve, although Julius had suspected him of it. Only Helena knew why.

Tom was still protecting her, albeit from a distance. Perhaps the acts of kindness were his way of making amends. If that was so, it was not working.

They drew up outside the shop, the horses nickering their protest. They would have to stand in the rain for a while now. Fleetingly, Helena felt sorry for them, but considering their shining coats and the bills for oats that passed through Julius's hands, she was probably wasting her time.

The same footman handed her down and held a canopy over them to protect their delicate heads from the rain on the short passage from the carriage door to the shop.

After a pleasant hour selecting and ordering their confections, the women were ready to leave. A footman opened the door for them, bowing them out.

The rain had stopped, but outside the street was still damp. The sun was doing its best, but the heavy cloud cover prevented it from making much of a difference. Bond Street was the haunt of the fashionable. Across the street was the notorious fencing hall belonging to an Italian, Domenici, so several men were gathered outside as the ladies left the milliner's shop. The footmen were burdened with boxes and parcels, containing the purchases they had decided to take home with them.

Eve laughed merrily. "I had never thought to spend such a sum on mere hats and caps before. I daresay my father would have considered the expense sinful."

Eve turned her attention to someone standing behind her. Before she looked, Helena knew who it must be. She turned to face her suitor, her heart sinking.

"Lord Everslade."

He swept his hat from his head and bowed. "Ladies. Lady Winterton, Lady Helena, it's a delight to see you. I trust you are both well?"

"Indeed." Eve stood her ground and lifted her chin. "I will pass your best wishes to my husband."

"I wish you would." He glanced at Helena, his brief perusal chilling her in a way she didn't completely understand. "I'm anticipating our first dance after our wedding."

Now she understood. He was upset that she had refused to see him when he'd called yesterday. "I fear I cannot give you that assurance." He was not the first persistent suitor she had suffered, but he was the most blatant. "I'm sorry you misunderstood me when we spoke the other day."

"I think not."

When she glanced away, trying to break any suggestion of intimacy between them, she caught the eye of the last person she would have wished present today.

Tom was watching her closely, his body poised, as if he would spring across the street to save her.

She turned her attention back to her unwanted suitor. "If you wish, you may call on my brother. He will, I'm sure, help to clarify the situation."

"I did better than that," he said. "Your parents have newly arrived in town, and I took the opportunity to call on them this morning." Not even Helena had heard that yet. Had he set spies outside their residence? Her senses went on alert, the hair on the back of her neck prickling.

"My parents do not have jurisdiction over my movements, sir. I have turned twenty-one."

He smiled, as if indulging a child's pet. "I beg to differ, ma'am. One's parents are always the first to be consulted. Your father was surprised to hear of our engagement, and your mother was pleased."

"She was?" Helena would have doubted that. Everslade lived too far away for her mother to feel comfortable having her marry him. Unless she had come to some kind of agreement with him, which she would not put past the annoying man. He had been nothing but friendly, not at all persistent. What had changed?

Obviously she needed to consult with Julius. Accordingly, she stepped forward. "If you will excuse me, I am presently on my way to my brother's house."

His voice hardened when he said, "To quote your good self, I beg to differ." Simultaneously he nodded to the driver of a carriage that had drawn up in the middle of the road and snaked his arm around her waist, dragging her close.

What was he about to do, kiss her in public? She would bite him first.

Instead, he whisked her off her feet. Helena lost her breath, did not even have the time to cry out. What in damnation was going on? That was all she could think of as he leaped through the open door of the carriage and dropped her on the seat.

Almost instinctively she made for the far door, lunging at full-length to open it and escape the other side. But the handle refused to give, and

Everslade threw himself on top of her, grasping her wrist and wrenching it away. The door on the other side slammed closed, and the carriage jerked into motion.

He still lay over her, and as she opened her mouth to scream, he slammed his mouth on hers, grinding his teeth against her lips. She tasted blood, but he had her too closely bound for her to bite him. She cried out anyway, but he swallowed her sound.

The carriage spun around the corner, and Helena found herself praying the vehicle would overturn. It might shower her with splinters of glass but at least it would stop. Terror and panic rose to stun her, but she was too busy fighting to breathe to force herself back to rational thought.

Clenching her fists, she pounded them against his shoulders, but he gave no sign of having registered her protests. Instead, he took her hands and dragged them down, pushing them to the seat either side of her head.

He drew back, gazing down at her in possessive triumph. "Maidenly protests are all very well, but you will not have that distinction for long." He glanced down, to where her breasts were pressing against her fichu. "I can wait until tonight. I will not have our first night spoiled by the incessant jolting of a coach, my love."

Some semblance of rationality returned to her. "Do you often abduct women in the middle of the day?"

"I knew I'd chosen well," he said with satisfaction.

She would never like green eyes again.

He never took his gaze from her. "You have wit and intelligence as well as beauty. You will be the perfect countess."

"Not for you." Should she mention that she was already a countess? Albeit to an earl who refused to acknowledge her. That, she realized, would prevent any contract Everslade wanted her to enter into with him. But it wouldn't prevent any unpleasantness that would precede it.

Wait—they had changed the marriage laws. "We cannot marry, sir."

"We can and we will. We are heading for the border, my darling one." Oh, damnation!

She wanted to spit in his face, had even begun the preparations for it, but she swallowed instead. Everslade had a wild look in his eyes. Although she would certainly bear it in mind for later, if she needed it. "Please let me up."

"One more kiss." He suited his actions to his words and gave her another painful kiss before he drew away and lifted up far enough to look out the window. Spots danced before her eyes, and she fought to retain consciousness.

"Ah, we are making good progress." He heaved his body off hers.

Helena gasped in relief and lay there until her vision cleared and she could be sure of sitting up without fainting. When she did, he stretched out a hand to help her, but she pretended not to notice. Glancing out of the window, she assessed their position. They had reached Spitalfields market, and that was too far for her liking.

Her panic subsided and she began to think. "I'll need to stop and collect necessary items," she said calmly.

"I have everything you need. Do you think I would have done this unprepared?"

"Who made you consider this?"

He sat opposite her, which came as a relief, but he leaned forward and rested his arms on his knees, clasping his hands together. "Your father told me you were considering living independently and your mother deeply disapproves. So do I. You have no right to do that, to deprive me of the wife I want above all others. Your mother forbade the match outright. I cannot allow that. I want you too much."

Did he intend to be romantic? Because what he said sounded threatening. "You think you know better than I do?"

"Naturally." His brows shot up; he appeared surprised she would even ask. "Sometimes a man needs to take matters into his own hands. I took your parents' displeasure and your brother's defiance of them as my cue. I have made inquiries, and I discovered your parents' relations with their son are not as good as it should be. His impulsive marriage has offended your mother. I am of every expectation that they will reconcile, once we are happily married."

Anger simmered low in Helena's gut. She bit back her initial response in favor of hard thinking. The carriage doors were locked. When they stopped to change horses was her best chance of getting away, but he might not let her. Instead, she might have to wait until they stopped for the night. Was he mad enough to offer her violence?

Yes. Young and handsome he might be, but he showed a disturbingly autocratic attitude. He probably believed in whipping his spouse into submission. Her flesh flinched in instinctive reaction. Appealing to the various people she met along the way would not help, because they would depend for their pay on Everslade. "My lord, can we not achieve the same ends the traditional way?" He appeared to believe that children should obey their parents; perhaps he was as traditional in outlook.

"We could, but it would take much longer, and by then the rift between your relatives could be permanent."

"It already is," she said without thought. Anger rose to blind her. How dare this man even dream of doing this to her? How could he subject her to such indignities? "Our family problems are none of your concern, sir, nor will they ever become so. How dare you interpose yourself?"

He broke into her protestations with a roar. "Be quiet, madam! By God you will learn to obey me!" Half rising, he swung his hand back and brought it across her face, knocking her sideways.

Blood flooded her mouth so she could not talk properly, and involuntary tears of pain sprang to her eyes. She lay there, eyes closed, forcing herself into as high an alert as she could.

This man was mad, or not far off it. Sadly, not mad enough for anyone to consider admitting him to an asylum, which was where he should be residing. He was full of himself and no doubt accustomed to believing himself the center of the universe.

She must get away, and to do that, she had to keep her wits about her. It would kill her to do it, but she might have to comply with his wishes. But if she spent a night under the same roof as him, he would claim that as proof they were intimate, and on that basis, her reputation could be destroyed. She'd taken chances before, but that was her choice. Having that choice taken away would spell lifelong imprisonment.

She would not stand for that. She would kill herself before that happened.

Chapter 11

The flash of a sword told Tom what Everslade was about. He was across the road as soon as he saw that tiny nod to the carriage driver, who before that moment had only been lingering, rather than showing any evidence of being with any of the people on the street. Dodging oncoming horses and ignoring the alarmed yells that surrounded him on all sides, he had nearly come within reach of the carriage before the driver whipped up the horses and it careened off.

He did not mutter curses; he yelled them, but continued to move, tromping over the piles of horse dung and cobbles until he reached Lady Winterton and her astonished group of manservants.

As the coach nearly took the corner at the end of the street on two wheels, a flash of movement made him whip his head around. Tom showed his teeth in a vicious grin. At least some good had come of his lunge. He had slowed the coach down enough to mark it.

He had no time to lose. Racing to the side of the road, he issued orders rapidly. He pointed at a footman carrying a heap of parcels. "Drop them, run back to your master's house, and tell him what has happened." He would not announce the events in the middle of the street. Who knew who was listening? God knew rumors enough would be racing around the city without him adding to them.

He needed a horse. He had to get to her before nightfall, otherwise she was done for. What was the idiotic man doing?

Lady Winterton took her place in the carriage and Tom leaped in after her. "Believe me, ma'am, I mean you no harm. I will see you safely back in your husband's arms and I will tell him what I saw. We have to catch the ruffian before he does any permanent damage to Lady Helena."

She stared at him, wide-eyed. "I have learned you are no friend of his, but I have also learned to think for myself, and I go by deeds, not mere words. I do not forget the good turn you did us. I do not pretend to know why you did so."

He nodded his thanks. "For the same reason I do this now." Because, despite his efforts to forget her, to think of Helena as a sister, he was still as in love with her as ever. He had vowed never to repeat his sin, but that did not stop him recalling his happiness before the terrible discovery. Although not a particularly religious man, he found himself praying under his breath. He had faced adversity and danger before but never like this. Would his spirited Helena have the sense to play along with Everslade, and if he did, would she agree to marry him? Stranger things had happened. Had she already accepted him?

When they arrived at the house in Brook Street, a mere ten minutes later, he escorted Lady Winterton inside personally, ignoring the disapproval of the superior person who opened the door to them.

He was not surprised to find a shirt-sleeved Lord Winterton standing in the hallway. He glanced at Tom but said nothing yet.

His wife flew into his arms, letting loose the tears that she had held back until now. He drew her away into the parlor at the front of the house, overlooking the street. Tom remained behind in the hall to issue orders. "If his lordship has not said so, he will require two horses, saddled and ready. In five minutes."

The butler exchanged a doubtful look with the footman. "He only said one," the footman said.

Tom shook his head, thought, and then followed the Wintertons into the parlor, pushing past another man who tried ineffectively to bar the door. "We have little time to argue," he said, as his lordship opened his mouth to speak. "I will go in instant pursuit. You stay here and arrange your formidable troops to follow. Your wife needs you and you may need to consider other strategies. But we must reach her before nightfall, or she could be irreparably ruined."

"Why would I trust you?"

"Why would I wish Lady Helena harm?" Tom demanded. "For God's sake, man, I'm not asking for your trust, only that you believe I am capable of performing this task. I swear, I will turn her over to whichever of your relatives you send, and I know them all. But I am here, and I am ready to leave."

Winterton helped his wife on to a sofa. The redoubtable lady was already recovering, mopping her face and blowing her nose. "You should both go," she said. "It's obvious Everslade did not want me."

"Did she accept his proposal?"

Winterton narrowed his eyes. "What do you think? I advised her to think about it, because I'm an utter fool, but she was firm in her refusal. She did not want him."

"Well he has her now."

Winterton studied him, his startlingly vivid blue eyes unfocused, and then nodded. "Very well. I've ordered horses and a groom to accompany me, one I would trust with my life. He will go with you."

"So I have to watch my back?"

"Only if you do anything that might displease me. Take it or leave it. Otherwise, I will go. But if you go in pursuit, I can organize matters here. I have sent a runner to my cousins' houses and ordered a carriage made ready. When you find her, keep her somewhere safe and send word, if you can. I will send the carriage to you."

He jerked his head to a green riding coat laid over a nearby chair. "Take that. You are hardly dressed for riding."

One glance at the gleaming boots standing by the side of the chair told Tom that he and Winterton were approximately the same size. He lost no time thrusting his arms through the sleeves of the coat and stamping into the remarkably practical boots. He found a cocked hat under the coat and crammed it on his head. Once he'd emptied the pockets of his sadly stained and probably ruined town coat, he transferred them to the riding coat, where he found a welcome addition. He drew the pair of pistols from the deep pockets and gave them a cursory examination. They were exactly as he liked—primed and ready for action. He wore his dress sword, which he retained.

"If you need a stronger weapon, I have it," Winterton said.

"No need," Tom replied. "I order fancy hilts but serviceable blades." Shoving his hand into his breeches' pocket, he drew out a short sheathed blade.

"There is a hidden blade in the side of the right boot," Winterton said tersely. He strode to the window, where a small writing table stood, and plucked a quill from the inkstand. "Here are the horses," he said, glancing out of the window.

"I'll send word if I can. If not, I'll escort her ladyship back here. She's as safe with me as she would be with you."

The realization struck him with the force of a punch. By all that was holy, he was speaking with his own brother. Half brother, it was true, but they shared a father. Except that Winterton was as yet unaware of the fact. Tom could put it off no longer. He would have to tell Winterton, at least. But not now. Explanations would have their time.

He turned back at the door, his hand on the gilded knob. "If I cannot return tonight, I will send word. That is, if he has traveled farther. I advise you to give out that she is safely back home. We'll find a way to contrive the truth. But I will do everything in my power to reach her in time. I have a man with the carriage. He discarded your livery and leaped on to the back of the vehicle as it was moving. Since he is a man of great resource, I trust him to do everything possible to stay with it. If he sends a message here, you will know him. His name is Lamaire."

Ignoring Winterton's shout, Tom left the room and went outside to mount the very fine mare Winterton had kindly put at his disposal.

* * * *

Helena was becoming heartily bored with Everslade's company. Once she righted herself, she tucked her hands under her cloak and refused to talk to him. He chose to believe she was sulking and called her charming, before he launched into a monologue of his plans, and since she was disinclined to agree with him, a discourse on his own cleverness.

Helena concentrated on keeping her tongue between her teeth and marking where they were going. As she had presumed, he had everything she would need to eat, drink, and even relieve herself, although she would be damned before she did that in his company. Instead, she preferred to hold her water until she was near to bursting with it. But even then she would not relent.

He kindly gave her his handkerchief to clean her poor face. She had cut the inside of her cheek with her teeth from his vicious blow, but had taken no other harm, except for a split lip from his bruising kisses, which he fondly described as "passionate."

How she could have ever imagined him handsome she did not understand. Her only solace was that he did not touch her again and he did not force himself on her. She took stock of her poor weapons, which consisted of her shoe buckles, hairpins, and a small fruit knife that she carried in a sheath in her pocket.

Wit and reason were probably her best defenses. She would let him talk himself to a standstill, and then she would try to persuade him not to take such a rash course.

"My love, you will adore my house in Italy. Indeed, I have rarely visited it myself, but it is as if time stood still there. It is quaint, in the countryside, although close to Rome, and a perfect place to honeymoon."

Helena repressed her shudder and risked another glance out of the window. They were undoubtedly to take the Great North Road, which she considered very foolish for a man trying to escape London. It was the first place Julius would look.

Then the import of what he had just said struck her hard. "Rome?"

"We are doubling back and going to the coast. I have a vessel waiting for me. And you, as it turns out." He patted his pocket. "We have a fortune here, my dear. We will have a merry time of it." He bestowed a roguish smile on her. "With any luck, I'll have given you a bellyful of my heir by the time we see your family again." He frowned. "Do you not wish to speak at all? Do I have to take all the burden of conversation?"

"What about Northumberland?"

He paused. "I will write to my mother and inform her of our change in plans."

"Do you not wish to show me your home?" At least it would not involve leaving the country if she agreed to go to Northumberland.

"Indeed I do, but Italy is as dear to me as England."

Wait—from the research Julius had done, Everslade had never left the country. He had not even been on the Grand Tour, because his mother had insisted on him not leaving her alone. She remembered that distinctly, because she had considered the fact another mark against him. A clinging mother she could do without.

"Tell me about your home."

"Have you ever been to Northumberland?"

Yes. "No. If I am to live there, I'd like to know more." Her mouth stung every time she spoke, but she fought not to show it.

"Ah." He pressed his fingertips together. "It is a lovely county. The best, of course. The lakes are beautiful, and the mountains provide the frame for them. My house is nestled between two of the highest, sheltered from the winds. A perfect love nest, one might say."

She remembered the lakes and mountains, but the last time she'd visited the Lake District, it had been in Cumberland, Westmoreland, and Lancashire. Most definitely not in Northumberland, which was the other side of the country.

"I have never been that far north," she said, further perjuring herself. "I know shamefully little about that part of the country." Just in case he recalled that he was talking about the wrong county, she could feign ignorance, too. Was he testing her? No, she decided, he was not, because he appeared in perfect harmony, leaning back, smiling as if he'd won.

His volatility alarmed Helena. She had only ever met one other person with moods that could flash from high to low in an instant, combined with a shocking lack of awareness of doing so, and that was Caroline, Julius's first wife. Caroline had also shown a similar lack of understanding of other people, even of her husband.

She could not get on that boat with him. If she did, she was lost. She must do everything in her power to get away. By this time, Helena had worked out an approach. Sullen but accepting with a side dish of fear would work best. He would find the fear flattering, in all likelihood. If she had a better weapon she wouldn't hesitate in trying to kill him, but even the holsters that usually contained carriage pistols were empty. "I must relieve myself."

"I have provided the means." He nodded to the small blue-and-white bourdaloue that sat on the floor of the carriage.

"I cannot." She wouldn't say why. Let him work it out for himself.

He groaned. "We are due to change carriages after we cross the Heath. I will allow you to stop then, but be warned. I will send a servant with you, and he will watch you."

That was almost worse, but she'd take the indignity of relieving herself in someone's presence for the chance to leave a note or a message. Oh, yes! She had her visiting cards with her. If she could drop a few, she could leave a trail of clues. Her propensity for privacy would have some benefits.

Swallowing her bile and her desire to tear his eyes out with her bare hands, Helena tried the meek feminine response. He would want that, and if she added a strong streak of shyness, she might delay the inevitable until someone came for her.

They reached Hampstead Heath. That was a blow. She had hoped her brother would have caught up with her before that time. Since three carriages were already waiting at the inn, they set forth in a train. The Heath was notorious for bold highwaymen, and footpads abounded there. Carriages would frequently wait at the Spaniards Inn until a few had gathered.

They negotiated the Heath, while Everslade tried to initiate conversation and Helena answered with softly spoken responses. "You will enjoy my house," he said, "and I mean to treat you carefully. I do not wish to wed you merely for your fortune, but your sweet self."

"Are you, then, short of funds, sir?" She'd pay him all she owned to get out of this mess. Before she killed him.

"Not at all. But any man of means must be delighted that his wife brings sufficient funds with her. You will no doubt wish me to dispose of your fortune for you. Indeed, many have come to me for advice."

How could she have not noticed how utterly pompous the man was? With every sentence he spoke, her hackles rose a bit more. For two pins she'd be backing into a corner and growling at the back of her throat, like the poor unfortunate cur that her father's gamekeeper caught on the estate last year. The beast now lived amiably with the other dogs in the kennel, so maybe it had just been hungry.

She was not hungry. Not for the man sitting opposite her, at any rate.

She almost wished for a highwayman, but they crossed the heath without incident. Nobody hid behind the trees or braved the rain that was pattering down on the coach roof. Outside all was bleak, the green of summer gone, the trees bedraggled, dripping soggy dead leaves.

The sight of a building ahead should have comforted Helena, but it did precisely the opposite. The light was dimming, preparing for full nightfall.

As if reading her mind, Everslade glanced out the window. "We have time to change horses and make a little headway before dark. At least, enough to confound our pursuers. I fear your brother is bound to send people in pursuit. A dead bore, but we need to at least make a show of confounding him."

"My father may not be pleased."

"Your excellent mother assures me that she will see that he causes no trouble."

He was altogether too complacent. In her experience, when her father wished to do something, he did it. The fact that he rarely troubled to do so fooled a lot of people, but not his family. Witness his determination to abide by the pact he'd made with his sisters to call the children outlandish names. He had stood firm on that resolve. However, now was not the time to voice her disagreement. Instead, she shifted in her seat and faced the window, gloomily watching the rush of the road under the wheels. At the end of the heath, the carriages which had traveled in a bunch steadily spaced themselves out once more.

Their coach halted at an inn. They did not stop at the usual place at the end of the heath, but another close by. This was her chance.

Before she could gather her resolve and humbly request that she be excused, he put a hand on the door, halting the footman who waited, head down, outside. The man probably expected to see terrible debauchery unfolding inside and averted his eyes.

"My dear," Everslade said, "please hand over your pocket."

She blinked in an attempt to mask her dismay. Her pocket held her little knife, her card case, even the tablet she used for making notes. Without it she would have little chance to leave a meaningful message. But he would not let her down without it.

What else was she carrying?

Helena had to lift her skirts to loosen the tape that fastened the pocket around her waist. She fumbled, trying to get the pocket undone and rescue something from inside, but before she could do so, he shoved his hand under her petticoats and grabbed it from her hand. Their faces were close enough for her to feel his breath and smell the onions he must have had with his breakfast.

He remained close and pressed his lips against hers, lover-like. "Here we are a married couple, traveling out of London. The coach has no crest, so nobody will be any the wiser. At the next stage, we will be leaving the coach behind and hiring a chaise. I am afraid we will be forced to do that a number of times before we eventually arrive at the coast, but better to make sure of our journey than to rush at it, eh, my love?"

She wished he would not call her that. When he kissed her again, she closed her eyes.

"That's better." After dropping the pocket on the floor, he spread his hand over her thigh and groaned. His fingers inched closer to her private parts. "I will not wait. I have to make you mine. I am sorry, my love, but a man has needs, and spending a week with you in this space will be the undoing of me unless I have you."

Helena summoned up all the curse words she could think of and said them to herself, in her mind. It did not help.

He withdrew his hand with a gentle smile. "I cannot wait for your return." The footman outside will escort you. Opening the door without attempting to straighten her gown, he addressed the footman. "Do not let her out of your sight for one moment. She is precious to me."

The footman touched his hat, which seemed a little large for him. "Yes, my lord."

The hint of an accent sounded familiar, but before Helena could demand that he show his face, he turned and led the way to the inn, pausing to usher her in front of him. "Private room for the lady!" he called to the landlord and tossed him a coin. "Only for her to freshen up!"

The landlord nodded to a boy standing at the side of the hall, who opened a door for her. She went inside to see one window and little else. Just a door, a window, an unpadded bench and a long table.

This was the best chance she would have. Her heart beating like a drum, Helena curled her fingers into claws and spun around, ready to go for the footman's eyes. She could not allow that pig of a lord anywhere near her.

She'd kill him first, and then she'd be hanged for murder, because the law would be bound to take his side. A footman? If she could scramble out of that window, she'd take her chances. This inn was busy.

But the man stepped back and lifted his head. That gave her enough pause to take his features in. "Don't I know you?"

"Parlez-vous français, madame?"

"Oui."

He spoke French without an accent, and fluidly. He continued in rapid French. "My name is Lamaire, and I am in the employ of Lord Alconbury."

"Then what were you doing in our livery? And how are you now in Everslade's livery?" Had the man sent him to spy on her? Then it was as well she had not clawed his eyes out, because he was probably ready for her.

"He sent me to Lord Winterton's house to ensure your safety. Lord Alconbury is a careful man. When Lord Everslade took you, I jumped on to the back of the coach." He twitched the ill-fitting rust-colored coat. "This I acquired when the carriage stopped to join the group at the Heath. Its owner is lying in the road there, or if he has recovered, he may have raised the alarm. I'm afraid I left Lord Winterton's coat with him."

Was it true? Helena frowned. "Why are we speaking French?"

"Spies," he said succinctly. "Doors and windows have ears. Did you think I would be the only footman Everslade would send? He would love you to try to escape. Then he may tie you down."

Helena swallowed.

"Come, my lady. Either you believe me or you do not." He thrust the bourdaloue at her. "I will turn my back, but for God's sake do not use the window. If I am correct, he will have stationed another man outside. We will find another way."

"He took my pocket. I was planning to leave a card here."

"I will take care of leaving messages for our pursuers. Count on it. They are arriving."

Was this a trap? "How can I believe you?"

"You either do or you do not. Think, madame."

She did. "Lamaire? Did my brother not have a valet of that name?"

He nodded. "I was an emissary from my master. Well, madame?"

"He plans to divert from the usual journey."

Lamaire nodded. "I thought as much. We will, I assure you, escape as soon as we may do it with relative safety. Can you ride?" He gave a tight smile at her astonished stare. "Very good. Then we will run tonight. You may have to please him. I am sorry, and I would spare you if I could, but he means to harm you if you do not." He paused. "He has a reputation among his servants, that man. He is not gentle."

"You heard that already?"

He nodded. "They think I am a new employ. The fact that they are not surprised tells me much. He does not keep servants for long." He turned his back. "I will give you what privacy I can."

That was just as well, because she was almost in pain from holding back. Quickly, she did what she needed to and shamefacedly put the vessel down on the floor. Lamaire did not even look at it. "I swear I will try to get you away before he takes you. Now back to English." He raised his voice and switched languages. "You have finished, ma'am?"

"Indeed." As she spoke, a man knocked and entered, bearing a bowl of water, a cake of soap, and a fresh towel. After her tears, the blow Everslade had dealt her, and her recent activity, Helena was delighted to have the opportunity to clean herself.

"Give him a vail," Helena said, putting on her best aristocratic tone. "I have no money on my person."

"Very well, ma'am." Lamaire handed the man a coin.

Helena also caught a curl of paper changing hands. No, card. She was not the only person to have calling cards. Had he found time to add a message? Please God, he had, but she could not even say anything, for fear the man standing outside the window and the one she glimpsed outside the door would hear her. When she had finished washing, he sent her a terse nod. "If you would come with me, ma'am."

Without a word, Helena stuck her hat back on her head and followed Lamaire. The man outside the door fell in behind, and like a little procession they trooped across the cobbled yard to the coach. Twilight had settled in now. It would be full dark in half an hour. Her reputation would be gone. If she did not marry Everslade, her mother would use her status as an excuse to call her back home, this time for good.

Except she was already married. One faint hope remained—that Tom would claim her. At least he had sent someone to watch her. He must still care for her, surely. Her poor shattered heart began to mend, like a destroyed iron statue being drawn together again by a powerful magnet.

She had fought her obsession for five years, and she was tired of it. One way or another they would reconcile their feelings and talk. She had to know why he would come nowhere near her, why he refused to speak to her, yet watched her. Oh, yes, she knew he watched her. She'd caught him and seen the way he turned away abruptly when he realized she'd seen him.

They had fallen so quickly for each other she had assumed what they shared was feverish infatuation, but she could not forget him.

Back to meek and obedient Lady Helena. Nobody would recognize her from that description. Only Lord Everslade, who appeared to believe he'd seen something in her that nobody else had.

Would she have to share a bed with him tonight? Would he try to take her in the carriage?

Helena swallowed and let Everslade help her into a new traveling chaise. In this one they would have to sit side by side.

"It was all they had," he said by way of explanation. "However, it will travel faster, and since we will be traveling ten miles in the dark, we will be better for speed. So come here, my beautiful bride, and kiss me."

* * * *

Tom traveled with two assistants, men who would send the messages to Winterton via runners, men who raced through the streets, faster than a vehicle could negotiate the congested center of the city. Farther out, he would have to use riders, but if he did not keep Winterton informed, the man would follow.

Although they had been at least nominal enemies for many years, Tom had never underestimated Winterton. More than any other man, he had harassed Tom's father and his brothers, infiltrating their networks and preventing them achieving their aims.

At the Spaniards Inn, Tom sent his man to inquire about the carriage. "Aye, sir," came the response. "We've had a busy day. People who come into London for the weekend travel out on Mondays. Must have had twelve coaches."

The innkeeper had come out to speak to him himself, despite Tom's relatively plain appearance. But gold coins spoke louder than silver, and he'd been generous.

The landlord rubbed his beard scruff, the bristles rasping against his grubby palm. "I can't say for sure, sir, but I did see a coach come down this way 'round about four o'clock with two people in it. The lady looked in a bad way, what I saw of her. The gen'leman had a satisfied look. He 'ad a lot of footmen, but no outriders. At least four big 'uns up, and two drivers."

Tom pulled out his half hunter and checked the time. He cursed. They were hours behind. If they stopped at a good inn and changed the horses before they tired significantly, they could gain even more ground. Would they hire a coach with lights and risk driving in the dark? The roads around London were probably in better heart than elsewhere, but that was not saying much.

Tom's heart leaped into his mouth when he saw the time. "Open the gates," he snapped to the toll-man, who had strolled over, probably to discover what the fuss might be.

"That poor young lady?" he murmured. "Saw 'er, I did. Bleedin' from 'er marf."

The accent was somewhat thick, but Tom had no problem understanding him. She'd been hurt. That bastard Everslade was going to die for this.

"Was she awake?" He tossed the man a half guinea.

The ruffian caught it deftly, bit it and pocketed it in one smooth movement. He'd probably had a misspent youth picking pockets in the city.

"Yes, and not 'appy at all."

"Open those gates," Tom repeated, and this time the man obliged.

"Shouldn't we wait for company?"

Tom glared at the footman who had dared suggest such a craven act. "We're armed, and I'm in the mood to kill somebody." As soon as they were through the gates, he broke into a canter, and then a gallop. Risky on such uneven ground, but he'd honed his reflexes, and he was on an excellent bay. Briefly he made a mental note to make Winterton an offer for the beast. Then he put his mind back on the task in hand and prayed he was in time.

Although the ground sped under his mount's hooves, everything went too slowly. Except for time. Dusk had settled in by the time they reached the far gates, and still they were behind.

He sent the two men with him to the local inns and he took the other. At the first one he reluctantly left his horse behind and had a fresh one saddled and two for his companions. Otherwise, he drew a blank there. They had not called at the inn, or the landlord had missed them. He was wondering whether to try a smaller establishment, when Worthing galloped toward him.

He drew his gray to a halt, the horse's flanks heaving with exertion. "My lord, they were at the Hawk in Hand."

"You're sure?"

The man leaned across and handed him a card, a cream board gleaming warmly in the orange-yellow lights emanating from the lanterns in the nearby tavern. The calling card was one of his own, the corner turned down and a rough scrawl on the back with, he guessed, a piece of charcoal from the fire. He tilted the card. Numbers.

The normal way of telling a person that the owner of the card was waiting for an answer, rather than leaving the pasteboard was to turn down the right corner. Lamaire had turned down the left, which meant he had not waited. They had moved on.

Those numbers marked a time! That meant two things. Lamaire was still with her, and he had the means to leave a trail. Grim-faced, he shoved the card in his pocket. "Did you question the landlord?"

"Yes, my lord. He was distressed to discover his part in the abduction."

"You told him?" Tom wanted to strike the idiot.

Worthing shrank back in his saddle. "He knew, or he'd guessed, but I told him this was your card. He doesn't know who the young lady was. She went inside while they changed to a chaise and came out again. He sent men in to guard her."

Otherwise, she'd have run away. A chill ran through his veins when he thought what Everslade would do to her if she tried to run and he caught her. The suspicion that he had only begun to uncover a truly sinister hidden life crept over him. Everslade had been a part of the London scene for years—suave, wealthy, considerate, and popular with the ladies. Not all females, it appeared. What Winterton had said before Tom had left in haste chimed with a few rumors he'd heard, but like many people, Tom had dismissed the stories as malicious gossip. Especially the one about Everslade being banned from the House of Correction in Covent Garden for flogging a woman half to death. He'd actually laughed at that one.

In a flash, he knew what Lamaire was telling him. "They went east. They're not taking the usual route to the Great North Road. Do either of you know this area?"

"My aunt used to live around here," Manning said. "I used to come here for weekends when I was little, when my parents were busy. They ran a city inn."

Thank Christ for London servants. "East. We need to find an inn with room for a chaise, preferably with more chaises to hire. My guess is that he will change the vehicle as often as possible, in an attempt to throw us off the trail." He spurred his horse, murmuring under his breath, "He'll have to try harder than that."

Once they stopped for the night, Everslade would not hesitate to make her his own. In any way he had to. He would delight in the scene if Helena fought back; that would give him the excuse he wanted. He'd brutalize her.

Fury and grief warred within Tom as he rode, but he had to fight his emotions down. He would be no good to her if he acted impulsively. He barely knew himself. He'd faced life-changing peril with hardly a qualm, and he was falling to pieces at the thought of Everslade even daring to touch Lady Helena Vernon. How he wished he had made her Lady Alconbury in truth.

Although that blissful outcome was not possible, he would never leave her again. He would always watch over her, care for her.

If she lived.

Chapter 12

Everslade had provided a variety of garments for Helena's use. One traveling gown, a plain brown one, but well made, jostled for space in the small portmanteau with a lighter gown, no doubt for the evenings, and a collection of clothes she doubted she would ever wear. The night rail was far too thin for any use, the fabric so fine it would tear if she turned over in bed. It had an equally thin robe to go over the top.

He meant to visit her tonight. He'd said as much. He'd mauled her so much in the carriage that she had almost been sick, but she had kept to her resolve and offered him no resistance. She was alone now, but not for long, she guessed.

She put on the night rail but added the traveling gown on top and kept her cloak handy. She had no clean shift, so the night rail would serve until she could find something more serviceable.

When a knock sounded on the door, her heart leaped to her throat, but she had barred it as securely as possible. Unfortunately the window was too high up for her to risk jumping. She would most likely break a limb if she tried. Neither was there a tree within jumping distance.

Only fighting held the answer. She could not let him do any more to her. She had discovered her limit about half an hour ago, when he'd fondled her between her legs and pinched her painfully. Would he know that she was no longer a virgin? He had treated her carefully, saying he would breach her there with the appropriate part of his body.

Perhaps she could offer to kiss it for him and bite it off.

Before today, Helena would never have thought herself possible of dreaming of such a thing. She spared a thought for the girls who arrived in London to become maids and ended in a stew or bagnio, serving several men a night, after having been raped into subservience.

How did they stand it? She would not have lasted one night.

The key rattled in the lock, and the latch lifted. She waited, praying the chair she had hopefully propped under the plank holding the door together would hold. Tears rose to her eyes and her heart beat so hard she had to fight for breath.

The door held.

Someone knocked, three gentle taps, and the word, "Madame," sounded softly.

It could be a trick. Lamaire could be a hired ruffian, bought to compel her into obedience or to fool her into trying a fruitless attempt at escape. Then Everslade could punish her. She had not missed the gleam in his eyes when he caused her pain. He liked it.

But what choice did she have? To wait here meekly like a lamb and allow the man who had snatched her off the street to rape her, or take a risk?

She went to the door. "I'm here."

"Madame, open the door. We have but five minutes, perhaps ten."

Helena made haste to move the chair away from the door. Lamaire barreled in on stockinged feet. "Collect your cloak, madame, you will need it."

"What do you propose?"

"The inn is full. If we can get downstairs, we may have a chance, but do not raise your head or let anyone get a good look at you. Then, I am afraid we must walk, probably across the fields. How far can you walk?"

She found her outdoor shoes that she had donned that morning, so long ago now. The hat, too, much the worse for wear, but if she went out in public without a hat, people would stare, and that was the last thing she needed. She could feign a semblance of respectability by bundling her hair up in it, since she had scarcely any hairpins left.

Everslade had pinched and fingered her so much that walking hurt, but she could still manage it. He must have left bruises, though she had not dared to examine the area, lest she find more.

Every floorboard creaked outside her room. A man sat outside, his head slumped, his chin touching his chest. He had obviously been put there by Everslade, otherwise why else would he be on a chair by her door? She held her breath but he did not move. A bottle rolled under his chair, and she smelled the strong odor of red wine.

When Lamaire held out his hand, she took it, and let him lead her, tiptoeing, a careful tread at a time, down the landing toward the stairs at the end. The floor was bare wood, well polished, the nails sticking proud of the surface. Small casement windows, diamond-paned, looked out over the yard where horses nickered and ostlers yelled. From downstairs came the murmur of patrons in the taproom, and the glow of lanterns and tapers. The stairs were lit by tapers stuck out from hooks in the walls, holding them clear of the worst of the fire hazards, but at the height of a tall man, so still not entirely safe. The whole place stank of beer, that sweet, hop-laden unmistakable odor. This inn was out of the way of the main roads, nestled in a village that in its turn was off the main high street of the place. And this was where her abductor had brought her to be raped.

As far as possible she tried to use his footsteps and timed her steps to coincide with his. When he moved forward, so did she.

A door to the left opened just after they'd inched past it. A grunt, then a "What the—" came, followed by a curse and the thump of heavy feet.

Lamaire pushed her in front of him. "Run! Scream! Tell them you are abducted!" Drawing his sword, he turned to face her tormentor.

Helena hurtled down the stairs, but as she did so, the door to the outside world burst open, admitting three men, swords and pistols drawn and hats pulled low over their foreheads. From above she could see no faces, but she knew, deep inside, these were Lamaire's men, sent to capture her and send her back.

The clash of swords sounded from above and then an explosion. A gunshot.

The man in front lifted his head. White-faced, his jaw spotted with the stubble of a day's growth, the man stared at her.

She knew what that stubble felt like against her skin. With a choked cry, Helena hurled herself down the last half dozen stairs into the arms of her husband. Her true husband.

* * * *

Sobbing, Helena clutched him. Tom felt like sobbing too, when her warm weight fell on to him. He'd only just dropped his sword in time, and he still held his pistol, cocked and ready to fire. She could have killed them both, but he would be the last person to castigate her. A cloak and pair of shoes were lying on the stairs where she'd dropped them. He gestured for his men to go upstairs, because much though he would like to, he could not deal with Everslade himself.

He had his arms full.

Except that the man himself appeared at the top of the stairs, wearing a positively garish banyan, and from what Tom could see, little else.

Tom did not stop to think. What was there to think about? Lifting his pistol, he fired.

The sound echoed around the restricted space and a few lights went out. So did the noise from the taproom, a moment of complete silence, before men cursed and the door was flung open.

Tom lowered his weapon and put his arms around Helena, who was still sobbing. He glanced at the men, who could not pass more than two at a time through the narrow archway that led from the public part of the inn to the residential part. Gesturing upstairs with his pistol, he said, as casually as he could manage, "Well, what did you expect me to do? The man is a positive disgrace. He attacked this lady and then threatened me." Since Lamaire had appeared briefly behind Everslade, relieving Tom's mind greatly, he knew he had a reliable witness.

His two henchmen rattled down the stairs. He paused for a word with one. "Get a coach and harness a couple of horses to it. Give the ostlers whatever they want." The man touched his hat and disappeared into the yard.

"I will take my woman home," he said, moving effortlessly from assassin to great lord. Swinging Helena into his arms, he tucked her face against his shoulder.

A man with all the pomposity of a magistrate came from the taproom. I am the coroner, sir. Pray, what has occurred here?"

Tom did not stop to answer him. He would have faced the man if it had only been him, but he could not bear Helena to be distressed any more, and the man emerging from the tap-room had the swagger of a pompous magistrate determined to make the most of the fracas. If it came to a court appearance, he could swear that he was rescuing Lady Helena on behalf of her brother, and Everslade had threatened him with his pistol first.

This affair would cost Tom a pretty penny, because he would pay anything to keep her name out of the scandal. They had a lot to manage, he and Winterton. He resented none of it, because he had her back in his arms.

Before anyone could protest, he had backed out of the inn.

He had them out of that place before the magistrate had thought of a way to detain him.

He and Winterton would have to put their heads together and devise some reason why Everslade had snatched Helena off the street and later had turned up dead in an obscure country inn, and why Tom had rescued her, and not her brother.

Sitting in the gig, which was all his servant had managed to find in time, swaying toward the Heath, Tom cradled Helena as she sobbed out her story. He bit his lip several times to keep from uttering curses that would not do anything to her peace of mind.

Until she looked up at him with reddened eyes and a tear-streaked face and said, "I hope you've killed him."

So did he.

* * *

Tom waited two days before he visited. He needed the time to rationalize his thoughts. Goddamn it, he ached for her. Every part of his body, every pore of his skin longed to take her. Keeping away from her, praying his inconvenient fever for her would abate had done no good at all.

Repeating to himself that he was her brother did absolutely no good. His body did not care who she was. It still wanted her under him, wanted to thrust into her until neither of them could take any more. Telling himself that love could take many forms helped not a whit, either.

But eventually he found a pair of breeches roomy enough not to give away his deeply inconvenient secret and made his way to the house in Brook Street, ordering Lamaire to accompany him. He had made a few discoveries that might not mean anything, but he needed to discuss them with his reluctant ally. But his first thought was for Helena. It always was, and he had resigned himself to the fact that she would always be his first concern.

Tom gained some amusement by the expression on the face of the man who opened the door to him. His face stiffened in shock, and then a resigned expression entered the dark eyes. "I will inform his lordship that you have arrived, my lord."

Tom handed his card to the man. "How is her ladyship?"

The man regarded him, all the expression drained from his face. Tom would appreciate a butler as good as this one. He glanced around, and beckoned to Lamaire. The Frenchman, smartly but inconspicuously dressed, bowed to the butler. "I have returned," he said.

"But not for good," the butler said, sounding, if anything, relieved.

"No, Watson, not for good," Tom said. "Lamaire is with me now." Without turning around, he added, "He always was."

"And you think I am unaware of that?" Winterton stood at the top of the stairs, hand on hip. Although at home, he was dressed immaculately, as always, with the touch of elegant extravagance that marked his personal style. "Come up."

Turning, he led the way to an elegant drawing room, throwing open the double doors with a flourish.

His mood far too eager, Tom followed him in, to find the owner of his heart sitting on a forget-me-not upholstered sofa in a gown of white sprigged with tiny blue flowers. A blue blanket was carelessly tossed aside, and she had found a book, the leather-upholstered volume propped elegantly between her carefully manicured hands. The nails were noticeably shorter than she usually wore them. But otherwise, she appeared as poised as her brother. That was, except for the tense lines around her mouth and the sadness haunting the deep blue of her eyes.

He basked in her presence, longed to seize her and kiss her, cradle her close and keep her safe. Instead, he took a seat by the fire and accepted the dish of tea the maid brought him with a gentle smile. Thus did enemies meet, parlay, and realign their allegiances. He had no idea if that would happen today, but they had to talk.

Gently he asked after Lady Helena's health, and equally smoothly, she assured him she was perfectly well. But her lower lip was thicker than usual, no doubt still swollen from the blow Everslade had dealt it.

The maid left the room. Julius took the matching chair to the one Tom occupied, on the other side of the fireplace. He sipped his tea before placing it on the small round table by his side. The delicate flower-sprigged china barely chinked as he laid it aside. He folded his hands together, the sapphire ring on his forefinger winking in the light from the windows behind Tom. "Did you call just to inquire after my sister's health?"

"I would appreciate knowing the truth." Tom addressed her directly.

"Only my mouth, and a few bruises" she said. "I slept for most of yesterday. Julius would not allow me out of bed."

"I'm glad to hear it." Tom nodded to his temporary ally. "I have made what inquiries I can."

"And do you have any conclusions?" Winterton picked up his tea once more, holding it in precisely the correct manner.

More than once Tom had wondered what lay beneath that perfect exterior. Now he knew some of it. Julius Vernon was a sensitive, deeply caring man who loved his new wife to distraction and would never allow any of the people he considered under his care to come to any harm. If they did, the perpetrators would not go unavenged.

They were oddly alike.

Winterton spared a glance at the manservant standing impassively by Tom's chair. "Sit down, do. And have some tea. It appears you are not the excellent valet I thought you."

"He is the best valet I have ever encountered," Tom said, "but from time to time he undertakes a few extracurricular tasks for me. He is devoted to me, not my family."

Lamaire found a seat on one of the other chairs, considerately taking a place where everyone could see him.

"Do I understand that you sent him to me last year?"

Tom nodded. "I told you I had a man on the scene. I needed to find the daughter of the Young Pretender before he did. The Pretender would have killed her."

"I see. And you do not wish for that?"

Tom turned his lip in a sneer. "What kind of man do you take me for?"

"A political one."

"And a mortal one. I can stomach no more killing." He'd told his father exactly the same thing. Whether Winterton understood it or not, that, for Tom, was the crux of the matter. "My father and I see family loyalty slightly differently."

"Is there a rift between father and son?" The inquiry sounded gentle.

Tom laughed derisively. "There has been ever since the old man ordered the son to turn back at Calais in the forty-five. He considers that his son took the Regency under false pretenses. Unfortunately the son has his own allies now. In public, and to their supporters, they do their best to present a united face."

"Then I take it you are no longer devoted to their cause?"

Tom took his time considering the question. If he answered, how much information would that give the family who were still his family's enemies? He glanced at Helena. Enemies no more, although he did not know what to call them now. However, he was not about to throw away every scrap of information in his possession. That way he would lose any usefulness and every edge he had. "I never was. In case you had not noticed, I have been trying to rebuild my family's wealth and reputation."

"Very successfully, by all accounts," Winterton drawled. He might appear at ease, but he was far from it.

Accustomed to observing opponents and allies closely, Tom had noted the tiny signs on Winterton a long time ago. His pupils dilated very slightly, for one thing. In someone with eyes as dark as Tom's own, that sign would barely be noticeable, but Winterton possessed pale blue eyes, and every shade was instantly apparent. If Tom offered any objections, Winterton would react. Tom could not blame him. Under this roof were the people who mattered most in the world to him. Tom would be edgy if Winterton had walked into his house, which he had a time or two.

"The Stuarts are, as always, their own worst enemies," Tom said. "If Prince Henry had not turned Cardinal, or if Prince Charles had married ten years ago and sired a healthy nursery full of children, their prospects would be much rosier. We both know that. They have a dwindling influence on world affairs, but that is fading as Europe realigns itself. We both know that too."

"War is coming," Winterton said, as if speaking of the weather.

"I know." Tom would have to be a fool if he hadn't noticed the subtle and not-so-subtle political maneuverings that were the precursor to a new conflict. He had made certain preparations against the event and realigned his own investments. He would not take odds against Winterton having done the same. But they were not here to discuss international politics. Not today, at any rate. He tilted his head to one side. "This war, however, will have little to do with the affairs of the Stuarts."

"You are not eaten up with a desire for justice? In my experience, most Jacobites use that as a reason for their continued allegiance."

Tom huffed a laugh. "Idealists, you mean? Spare me idealists, please. Some have resigned themselves to having lost everything at home, so they have nothing else to lose. Others are more interested in what they can lever for themselves. The idealists involved in the Cause are invariably disappointed." He changed position, crossing his ankle over his knee. "At the moment, revenge is uppermost in my mind. Everslade has disappeared. I knew I should have killed him while I had the opportunity." He had just revealed his own propensity to fidget when he was agitated, but Winterton would surely know that.

"Perhaps you should have, but that would have branded you a possible murderer in the eyes of the public." Winterton placed his empty tea-dish in its saucer with precision but without looking. A casual reminder of his talents, as if Tom needed reminding of them. He had talents too, not all of them on blatant display.

Tom spared a glance at Helena and caught her looking at him. "Thank you for rescuing me," she said softly.

He bowed his head, smiling, as if he had offered her some small service. "Think nothing of it. Of course I did." In everything but words, he let her know he cared for her. Just not how much.

She glanced down at her book, as if surprised to discover it still there. Gently, she closed it and set it aside, concentrating on laying it down, as if she was anxious not to meet his gaze.

"I sent a man to the inn the next morning," Winterton said.

Tom tore his eyes away from her and back to his host.

"Everslade complained loudly about his hurts. The landlord reluctantly permitted him to stay, but he slipped away in the night. I assume because he was afraid he might be found out." Winterton glanced at his sister, his gaze grave. "I owe my sister a deep apology. It appears the man we knew as Lord Everslade may not have been the right one." He turned his attention back to Tom. "In short, he was an impostor."

"The devil, you say!" Tom got to his feet and paced before the window before taking his seat again. Devil take it, why had he not thought of that? "How did I miss that?"

"You investigated him?" Helena demanded in a voice of great horror.

"Yes, of course. Why would I not? He arrived back in town a month ago and showed you distinctive attention from the start. I could tell he was making a play for you, so yes, I had him investigated."

"And what did you find?" Winterton drawled.

He was showing more of his hand than he'd intended. But the deed was done now, and he would not reveal his error. "I presume you investigated too. Everslade is an earl living in the north of England. He has no siblings. His mother adored him and rarely allowed him out of her sight, but he got away this autumn."

Winterton nodded. "That more or less matches what I discovered. Everslade is also wealthy, due to the number of coal mines on his modest estate. He has not been back there for a number of years. Five, to be precise. Before that, he was assiduous in the management of his estate. Local opinion has it that his mother's death sent him away. I am not so sure. None of his servants have worked for him for more than five years. His behavior has changed utterly in the last five years. He seeks the most vicious pleasures where before he was gentle and considerate. He dresses well, where he used to be almost slovenly with his costume. From the descriptions I have, some extremely detailed, we could be talking about two separate men. Even the color of his hair has changed."

"Indeed." His stomach churned, as he took in what Winterton was telling him. "Do you know who he was?"

Winterton shook his head. "Not yet."

"I may know something," Lamaire said.

The damned man sat so quietly, Tom had nearly forgotten he was there. He had brought him because of his involvement in the affair, but he had not expected any extra information to come from him.

But now he dug his hand into his pocket and came out with a crumpled piece of paper. "I had little time before we were interrupted, but if you recall, sir, I had a brief golden moment with the man we knew as Lord Everslade."

Tom took the paper and listened to Everslade. He glanced at the writing as the man spoke. What he saw made him stiffen in alarm.

"He shot at me, but his preparations were clumsy, and the attack was easy to evade. I shot at him, but I fear my aim was not true. I was facing the stairs and concerned any stray shot would hit the wrong person." A wicked grin flitted over his mouth. "So I used the butt of my pistol instead. It served its purpose. After that, I had a moment, thanks to you, my lord, when I could search him. The man was wearing nothing but a banyan. Apart from a few personal items, I discovered this." He nodded in the direction of the note.

Tom read the brief note aloud. "I must charge you to adhere to our agreement. I will send you details of the person in the next dispatch." He looked up. "That is all it says, but it is not all this note tells me. It's execrably spelled, and whoever wrote it has a spider's scrawl. One that I know."

"I see." Winterton held out his hand.

Lamaire got to his feet, took the note from Tom, and handed it to his erstwhile master, who gave him a long considering look.

"Work for me, and I will pay you double what Lord Alconbury does."

"I thank you, sir. I will bear your offer in mind." Lamaire bowed.

"Not many people fool me so convincingly," Winterton said, turning his attention to the note. "Ah, yes. Our mutual acquaintance." He closed his eyes.

Tom knew they were thinking the same thing, and controlling themselves just as rigidly.

"The Pretender. The younger, I believe."

"His father has the better hand but never puts such sensitive information in writing," Tom murmured. He flicked another glance at Helena and caught her watching him, eyes wide. "I'm sorry. I should never have allowed the man past my inspection. I cannot believe he fooled us both."

"Neither can I," Winterton said grimly. "I believe I will send for Everslade's servants, the ones who knew him in his youth. I will send them a generous remuneration."

"You will allow me to add to that sum," Tom said, his hands clenching in frustration.

Winterton looked up. "You did not know that this unknown person was an agent of the Young Pretender's?"

"Of course not."

"I see no 'of course' about the matter. You could have fallen out with him. A spy in the top echelons of society would prove useful if you were prosecuting the interests of the Stuarts."

Tom made a sound of derision at the back of his throat. "And how do you suppose I would set a spy there? How did this man gain the title? As far as I could ascertain, the true Everslade had no interest in the Stuarts, and neither did his family. That is a considerable and foolish risk."

"Unless the true Everslade is dead," Winterton said softly.

Helena's small gasp made both men turn to her, but she had recovered her calm demeanor by the time they had her under observation. But with the eyes of an erstwhile lover, Tom saw her complexion pale, and her eyes widen.

"Do you truly think the man who abducted me had killed a man?"

"Yes," Winterton said. "He could have done so."

Tom refused to allow anyone to distress Helena in that way. He got to his feet, only pausing when he reminded himself that he had no right to claim her as he wished. But he could tell her the truth.

He would not tell brother and sister that they had gained another brother. He could not bear to have Helena upset in the presence of anyone else. So soon after her distressing ordeal, how could he pile even more bad news on her head?

He could not. The secret was still his to bear. He would wait until a more propitious time.

"I wish to speak to Lord Alconbury alone," she said, her voice firm. She met Winterton's gaze. "I have something particular to ask him."

Winterton's calculating stare went from his sister to Tom and back again. "I have to trust him with you because of his signal service on Monday, but I cannot leave you alone for long."

Helena snorted. "Because of the proprieties?"

"Even more so now," Winterton said softly, and turned his attention to Tom. "You understand?"

"Nobody better." If he did but know it, Tom had as much at stake here as Winterton did. Helena would not suffer publicly because of this. "I take it you have a story to cover the incident?"

"Helena tells me you kept her face hidden." Winterton sighed. "Her hair, however, is one of her most distinctive features. Stories are already circulating. I have not yet met them with an outright lie, but I fear I will have to devise something soon. I have said she was visiting a sick relative on Monday, but that might not serve. I will need to strengthen the tale, but Helena will not allow it."

Rumors were vicious things. They could undeservedly ruin a blameless reputation. Helena must allow them to work to regain her good name. Otherwise, despite her family's connections and their influence, the rumors would never die.

"I have a story, but I need to speak to Lord Alconbury to obtain his agreement," Helena said calmly.

Winterton sighed heavily. "You have fifteen minutes. I cannot allow more. I will take myself off and consult Lamaire about a new coat I bought last week. I value his taste."

And no doubt, work even harder to poach him. Tom was almost sure he would not succeed, but he did not like Lamaire going off with him. He should never have allowed the man to display his considerable skills to one of the finest arbiters of fashion London had to offer. He would sacrifice even Lamaire for the chance of ten minutes alone with Helena. He had been granted fifteen, so he was more than recompensed.

The door closed and silence fell. Tom, accepting he was a besotted fool, could watch her for all that time, but he must make the most of the minutes he had with her.

She folded her hands neatly in her lap. Ruthlessly, Tom squashed the notion of laying his head there.

"If my reputation is ruined, my mother will insist on me returning to her side," Helena said, her voice slightly higher pitched than normal. "I will spend the rest of my life pandering to her needs. Julius is in the process of settling an annuity on me. I had planned to buy a Thames-side villa, find a convenient relative who needs a home, and spend my time in genteel seclusion. I was almost looking forward to it. I believed you did not care for me, or that you had decided against allying yourself to your enemies."

He would have spoken, but she held up her hand to stop him. It was not entirely steady. She returned it to her lap.

"Recent events have suggested to me that I was wrong. Oh, I don't doubt that you would have done everything in your power to rescue me. You're a chivalrous man. If Julius does not know that, I certainly do."

She closed her eyes, but as he rose from his chair, she shook her head and he subsided once more.

"Helena…"

She continued as if he had said nothing. "But to call me your darling when you thought I was asleep, and to hold me all the way back to London? You would not have done that if I had been another woman. Therefore, I have a solution, at least to the suggestion that my reputation might finally be in tatters."

"You know I'll do anything to help you."

"Then be my husband again, and do it in public. If we are seen together in an out-of-the-way country inn, what of that? We are married, so nobody will think it odd. That you wanted to take me away when a drunken fracas ensued? That too."

He closed his eyes, agony wringing his guts. "Anything but that."

Now her expression was anything but serene. The mask dropped away, leaving a distressed vital woman beneath. "Why not? Why have you so carefully kept away from me? So much that I thought your initial passion for me was mistaken and you regretted your actions."

"I do, but not because of that."

"Then why make both of us miserable? Why not face our families and have done?" She gripped her hands together until the knuckles whitened; tears sparkled in her eyes.

"You're killing me, Helena. I cannot see you so distressed."

"Then go, like the coward you are, and leave me to grieve." She shook her head. "No, don't. You have been doing that for the past five years, have you not? Why?"

He swallowed. He would have to confess some of the truth. "Because to tell you the truth would distress you even more."

"Our marriage is legal. I made sure of it, and I have a copy of the certificate."

He had thought of claiming that and then destroying what records he could bribe out of the Fleet or steal from it, but he had put off the task until, it appeared, he'd left it too late. Why had he not already done that?

Because he did not want the truth to be real. He didn't want to lose the one connection to the woman he would always love. Where did he begin?

"Will you not just accept that our marriage is not valid?"

"No. If I marry anyone else, I will always have that certificate in my keeping. I will know that I am doing my husband a deep disservice and that my children with anyone but you must be illegitimate. How can I burden anyone else with that?" She bit her lip before adding, "I have not met another man I am desirous of marrying. Not after you."

Tom groaned and put his head in his hands. "Helena, what am I to do with you?"

"I already told you."

"Not that. We cannot." There was no hope for it; he would have to tell her the truth. But not here and not now. Winterton would send a servant in far too soon, and the truth would distress Helena even more. He lifted his head. "If I prove to your satisfaction that a forbidden level of consanguinity lies between us, will you then leave this matter alone?"

Her eyes widened. Why in heaven's name had he given voice to the word that had haunted him day and night? But it was done. She brought far more out of him than he meant to say. Tom was notoriously close-mouthed when he wished to be. Nobody pried secrets from him, but he was babbling like a baby now. He clamped his mouth shut and waited for her response.

"Yes." She folded her arms, the lace at her elbows falling over her pale skin. "Prove it beyond doubt."

"Not here. Will you risk your reputation one more time? Come to the house a week from now."

She shook her head. "No. I will not go another week until I know. Thursday."

"But you are only just recovering from your ordeal." He could not lay another on her so soon.

"Next Thursday. At eleven. I will, however, bring a coach and footmen, so the visit will not be covert. I cannot cause my brother such distress as to give my protectors the slip."

So the house in Folgate Street would no longer be a secret. He would accept that. He had other establishments, but none as precious as this one. He never used it, never allowed anyone else to use it, but kept it maintained. After next Thursday they could both move on and the house could become something else, instead of a mausoleum to events that should never have occurred in the first place. "Very well. Then I might make you a gift of the house, to use as you will."

She closed her eyes and sighed. "Once, that was all I wanted. That and you." She spoke quietly, her voice vibrating with longing. Opening her eyes, she said, "Thursday, at eleven."

Tom left shortly after. He couldn't bear to look at her any longer. After Thursday, she would not look at him again. Or she would tell Winterton and he would kill her. He no longer cared.

Chapter 13

Julius pressed Helena for answers, but she had not allowed any. Risking everything on her belief, she had calmly done her research and collected what she needed to. When Julius asked her what she was about, she told him and waited for his response.

"There is only one way out of this pickle now," she said, "and you know what that is. I will meet Lord Alconbury and discover what he has to tell me."

"Risking your reputation even more?" Standing at the window of the breakfast parlor, staring out at the rain-soaked day, Julius had sounded almost resigned. She had not allowed him to tell lies on her behalf. She was sick of them and wanted them done. After she had confronted Tom, her future was clear, and the road had only two forks. She could live with him as his wife or return to her mother and dwindle into the shadows.

Because the rumors were spreading around London like wildfire. On the Tuesday before her visit to Folgate Street, the journals and gossip-sheets were rife with speculation. The worst had happened, and "someone" had seen her half dressed in the arms of Lord Alconbury in a country inn, just as if they were hiding from notice. Who had spread the rumors, she had no idea.

"I'm sorry to bring you such disturbance, especially at such a time." Her dreams of a villa by the Thames had shattered and fallen into dust. If she did that, not only her reputation, but by association, her family's, would suffer badly. She could no longer consider the prospect of living independently. Not once she had been branded a harlot. Her mother would lose no time dusting her hands and turning her back on her eldest daughter, but Helena knew her siblings and her father would refuse to take that course. A pity, really.

Everything hinged on her seemingly innocuous visit today. If the footmen, at least not wearing their livery today, thought it odd that Helena used her own key to gain access to the property, they did not comment. Nor did they remark on her eccentric lack of a companion. After all, she was visiting a respectable widow.

She arrived half an hour early, because she wanted to explore, but she didn't want Tom to know. Craving the short minutes of solitude, she entered the hallway and softly closed the door. She had never forgotten a moment of their short time here.

Papers crackled in her pocket. That one word, "consanguinity" had given her the clue. In order for a marriage to be invalidated for that reason, the bride and groom had to be very closely related. Parents, uncles and aunts, siblings and the spouses of siblings. That close. Carefully, Helena had considered each possibility, and just as carefully, collected what evidence she could find. When she had discounted the ridiculous possibilities, only a few remained, and one had made itself clear to her. But she needed to see what he claimed was proof first.

* * * *

Helena opened the door of the little house in Folgate Street and was instantly transported back five years. The hallway was not covered with dust, as she'd expected, or changed in any significant way. She wrinkled her nose at the scent of furniture polish, and the slight fustiness that old houses often carried. Carriages rattled by and outside a church clock struck the half-hour. The tiny hall still held a row of coat hooks, a small table by the door and little else. No clock ticked, no servant bumbled about in the kitchen downstairs. But the place was perfectly, eerily clean and free of dust.

The remnants of that impulsive, happy girl remained here, her laughter captured in the atmosphere, her bright expectations for the future trapped here, like a fly in amber. She had left them here, and here they had remained.

Gingerly, she opened the door to the downstairs parlor. The furniture was not shrouded under covers, but open and polished. It looked as if someone had left the room only a moment ago. A few prints hung on the walls, the ones of King James and King George side by side, staring at each other. It had amused her to put them there and sent Tom into gales of laughter when he'd seen them. The man she had married.

She had the assurance of the prison that Clegg was qualified to marry people, and she had a copy of the certificate. What else did they need? Perhaps Tom thought that the new law, enacted two years ago, making such irregular marriages illegal, was enough to annul their marriage, but if he did, he was misinformed. Marriages enacted before the law came into force last year were still valid. The one word, "consanguinity" had given her a clue, and over the last week, when she'd been convalescing and basically hiding from the increasingly vicious rumors flying around town, she'd done some useful research.

She left the front parlor and went into the one at the back. It was in the same condition as the front. A row of clean glasses stood by the decanter on the sideboard. Was Tom still using this place? She touched the rim of a glass. Had he used it recently? Or had he turned this place into a monument for youthful folly?

He had torn her heart out of her chest and stamped on it. Now she was about to discover why. Another hour and she might feel completely different. She held on to that notion, clutched it for all she was worth. What would he bring, if anything? Would he come at all?

Lifting her skirts, Helena climbed the steep, narrow staircase, bypassing the main rooms to climb to the next floor and enter the bedroom where they had spent so many happy hours. Facing it was a kind of dare. If she could do this and feel nothing, perhaps what she felt for him was truly over. Perhaps then she could exorcise the final ghosts and move on. A chair was drawn up to the dressing table, a lacy shawl flung over the back, as if recently discarded. A modest toilet set was laid with military precision on the small glass-covered surface, the brushes at right angles to the clothes brush at the top, and a silver-backed hand mirror on one side. Unused pots of powders and unguents lay at precise distances from each other, and an empty molded glass pin tray capped the arrangement. It appeared more like a still-life, something an artist would paint, than a real set.

So she had allayed her other secret fear, that he had used the house for a succession of mistresses. It would be a convenient place for him to keep a woman. The highest sticklers would not abide it, but a more modest woman would find a comfortable home here. However, despite the careful arrangements and the absence of dust, no evidence lay of anyone actually living here. Perhaps the last occupant had moved on, and he'd had the place cleaned out.

The sounds and scents of their lovemaking were long gone, except in her mind. The bed was re-dressed, with new drapes and covers in a heavenly shade of blue. But here she had lost her heart. More fool she. Evidently, he had moved on.

As the clock chimed eleven, a key scraped in the lock downstairs, the sound loud in the eerie silence. Turning, panic rising in her breast, Helena ran outside the room, the worn boards creaking under her weight. She didn't have time to run all the way downstairs, but she would not let him catch her here. This room would remain sacred in her memories, if not in his. She ran down a floor to the main rooms.

The front parlor here was formally furnished in an old-fashioned style that reminded her of a little-used room in the family seat at Edensor Abbey. It meant little to her, since they had never spent much time there. Here she would close the door on this business. Either she would leave a disgraced woman, or an acknowledged wife. She prepared to fight the battle of her life.

His tread sounded on the stairs. He didn't call her name or check the rooms downstairs. He came straight to her. She stood on the far side of the room to the door, a circular table between her and the doorway.

As always the sight of him made her heart leap, but she was accustomed to that, and she had braced herself for the impact. Two steps into the room, he halted and gazed at her, his eyes hungry, his face calm. He bowed formally, cutting her to the bone.

"We're not in public now," she said softly. "You don't have to do that."

"I do," he said, straightening. "I owe you much more than that."

"How so?" She tilted her head to one side, studying him. He appeared haggard, as if he had not slept, shadows like thumbprints under his eyes. She would not give him pity. He did not deserve it for leaving her heartbroken five years before. But facing him now, remembering all they had said and done, she had to work to recall that terrible moment when her world had collapsed around her.

"I admire your forbearance and your understanding." His voice held the slightest quaver, and when he spoke again, he'd pitched the tone deeper, no doubt to cover up any trace of weakness. "What I did to you was unforgivable. But I had made a discovery and I could not share it with you. I could hardly understand it myself at the time."

"Why could you not share it with me?"

"Because it nearly killed me to learn it. How could I do that to you?"

He sounded almost caring. She curled her lip. "What is so terrible? Why would you break all your promises?"

He did not answer immediately, but glanced away. Dipping a hand into the pocket of his deep crimson coat, he drew out a paper. So he'd come prepared, too. "Look at this." Placing two fingers on the paper, he shoved it across the table.

She stepped close enough to see it. Even touching something that had left his possession so recently made her heart beat a little faster. She was a fool, no doubt about it.

Someone had crumpled this sheet, but the creases were faint. After she read it through, she read it again. He had given her a statement from his mother that she'd had an affair with the Duke of Kirkburton and he, Tom, was the result.

Horror swept through her, and then a building sense of triumph, glowing deep in her belly. "So you think you took your sister to bed?" Before she read the document through again, she glanced up at him.

All the color had leached from his face. He gave a terse nod.

"Who wrote this?" she asked.

"My mother."

"You're certain it's not a forgery?"

"I know her writing too well for anyone to deceive me."

She folded her arms. "Tell me what you know." Before she showed him what she had, she must hear his story in full and know what she had to contend with.

"My mother was pregnant before my father bedded her. It's known that she was courted by both men, Northwich and Kirkburton. Society was abuzz with it at the time. You cannot deny that."

She shrugged. "Of course not. It's one of the reasons our families are at odds. Your father won her."

His lips twisted into a wry grin. "In a way. She did not tell him until they were in Rome. He wanted the blessing of his Pope and his king before he bedded her, and it was then that she told him. He made her write that confession, but the King prevailed on him not to deny her or the child."

"Of course he did," she said, her lip curling in a sneer. "I assume when you say 'the King,' you are referring to the Old Pretender?"

He shrugged in his turn. "If you wish to call him that. We won't fall out over that here."

"That seems tolerant from a lifelong Jacobite."

He met her gaze coolly. "I was born into it. It is not necessarily where my heart lies." He stopped and looked away, visibly collecting himself before he came back to her. "The Stuarts have done us no favors. They took all and gave little back. I told you and your brother that."

Folding her hands together, gripping them hard, she said, "Go on. Tell me what you know."

"You seem remarkably collected for a woman who has just met her brother."

"Who has slept with her brother, you mean." Even saying it aloud did not make her believe it. Putting her hand in her pocket, she touched the fat sheaf of papers resting there. But there was still a possibility that Tom had told her the truth. It depended on the date. "When is your birthday?"

His dark brows slashed together. "Why is that important?"

"It's vital. Tell me."

"September the twentieth."

"Then you sacrificed our love for nothing. We are truly married."

* * * *

Disbelief hammered its way through Tom. Facing her had been bad enough, but now she refused to believe him? He needed to convince her, or she would never move on. The notion made his heart bleed, but they had to get past this. "You cannot do this, Helena. Your life is worth more than pining for a mistake we made in our youth. Our marriage may have been conducted properly, but we are not married. Siblings cannot marry."

"We are not siblings."

He was coming to the end of his rope. "Tell me." The words came out as an order, but he was past politeness. Facing her, telling her the terrible thing they had unwittingly done was bad enough, but her disbelief made his task exponentially more difficult. "We cannot possibly sue for annulment, for that would be to tell everyone our mistake, but we can agree to disregard this mistake and provide the truth, should anyone require it in the future."

She flicked away his concern with a delicate brush of her hand. "You were born in September, so the earliest you could have been conceived was December, is it not?"

He nodded, waiting to see where she would take this.

She paused to draw a sheaf of papers out of her pocket. Spreading them before her, she sorted through them, and selected a few. A small smile curled her delectable lips. If he had to spend much more time alone in this room with her, he would surely go mad.

She lifted her head, addressing him coolly. "According to that note and your father's account, your mother and my father had an affair, which ended with your mother's pregnancy."

He nodded. "Succinct and to the point, but yes."

"When your parents married, your father took your mother to Rome."

He nodded again, but said nothing this time.

"When did your parents marry?"

"In July 1720."

"So in order for you to be my father's son, the affair must have continued after our parents married, since my parents married in August." She shook her head. "They were at odds, even then. How sad that they did not follow their hearts."

"Then you don't deny that they were lovers?"

She shrugged, the shoulder of her green gown slipping fractionally. When she turned her head, her silvery hair caught the light from the single window, sending a shaft of sunlight to pierce his heart. "My father certainly loved her, and it is true that he wanted to marry her, but his parents refused to countenance the union and arranged the marriage with my mother. They did not have the courage to defy their parents." She turned a face as hard as marble to him, asking the question without words.

"Yes," he said, in answer. "Yes, if we were married in truth, I would have done anything to keep you, defied anyone. Is that what you wanted to hear?"

Her delicately arched brows, several shades darker than her hair, rose. "Yes, I did need to hear that. To continue." She glanced at one of the papers she'd spread on the table. It was a letter of some kind, but he could not read it from the other side of the table. "You obviously know that my father took my mother abroad. He wished to present her at Versailles. First they sailed to Italy and visited the centers of classical culture. Your parents were in Rome for a different reason."

"My parents did not return to England until March the following year. Yours returned in time for the Season the year after that, with their son."

"After my grandmother died, the King persuaded him to claim the title and to rebuild his fortune. He said my father would be of more use if he were not attainted, and he provided a firm base in England. Reluctantly, my parents returned."

She had found some loophole that appeared to explain he was not there. But his mother would not have lied to his father about such an important matter. Her father adored her, and that admission had nearly driven him to leave her or at the least disown his son. If it were not that the King had ordered him to keep both wife and child, he might have left her in Rome.

Helena seemed at her coolest, the mask of elegant calm firmly in place. She gave a sharp businesslike nod and then put her fingers on two of the papers and pushed them over to him in a mirror of his earlier gesture. As if in a dream, he picked them up and glanced at them. A letter and a receipt. He returned his attention to her.

Helena allowed herself a grin, although he had no idea what she had to smile about. Perhaps it was relief that at last they were facing reality. "Do you remember what else happened in 1720?"

He would play along with her. If she needed to recite events from the year in question to put the circumstances into context, so be it. "Many things. The most notable is probably the South Sea Bubble." His father had lost no money in the crash of the stocks, because he had no money to invest, but the scandal had cost many people dearly. The South Sea Company had purchased the national debt, so when the company collapsed, the country had nearly followed suit.

"Exactly. Do you remember the timing?"

He frowned. Surely they had dealt with that sideline. "The company collapsed in the autumn of 1720."

"Exactly. Because of that, my parents never set foot on the Continent in that year, or the year after, for that matter. That was a ruse."

Wait, what had she said? His heart jolted. He forced his control back to what it should be, but the papers he held trembled.

She glanced at the other papers and then met his eyes once more. "My father's wedding was timed so that his leaving England would not be remarked as more than a bride-trip. He married my mother and took her to the South Seas. They were on a mission on behalf of Sir Robert Walpole and other investors, but when they left in August, the South Sea Company was still going strong, so they did not wish to alarm a volatile market. It was given out that they had gone abroad on their honeymoon, but they never set foot on the continent."

He heard the words with dull shock. Each echoed around his brain as if they had no meaning. Eventually he roused himself enough to ask, "When did they return?"

"The market collapsed in September, so my father used the visit to conduct other matters. He bought land, and businesses. We have ample proof of his visit." She nodded to the bundle of papers on the table and glanced at the two in his hands. "Here's what proof I could gather quickly."

He spread the papers out on the table. One was a letter, briefly saying they had arrived safely. It was dated and sealed, but on its own it was no proof. Another, however, was a bill of sale for a parcel of land in Jamaica. That was a formal document, and it was dated and signed in December 1720.

"And this is your father's signature?"

"Indubitably."

The signature was the same as the one on the letter. "This is true?"

She nodded again. "They did not arrive back in Britain until the following April."

It was true. The Duke of Kirkburton was not his father.

His knees gave way, and he grabbed the table for support. It wobbled, and he snatched it back. Helena rounded the table quickly and grabbed his elbow, guiding him to a heavy wing back chair that stood by the fireplace.

He slumped into it, but gripped her hand tightly. "You have more proof?" Not that he needed it. He needed time to assimilate what had just happened here.

"Land deeds, letters, certificates of employment..." She laughed shakily. "My father never throws anything away. They sold out of the South Sea Company before they left, which was just as well, as it turned out."

He nodded and grinned wryly. "Your family is always on the winning side, is it not?"

"I wouldn't say that. They lost a great deal in the Civil War. They were royalists, too."

Staring at the papers on the table, mocking his own contribution, the sheet of writing that had cost him his happiness, he swallowed. "My mother lied? Why would she lie?"

"Any number of reasons. I never knew the lady, so I cannot say."

"She was a good woman. I remember her. She died when I was thirteen. She was a society beauty, but so much more than that." He let his melancholy free. If she had lied, why would she do so? "What reason would she have for lying?"

In a swish of skirts she bent down, sitting on her heels so they faced each other. They still only touched where their hands were linked. "I cannot say," she repeated carefully and slowly. "Perhaps your father knows."

He met her gaze. "He believes it too. He made her confess and write the note. Then he accepted me as his."

She frowned. "Why would he do that? From what I know of your father, he is as much a family man as mine. My father would have sent his wife away to have the child in secret. He would never have accepted him as his heir. Later children, maybe, but not the heir!"

He was as puzzled as she was. "I do not know," he said. "But I mean to find out. You swear this is true?"

Without hesitation, she nodded. "Walpole and the group of men who were concerned about the Bubble deliberately confused anyone asking where my father was. They said he went abroad on his marriage, because they did not want people to know they were concerned. The market was volatile to the point of madness. One word in the wrong direction would have forced the collapse. As it happened, it collapsed anyway, but only after my father had arrived in the South Seas."

"Dear God," he said, his words scarcely more than a breath. "This is hard to believe. For the last five years, I've thought of us as siblings. Or tried to." With her so close he could not deny the truth. "I never succeeded. I told myself that love is love, that I had mistaken romantic love for a different kind of connection."

He gripped her hand so tightly that he must be hurting her but she never showed, by a twitch or a change in her lovely eyes, that he was doing so.

With an effort, he relaxed his hold. She did not pull her hand away but left it there, resting in his. That small gesture meant so much to him.

"I lied to myself and kept on lying, but it didn't work. It was still a lie."

She nodded. "My feelings were never confused, not after the first shock."

"I'm so sorry." His words were so inadequate, but he had to start somewhere.

"At first I believed what you said in the letter. Then I thought again, and remembered. You didn't lie here, not in this house. I know that for certain. But I was young and I had no way of getting through to you. I thought of barging into your house and demanding an answer. I thought of confessing all to my parents. But what would those tactics do? Where would they leave me? So I did nothing and waited."

"You were wiser than I, love." The word had just slipped out, but he would not take it back now. "I made inquiries, but everything I discovered spoke to the truth of what my mother said. I went to Rome—"

"You did?"

"What else could I do? I needed the truth. There, I discovered exactly nothing. No evidence that your parents had been there all that time ago, but that proved nothing."

He got to his feet. She came with him, rising like Venus from the waves in a froth of green silk.

"Do we speak of everything now?"

A smile toyed with the corners of her mouth. "Do we have to? Or will we meet again?"

"We have to." Clasping her hands between his, he drew her closer. "It appears we are married, after all. But give me some time, love. I need to talk to my father, to discover why my mother could lie to him in that way." He closed his eyes. "He told me five years ago."

Her eyes widened. "You told him about us?"

"I didn't have to. He'd been watching us. He knew I felt more than I should for you. He told me that my mother confessed she was carrying another man's child in Rome. He said that he left her and traveled around Italy, trying to decide on his course of action. He loved her, you see. When he returned, the child had been born. He was ready to leave me with guardians in Rome, but the King feared the gossip would be damaging and prevailed on him to keep me."

So often children born that way, illicit, unwanted children disappeared as if they had never existed. "He loved her, so he kept me." He paused. "There was another reason. At the time he believed himself incapable of siring children. Although he'd had mistresses, he'd never sired a child."

He shook his head. "My father must have been remarkably naive at the time. He discovered how fertile he was when my brothers and sisters came along. I believed it because he believed it."

They gazed at each other. He had never dreamed she would be this close again, or if she was, that he would have her in his grasp. "Every time I saw you I wanted you. Always and ever, I desired you. How could I stay in the same room as you when I felt like that? How could I share such a terrible secret with you?"

"I saw it, but you would not let me anywhere near you."

"I dared not. Or I might have done this."

Even though the matter was far from settled, he could not resist drawing her close and bringing his mouth down on hers.

She opened to him immediately and it was as if the last five years melted away as they kissed. He moaned into her mouth, his shaft rising, and all his primitive instincts rose, shrieking, "Take her! Take her!" into his mind.

He pushed her away, gasping. "To touch you is to want you. We cannot."

"Why not?" She moved closer, nestling against his chest. "I forgive you. Your reasons were perfectly correct, although I will probably punish you for not telling me sooner. Except for when I want to hit you, of course." Sliding her hand into her pocket, she drew out an object he had not seen for five years. His signet ring. "This is still valid."

He blinked away a tear as he took it and fitted it on her finger. "It is also still too big for you."

She folded her fingers over it. "It's mine. You gave it to me."

"It is always yours. But I will get you another. One that fits."

Her smile warmed him right to his heart. "Why did you wait this long?"

"I told myself more than once that I should tell you, but I was a coward. I told myself I wanted to spare you the agony. I searched the family records, and while I did not find absolute proof, everything pointed to my mother telling the truth. Your father's friends concealed his mission so effectively that not one of the publications from that time reported that he had gone to the Americas. I went to the newspaper offices and demanded to see their archives. I did everything I could think of to disprove what she said, but I could not. And I could not come near you without wanting you, so I kept away. I vowed that when I saw you marry another man, I would give you my blessing. I told myself when you moved on, so would I. And there was the other matter."

"Ah, yes," she said. "That." She rested her forehead against his chest. "It seems unfair that political matters affect us so closely, but that's the nature of the beast, is it not?"

He touched her cheek, marveling at his right to do so. "And you did not move on. This week it became clear to me that you had to know. I didn't want you to feel what I did when I learned what we were to each other. That I had taken my sister to my bed."

She shuddered. "If that had been true, I would have wanted to know. I could have fallen pregnant. What then?"

He stared at her, a chill spreading through him. "I don't know. Would we have sacrificed ourselves for our child?"

Her little head shake told him everything and nothing. "I don't know either. But it didn't happen."

He clasped her closer. "I know what would have happened. I would have claimed you, and we would have been forced to investigate my mother's claims sooner. All this would have come out into the open."

"But we didn't know that."

No, they didn't. Speculating on would haves and should haves was nonsense. They were here now, after throwing so much time away. He didn't want to waste another moment. "Shall we carry on where we left off?"

She stared at him, eyes dancing.

"If you say yes, we'll leave England today, tonight. No going home to pack, no looking back." Even as he said it, the mental pictures of the people he would hurt and those he would let down danced before his eyes.

"We can't."

"No." The visions of freedom crashed and burned, never to return. "We have to face people, do we not? Tell them what we've done."

"It won't be so bad," she said softly, cradling his jaw in her hand.

"Not if we do it together. We might even go to live in that house in France after all."

"Perhaps. But we were foolish to think we could do that in the first place."

He nodded. "You're right. We cannot do such a thing."

She gave a sudden spurt of laughter. "My brother would have hunted us down. He would not have rested. It was foolish of me to even imagine that he would."

"Why are you laughing?"

"Because we are here, and married, and we cannot fail. Not now."

He wished he had such lightness of spirit because he had no such expectation. But at least he knew he would fight for her. "Make love with me." Nothing mattered more. He hungered to know how she had changed and what she looked like now. Her skin was still dewy-soft. The thought of waking with that perfection within reach every morning for the rest of his life made him giddy.

"Yes."

Right then and there he tumbled even deeper in love with her. Her faith, her lack of doubt, humbled him. With her, he could be a better person. The last five years had completed his education. He had delved into deeper cynicism and at the bottom, to his surprise, found answers. Practical answers that served to keep the balance between their two families level.

He led her upstairs and pushed open the door to the bedroom. "You've already been up here," he said.

"Yes. How did you know?"

"Your perfume."

"I'm not wearing any perfume."

He drew her close and breathed in deep. "I beg to differ." He glanced down at her gown. "You look lovely, but I wager you'll look better with this off."

"Are we not rushing into this?"

"Yes." He had to confess all. "But I am afraid, sweetheart. I'm afraid you will change your mind, or disappear, and I'll never have this chance again. I'm afraid I'll never touch you again, never hold you or call you mine."

Who knew what waited for them outside these doors?

"No more talk. We'll decide what to do after. Later. Should I send your carriage away?"

Another laugh. "Good lord, no! Julius would only send another to collect me."

Undressing her proved a delight he should perhaps have lingered over, but he could not. Now she was here, now he was with her, he couldn't wait to see her, to touch her. As he revealed more, he became more intoxicated. When he urged her to turn around so he could unfasten her stays, she wagged a finger at him mischievously.

"Watch." She unhooked her stays from the front. "My mother thinks it's scandalous that I've taken to using this style. Of course for formal wear, I use the back lacing, but this way I can undress myself and get dressed again." She paused, her hands on the last hook. "Which is of course why it is scandalous."

"You should let me unlace you sometimes." There he went, speaking as if their staying together was a foregone conclusion, but he could not imagine any other outcome.

"I will." Then his certainty was reflected in her.

When she was in her shift and nothing else, he reached for her and helped her with her last garment. He was naked and rampantly aroused, his cock hard and aching for her, their clothes scattered haphazardly over the floor, the chair by the dressing table, and the one by the window.

He'd dragged the curtains across but had not bothered to arrange them, only to cover their actions from prying eyes. He hid nothing from her, but revelled in her possessive gaze. With the fine lawn whisked over her head, she was naked too.

"Here we are equals. But we were wrong before." He murmured the words against her hair, rippling down now it was free of the restraining pins. "We cannot shut the world out. We have to let it in." If he had learned anything while they'd been apart, it was this. "All that you are makes you more precious to me."

How could he have ever imagined they were brother and sister? She was his love, the only person meant for him, and he for her. That was why— "I took no mistresses. I shared my bed with nobody while we were apart."

She stared up at him, blinking. "Truly?"

He smiled at her amazement. "Yes, truly. I wanted nobody else. Every woman I met I compared to you, and they all came up wanting."

She laughed and lowered her head. "I am not so perfect. My sister is considered the beauty."

"Then they are mad or blind. You are perfect for me, Helena, and you are the only woman I want."

Her sigh sent a hot breath of air across his chest. "You're perfect too. That's why I didn't accept any offers. That, and knowing I was already married." She lifted her chin. "How could you ever have expected me to move on just with your say-so? After I obtained our certificate of marriage, do you know how many times I tried to see you?"

"I contrived never to be alone with you," he confessed. "It was too dangerous." Bending his head, he brushed his lips across hers. "Now get into that bed before I burst."

His confession sent her into gales of laughter. She was still laughing when he joined her, but he put paid to that when he rolled over her and kissed her.

"Sweetheart, this is what I dreamed of."

The years melted away. He had a lot to make up for, and he would devote every waking moment to it. Starting today.

When he touched her, he discovered how wet she was. He lifted his fingers to his mouth and tasted them, watched her eyes widen.

"Let me reacquaint myself with you and assure myself that this really is my wife in bed with me."

Kissing her was to taste heaven. He kissed down her neck, stroking his lips over her shoulders. The glory of her breasts awaited him, twin cushions of bounty tipped with rosettes that hardened into stiff peaks when he took them into his mouth and sucked, and then licked around them. Her gasps and tiny moans of delight fed his need to please her, to give her everything he could.

He could have feasted on them all day, but more luscious delights awaited him, and he did not want to miss them. Kissing down, he dipped his tongue into the sweet indentation of her navel and then farther. She gripped his hair. Now it was long she could grasp handfuls of it. She tugged.

"Tom, you cannot…"

"Watch me." He lifted his head and met her wide-eyed blue gaze. "I want to. I need to claim you, every part of you."

"Tom, how…?"

He took his first lick of her intimate juices. "Now be quiet and enjoy."

Her sighs and moans delighted and enthralled him. He explored her fully, tasting every part of her. She needed no preparation, but he urged her anyway, determined he would give her pleasure this way first.

She did not need telling this time. Spreading her legs, she lifted her knees to give him greater access. When she pushed her cleft at him, he rejoiced and did as she bade him, sucking and teasing. He inserted a finger into her silky heat, urging her to greater heights.

She cried out, her body clamping down on him, the pulses signaling her release. Her first release. He did not return to her until he had wrung every last spasm from her, and then he surged back up the bed, unable to wait a moment longer.

He notched his shaft into her wet heat and plunged. Then gasped. She was so tight, but so lusciously welcoming. When he was embedded as deeply as possible, he stopped. "If I move I'll end this too soon, and I want to make you come once more at least."

"Come?" Her eyes were shining.

"That's what it is generally called. I used that word with you before."

"You remember that?"

"Every moment. Every second. Every thrust," he said, matching action to words.

As he drove deeply, and she caught the rhythm, she gripped his shoulders, her mouth dropping open as she gasped his name.

He claimed her mouth, kissing her fiercely as he took her further and harder, until they were working as one. As he stroked into her, she met him, grinding her body against his. Her breasts quivered with each stroke, her nipples grazing his chest every time he came down on her.

When he found that spot inside her, he ensured his cock nudged it with every thrust. The effect stunned and delighted him. Clutching him so hard that she would leave marks, she quivered and pulsed, her body fiercely responding to him.

He could hold back no longer.

He barely drew out of her in time, and with a groan, spent himself on her stomach, each throb wrenching the soul from his body.

Hovering above her, his arms shook. Hair fell over his face when he hung his head, panting, trying to recover enough to grab the towel that lay within reach on the washstand. With an effort, he managed the feat, and wiped her clean before lying next to her and pulling her into his arms.

"Why did you do that?" Her features reflected her bewildered tone.

"What, sweetheart?" Sleep swept over him, the slumber of the sated male, but her question kept him awake.

"You know—on my stomach."

"Ah. Well, we've agreed that we are not running away this time. Reconciling ourselves to our families could take some time and if—when—we have a child, I would prefer that its legitimacy is unquestioned. There's still a risk of pregnancy, but I've done my best to reduce it." Since he was awake now he kissed her.

Her fingers around his chin, the pressure of her body against him gave him more than enough to fight for.

Their lips parted and she sighed and rested against him. "I should like to remain here always."

"The outside world would come knocking. Indeed, it's a wonder this place has remained hidden from our people, since both our families are experts at uncovering matters people prefer to keep secret."

"Yes." She curved her arm around his waist. "Until recently Julius put all his energies into—" She broke off with a guilty gasp.

He chuckled. "I'll say it first, shall I? My father knows that King James married Maria Rubio prior to his official marriage to Queen Maria Clementina. Then, after the Queen left him, he went back to his first love. Which makes the children from the marriage to Maria legitimate. Does that ease your mind that I know?"

"In a way," she admitted. She stroked his stomach in a very distracting way. "But that was not all. Julius knows that you know. Our family and yours have different aims."

"Not so much." He glanced down and dragged the covers over their cooling bodies. "My father wants my brother or my sisters to marry one of the candidates, giving them a claim to the throne. Your family has been marrying them with alarming rapidity."

"But we don't want them to be monarchs."

"True." He should tell her the truth. "Which is why I've been helping your brother covertly. Although if you tell him, I doubt he'll be grateful."

She mumbled something into his shoulder, which he didn't catch, and then moved her head away. "I think he knows. He's puzzled."

After smiling down at her like a loon, he kissed her.

"He found love again recently."

"She's not a daughter of the Old Pretender." That was the original reason Julius had sought Eve out.

"I know. Your brother kindly let me know, in a roundabout way." He sighed. "If I could find the original birth certificate between Maria and the King, I'd toss it into the flames. It has diverted my father badly. I would rather accept what we have and work with that. He still has the idealism of his youth."

"Would you truly destroy it?"

He nodded. "The Stuarts will not come back. I'm convinced of that. Forcing a candidate from a dubiously legitimate marriage on to an unwilling populace is not the way to achieve it. She was a wise woman, Maria Rubio."

"How so?"

"She loved King James, but she did not trust him or his advisors, so she sent the children away to be raised in secret. I believe she loved her children too much to force the issue. Don't forget that at any time, she could have presented her certificate of marriage and claimed legitimacy for her children, but she chose not to."

Helena raised a brow. "Chose? Or perhaps she was made to send them into exile to keep them secret? Now the secret is known in certain circles, the Young Pretender seems determined to find them first."

He nodded. "And his intentions are murderous. Another reason to discover them before he does. What is done, is done, my sweet. We cannot go back, only go on, but the Restoration of the last century gave my father more ideas. It might happen. Who knows?" He gazed at her, his recovery well under way. His shaft sprang back into awareness, demanding attention like an eager child after a sweetmeat.

Regretfully he would have to deny it. "If we stay here, we'll be doing more than discussing politics. We need a plan, sweetheart. I'm claiming you as my wife. No waiting, not anymore. I will speak to my father today."

"I can find you more proof, if you wish."

He turned her in his arms, bending to kiss her once more. "This will not be an easy path. We cannot expect to announce our marriage to our families and have them welcome us with open arms. It will take time, my love, for them to accept us. Are you ready for that?"

She nodded. "I don't want to give my family up. If we have to live at a distance, so be it, but I can't reject them completely. We might be able to mend the feud, or we might cause a temporary lull, but that is not likely, love. I suspect both our families will do all they can to reject us or negate the marriage."

He hated the twinge of pain that crossed her features and the frown it put between her eyes. "Perhaps. But I will not give you up."

"Nor I you."

Chapter 14

Helena arrived back at Julius's London house in time to dress for dinner. Still bathing in the glow of reconciling with Tom, she had hoped to gain her room without interruption, but as she passed the main salon on the first floor, Eve came out.

"Ah, Helena, I thought I heard you come in." She appeared harassed, her usually smiling mouth in a thin line, and her eyes wary. "Could you spare a moment?"

Wondering what had happened, Helena followed Eve in. The gracious drawing room contained delicate French furniture upholstered in forget-me-not blue, and the wide windows let in any daylight available. In the midafternoon, the sun was beginning its decline to the horizon, but there was still plenty of light, enough for the wax candles in the sconces to remain unlit.

Unfortunately, the room also contained her mother and Julius, arms folded, grim-faced.

"I said an hour," he said.

"You sound like my father."

"He is upstairs. He'll be joining us shortly," her mother said.

Helena made her curtsey to her mother, who regarded her daughter with a jaundiced eye.

"Sir George is in Derbyshire, awaiting the birth of his firstborn. That child should have been yours."

The notion repelled her even more now. "I'm happy for him, Mother. I'm also delighted that I had the good sense to reject him. We would never have suited." She changed the subject briskly. "I am surprised to see you here, ma'am. Is this not a distinctly unfashionable time of year to come to town?"

"Nevertheless, I know my duty," her mother said. She folded her hands in the lap of her dark red afternoon gown. "I have come to take you home. I have had enough shilly-shallying, my girl. You have had all the time in the world to sort out your affairs, and you have failed to do so. Since you will have it, I have come to save you from yourself."

Helena glanced at Julius, who motioned to a chair by the fire. Feeling trapped, she sat. Matters were coming to a head much faster than she had imagined. On the way home, she'd made her plan. She would tell Julius and Eve tomorrow morning and then let them prove anything they wanted, but she agreed with Tom. They would wait only as long as needful to inform their families of their intentions.

Sooner than that, if tonight was any indication. She lifted her chin defiantly. She would lie no more.

"The rumors have spread to Derbyshire," Julius said gloomily. He strolled to the window, hands in the capacious pockets of his coat. "I can do no more. If you wish to continue with your plan to move to your own establishment, I will support you, but I cannot think it wise."

"What rumors?" she demanded. "Oh, I know why, but I want to know precisely what they are saying."

Julius turned around, the light casting him into shadow, but she could still see that his mouth was set in a grim line. "That you were trysting with Lord Alconbury in that inn last week. I have, at your request, neither confirmed nor denied the stories, but they have gone too far now for me to nip them in the bud."

Her father stood in the doorway. He did not usually intervene in his wife's management of the household and their children, but this time, here he was. "If you come home with us, I swear I will do everything in my power to protect you from malicious gossip. I will not have you subjected to that viciousness."

"You are always welcome to stay with us, Helena," Julius said softly from the other side of the room. "But things must necessarily change."

"By which you mean I may no longer expect to attract a husband I may be comfortable with," she said primly and then broke into a smile. She was bursting to tell them, but even more she wanted her mother to condemn herself even more.

"Are you glad?" The duchess bridled, positively drew herself up and trembled with rage. "Can you be happy that you are about to dwindle into overlooked and never-thanked spinsterhood? I daresay your father could find someone to marry you. After all, your portion is generous. But you can expect no more favors, and you will not have the pick of the crop, as you have before. We must work to restore your reputation, but it will not be easy, and by the time we have achieved it, you will be well past marriageable age. Is that clear enough for you, Helena?"

Julius groaned. "Why did you not allow me to cover this story? I have done it before."

Ah, yes, with Connie, their cousin Alex's wife. Connie was in direr straits than Helena had ever found herself, and not through any fault of her own. Julius had restored her reputation, simply by denying the events had ever taken place. He could not do that with Helena, not now. His silence had given tacit acceptance to the rumors flying around town, and obviously, the country, too. But they did not matter because she had won.

Julius deserved an answer. "Julius you've been unfailingly kind and patient with me. Thank you."

Her brother inclined his head, but he stayed silent, giving her the floor.

"But you do not have to worry about me any longer." She encompassed her mother in her glance and then fixed her attention on her father. "I am already married. I have been so for the last five years."

* * * *

Tom waited until the following day to break the news to his father. While he grieved to bring any more distress to him, this task would not wait. Nor should it. He intended to busy himself finding a house for them for a few weeks, until they could decide what they wanted to do next. He had to admit that would depend on what their families wanted, because, although he would prefer to whisk his wife away to a private paradise of their own, that would have to wait.

Accordingly, he sought an interview with him before his father left the house the following morning. Breakfast was served at noon in London, but they were out and about before that. Tom had lodged a copy of the marriage certificate with the family's London lawyer, apologizing for the late delivery. He would carry a picture of the way the clerk had reacted to the end of his days. The man had glanced at it, picked up his spectacles from the debris on his desk to take a closer look, and then glanced at Tom and back at the paper before he'd said, "Yes, my lord," in such a wooden tone that Tom knew he was deeply affected.

The murmurs began even before he had cleared the office. The news would not be circulated from there, but by tomorrow London would know.

His father tended to remain in the house before breakfast, attending to necessary business and writing letters, so Tom was fairly confident of finding him the small office on the first floor, behind the main rooms.

Sure enough when he tapped on the door, the irritable "Come!" told him his father was at home and not happy with whatever he was dealing with.

He would be even unhappier when Tom told him his news. However, if he heard the tidings from anyone else, the duke would probably have the kind of apoplexy that would affect his health. Tom loved him too much to risk that occurrence.

His father's usually stern expression softened when Tom entered the room. He gestured to a chair. "Good morning, Alconbury. You have saved me from the tedious task of checking the list of candidates for the position of second footman." He sighed. "I should leave such matters to Richardson, but I cannot say that I altogether trust him."

"You trust nobody, Papa." Tom drew up a chair and sat, holding the papers he'd brought with him.

"I have good reason. Kirkburton constantly sends spies to me."

"And you do not send them to him? Or rather, to his son."

His father carefully placed his pen in the stand and rolled his shoulders, leaning back in his well-worn but supremely comfortable chair. He refused to allow the dowager to replace it, claiming it was the best chair he'd ever sat in, and he would never find another. "I see you came armed. Is this new information, or something I've forgotten to discuss with you?"

Tom shook his head. He took his last look at his father, because in a moment their whole relationship would change. He greatly respected his parent for refusing to deny his wife and the cuckoo in his nest, but now he loved him more. "I'm sorry I have to bring this matter to your attention, sir."

His father regarded the pile of unopened correspondence next to him with a grimace. "One more will not make a great difference. Out with it, boy!"

Tom could not resist a grin, despite the tension turning his insides into a small, painful knot. The epithet told him that his father was in an averagely good mood. "Do you remember when, five years ago, you told me the story of my birth?"

All notions of good temper disappeared. The duke took on the mien of an icicle. "Yes."

"Because of that information, I terminated a relationship with someone I cared for very much."

A little of the icicle thawed. The duke raised a brow. "I hope you were not shamed into it. You have nothing to be ashamed of, my son."

Now that epithet he had used deliberately. "I know that. But thank you." Now he was here, he did not know how to begin. He'd rehearsed a speech, but it left him now. His mind went blank to all but one fact. "Five years ago I married Helena Vernon."

His father had rested his hands on his desk. Both hands clenched into tight fists.

"When you told me of my parentage, I immediately cut the relationship." The remembrance of what giving up all his hopes had done returned to him with a sharp pang.

"Why would you marry her without asking me?"

The duke spoke mildly, but Tom was not deceived.

"Papa, we fell in love before we realized who we were. I saw her and wanted her. She felt the same. Once I learned your secret, I assumed I had mistaken love of a brother for his sister. Obviously applying for an annulment was out of the question. I fell deeply in love with her. Then her mother tried to compel her to marry a man of her choosing, and she was deeply distressed. I claimed her before anyone else could."

"Like picking a kitten from a litter?" The duke's dry words pierced Tom to the heart.

"Like making sure of the woman who already had my heart."

"But you cut off the connection? Then there is no harm done, is there?" his father said. "Is that why you refused to accept any of the young ladies your grandmother pushed your way?"

Tom nodded. "I tried, but I could not forget her. I kept away from her, but I knew I had hurt her greatly. I did not tell her why I had cut the connection. I only told her that our marriage was a sham. I could not bring that to her." He looked away. Even recalling that time brought back the gnawing agony that had sliced into him for the last five years. "Why would I cause another person the same pain that I felt? I let her believe I'd had second thoughts, thinking the reputation our family has with hers would persuade her of my perfidy. It did not, but I still kept away."

This time his father just nodded, but his hands relaxed a little.

"However, the recent incident brought us together again."

"About that…" his father said.

"She was abducted by a man determined to take her to the border and marry her. I happened to be there when it happened, so I went in immediate pursuit. I could do nothing else."

"In that I agree. No young woman deserves that fate."

"Unfortunately I did not catch up with her until later, after dark, so her reputation was endangered. There was a fracas, which Lamaire and I did our best to quell, but the occupants of the taproom in the inn saw some of it and recognized Helena. I never made any secret of my identity."

"So someone recognized you both?" the duke said.

Tom saw the point. "I had not thought that far."

"But it is interesting, is it not, that you were so easily recognized? What was the name of the man who took her?"

"Everslade. However, Winterton claims he is not Lord Everslade, but an impostor. Is he one of ours?" They had agents everywhere, but Tom had never seen the man before he had come to London.

"No."

"The current whereabouts of the real Lord Everslade are not known."

"Hmm." The duke plucked his pen from the tray, dipped it in the ink, and made a note. "I'll make inquiries."

"We left the impostor at the inn. I was more concerned with getting Helena to safety. What she said then, on the way back to town, convinced me that I was doing her a disservice to let her believe anything but the truth about us. I arranged to meet her privately and tell her."

"Why did you not tell her immediately?"

Tom sent his father a sharp look. "She was distressed. You would want me to tell her that she had married her brother?"

The duke pursed his lips and frowned. "I see your point."

"I met her and told her. Only then did she prove to me that her father could not have sired me." He pushed the documents that Helena had given him to his father.

The duke took his time reading through the papers. Tom clasped his hands together to prevent drumming his fingers or fidgeting. His father could not abide fidgeting.

Eventually, his father raised his head, his face a careful mask of imperturbability. "So it appears we still do not know who fathered you. I would love to acknowledge you as my true son, but in truth, I cannot. I did not have intimate relations with your mother until after she gave birth to you, and that is the absolute truth. Someone else got there before I did. I will undertake to discover all I can, but we may never know."

"Who would she be hiding? Who is so important that their identity must be kept secret?"

His father's heavy-lidded eyes flickered just for a moment. "I do not know, but I will do all in my power to discover. I loved your mother very much, and she reciprocated the emotion. By telling me what she did, she risked everything we had."

But his father had forgiven her, where most men would not have. He had even acknowledged Tom as his son.

The duke sighed. "Enough. Of course this means that you are still legitimately married to Lady Helena Vernon. That makes mincemeat of the rumors currently infesting every quarter of town."

"Yes it does." Tom felt a smile twitch at the corner of his mouth, but he would not give way to it here. The happiness he felt was not appropriate for this place or time. "I mean to claim her as soon as possible. She is my wife, and I will acknowledge her as such. We will say we married quietly and chose to keep our union from prying eyes."

"That will do," the duke said. "I suppose there is no hope for it. But I cannot accept her into this house, Thomas. You must know that. I cannot risk her discovering anything she should not. She must become a Dankworth and cleave to you."

Recalling Helena's relationship with her family, Tom doubted that would ever come to pass, except nominally. He got to his feet. "I meant to hire a house for us until we have resolved the matter of the scandal. We can only scotch it by appearing in public, I believe. I was hoping for your support."

His father was notorious for his cold behavior, particularly in public. In private he possessed a vicious temper, but very few people saw that, and he did his best to curtail it, having decided that matters undertaken in that state stood little chance of success. "A man," he said once, "finding me in a temper has stolen a march on me. I have lost before I have begun."

But fire burned in the Duke of Northwich's eyes.

"You may disown me, sir," Tom said.

"That is the devil of it," his father replied. "I cannot. I have acknowledged you for many years, and I cannot cast you off now. Legally, you are my son and heir, and you will remain so. Until your dying day."

Tom felt a chill, shivering through his very bones, despite the cozy warmth of the room they sat in. The fire spat, and the sound made him start in shock.

The doorbell clanged.

Premonition ate into Tom's heart, and he left the room to stand at the top of the stairs.

Helena stood there. She had a hat crammed on her head, with curls tumbling down in glorious disarray, and a cloak was wrapped around her, completely hiding whatever she was wearing beneath.

Tom raced down the stairs and dragged her into his arms, kicking the door closed behind her. It slammed, the sound echoing through the house.

The duke appeared above, his voice blending with the sound of the slammed door. "What is the meaning of this?"

Tom ignored him, as well as the butler, who stood nonplussed in the hall. "Tea for her ladyship," he rapped out, not caring who answered the call. He swung her up and headed for the stairs.

Helena gripped his coat, holding it to her eyes. Somewhere on the stairs she lost her hat, and her hair flowed down, streaming over her as it had that night at the inn. He would not let her go this time. Or ever, come to that. Tom took her into the drawing room, under the astonished eyes of his grandmother, who was taking tea in solitary splendor.

He took a seat, cradling her against him. "Grandmamma, this is probably not the right time, but I'd like you to meet my wife."

"Well!" Getting to her feet, the dowager swept out of the room. A maid came in and placed her hands on the tea tray, but Tom curtly ordered her to pour a fresh dish for his wife. After she had done so, she left the room, closing the door quietly behind her.

Helena had almost stopped shaking. Smoothing back her hair, he kissed her forehead, which was too hot for his liking. "What is it, my love? Who has done this to you?" With a little contortion, he managed to drag his handkerchief out of his pocket. Instead of giving it to her, he cleaned her up himself, mopping the tear stains from her face and holding it to her nose, commanding her to blow.

Her first effort was too feeble to have any effect, but after the second, the light returned to her eyes. She released her death grip on his coat, but did not try to leave him. That was just as well, because he would not have let her go. "My mother," she said, her voice heavy with tears.

"Ah. Where was your brother?"

"He left the house earlier, making some inquiries on my behalf, he said. Eve was lying down in her room. My mother chooses her moments. Apparently she ordered the coach put to." She swallowed. "She was determined to take me back to the country. She said"—she gulped—"she said I was not to worry, she would take care of everything. If necessary, she would have my father take you to the House of Lords for a divorce. I said I did not want that, and she said she would accuse you of forcible abduction. She wanted to sue you."

Tom had not been aware that the door had opened, but his father had entered the room. He walked on silent feet to where Tom could see him.

"I have changed my mind," he said softly. "Naturally your wife is welcome here, with us."

"Why?" Tom could not believe his father did not have a scheme in mind.

"She is your wife," he said simply. "Do you require anything?"

"We'll let you know. Thank you, Papa."

He cradled Helena's head in his hand. "What did she do?"

"My mother had the traveling coach prepared. She told me to go to my room and dress for travel. I locked myself in and got out by the jib door and the servants' quarters."

"You walked here?" Astounded, Tom drew back to gaze at her face, and then he looked at his father.

"The duchess of Kirkburton is a determined woman." Sighing, his father perched on the arm of a nearby chair. "I believe she has fostered some ill-feeling between our families, but I cannot blame her for that."

"She's more than that. If she had me in the country she would never let me go."

When Helena tried to knuckle her eyes, Tom shushed her and wiped away the fresh tears carefully.

"Believe it, my son," the duke said. "If I were married to her, I'd be tempted to put paid to my existence. She is an interfering, designing woman. Years ago, she determined that Lady Helena would be her support in her old age and determinedly set about making it so. The matter was none of my concern, but it is now." He got to his feet. "Please assure her ladyship that she is perfectly safe here. I will find a maid to serve her."

"Thank you."

"I thought he would turn me out of doors," she said.

Subdued now, her face pink, her eyes bloodshot, Helena was still the most beautiful woman Tom had ever seen.

"My father is a loving man, but sometimes his ideals get in the way. He has had to trim his sails, but at heart he's still a romantic."

"I never thought of him that way."

"Not many people do. Come, drink your tea." Easing her on to the sofa, he got up and handed her the dish in its saucer.

"That is pretty," she remarked, just as if she were taking tea in the afternoon.

Her breeding went bone deep. The tea set was one of his grandmother's favorites, a Meissen set decorated with spring flowers. Snowdrops and primroses rioted over the polished, delicate porcelain.

"I shall buy you a set," he promised.

At least he managed to invoke a smile, watery though it was. Sitting back against the dark green upholstery, her silver-gilt hair flowing over her loose white-and-pink gown, she appeared like nothing so much as a fairy come down to earth.

"Come, love, that's better."

She finished her tea before she spoke. Her imperious gesture when she thrust the porcelain at him brought a smile to his lips.

"My mother has always been able to drive me into a complete pet," she said. Her voice had almost regained its usual mellifluous tones. "My tears were as much frustration and anger as distress. At least, this time. I do have a lamentable temper. You should probably know that."

"In this case it has driven you to exactly the right action." He frowned. "Except running through the streets completely unattended. After your ordeal, my love, I cannot allow that."

"I doubt anyone would have recognized the madwoman rushing past them as the prim and proper Lady Helena Vernon." She tried for a smile.

"That is just as well, since you are Lady Alconbury."

She paused, gazing at him in wonder. "So I am."

"Would you like to rest? My room is your room. At least, until they make one ready for you."

"Tell them not to bother."

He burst into laughter, a note of shrillness marring the tone. "You will need somewhere for your belongings, at the very least."

She spread her arms. "I come to you with what you see. Nothing more." Plunging her hand down the front of her gown, she tugged out a gold chain. On it she had threaded his signet ring. "And my wedding ring."

"I must see about getting you a proper one. And I will arrange for all the mantua makers, haberdashers, cobblers, and God knows who else to call. You are not leaving this house until I know more of the situation, so they will come here."

"Ah, another managing man." She put her hand to her heart and cast her gaze to the ceiling. "Will I ever be done with them?"

She could still make him smile. "You have recovered remarkably quickly," he said. "But I know you, my love. Never do that with me."

"What?" She swallowed.

"That mask of yours is remarkable, almost as effective as your brother's. Do not show it to me." He gentled his voice. He wanted to hear her laughter again, but only when it was sincerely meant. "I am your husband, and we will have no artifice between us."

Her eyes rounded. "What, none?"

"No deception." He would remain firm on this. "Only truth. Don't you think our families have suffered enough from deceit and plotting?"

She nodded. "Yes. I think that too. That was why I refused to allow Julius to limit the damage, as he put it. We have lived a lie for the past five years, Tom, even though some of it was none of our doing. No more."

"In that, my sweet, we are in accord." He got to his feet. "Do you wish to dine in our room?"

"No. But I have nothing suitable to wear for dinner."

"I'm sure we can find something for you. My sisters will have gowns aplenty. Chloe is nearer your coloring, but Emilia is more your size." He assessed her figure, but found himself lost in her charms. The swell of her breasts, the lovely waist he knew from experience he could almost span with his hands and the curves her gown hid, her bottom and the graceful line of her thighs came to mind. His mouth went dry when he realized that was all his now. But the last thing she needed was a man lusting all over her. She needed care and consideration. Her fragile state was his to minister to, and he would ensure she had everything he could give her. "Would you like me to carry you?"

In an elegant swoop, she got to her feet. "Absolutely not. When I arrived, I was tired from running. That was all. I must thank your sisters kindly for the loan. I will not go back. I will not give my mother any opportunity to take me. She would have taken me with or without my permission, and frankly, I am tired of being abducted. I am not a sack of potatoes to be thrown from hand to hand."

Crooking his arm, he watched as she laid her fingers on it in the exactly approved manner. Throwing her head back, her hair in glorious disarray, she accompanied him upstairs to his suite.

Chapter 15

Since he was the heir, Tom had a fine suite. Helena approved of it. Whether he had chosen the dark blue upholstery at the bed and the windows or had it chosen for him, the color went well with her complexion and appearance. The Countess of Alconbury would receive her visitors here, hold her levees here, and perhaps even give birth here. She moved around the room, trailing her fingers along the polished mahogany of the dressing table, the soft padding of the daybed, and the waxed perfection of the marquetry tallboy.

"That's a large bed for one," she said.

"It will be for two, now."

"Julius shares a bed with Eve every night. He never did that with Caroline, although he would have done at first." She stopped, aware she was giving away family secrets. Then continued, because she would not deny that part of her. "He adored Caroline when they were first married, but it is not like the passion he feels for Eve. That is fathoms deep."

He came up behind her and rested his hands on her shoulders. "Then we have that much in common. We are both completely in love with our wives." He kissed the side of her neck. "When we first met, I had my doubts. Who believes in love at first sight? But it happened. I have never stopped loving you, Helena. Why do you think I kept my distance from you? To touch you, to hold you, that was all I wanted, and I thought it sinful. It is not."

"No." She put one hand over the one on her left shoulder.

Downstairs she had made herself a resolution. She would only look forward, not back. What had gone would not return. With that in mind, she could go on and forget her mother's terrible words. She would not even repeat them to Tom.

"You are plain and old. Nobody wants you, least of all your father and myself. I will tolerate you, however. But you must accompany me back to the countryside now. We will not go to the Abbey immediately. Your last hope was Lord Everslade, but you ruined that. Why could you not go with him?"

The last part of her speech had shocked Helena to her core. Even now she shied away from the implications of what was said.

A knock at the door heralded a welcome interruption. Tom called out, "Come in!" but stayed where he was, his hands on her shoulders.

He turned her to face a red-faced maid. The woman bobbed a curtsey, tricky because she carried an armful of fabric.

"If it please my lady, Lady Emilia has sent a gown for this evening and one for the morning. She says she will be pleased to lend you anything you might need."

"That doesn't sound like Emilia," Tom said with a smile. "What she has, she holds on to. My father probably bribed her with the promise of a visit to the draper's."

Helena shot him a quelling glance. "I am much obliged to Lady Emilia. She has excellent taste." Even though the gowns would suit someone of darker coloring, which was only to be expected, because Lady Emilia was a dark beauty. One was of a deep crimson color, a dinner gown of brocaded silk, with a petticoat of white, embroidered in crimson. Helena had seen that gown last season, so she was probably planning to have it made over for April. The day gown was a soft moss green, again not Helena's best color, but she would wear anything at the moment.

"It will be awkward, using the same room," she said, "but I will be interested in your preparations for dinner." She smiled at Tom, who returned the favor.

"If you please, ma'am," the maid said, "her grace suggested you might like to use the bedroom adjoining this one. She says she fears it is very old-fashioned, since it is only used as an occasional guest room, but you might like it."

"Her grace is very obliging," Tom sounded surprised, his voice lifting, but Helena appreciated the consideration.

The dowager duchess had brought up Tom and his siblings after the sad death of their mother, done double duty, so to speak. She deserved respect for that, and for refraining from voicing her opinions on the family obsession with the Stuarts.

"I wish her ladyship here tonight," said Tom. "If you do not object, my love."

His endearment spoken before someone else gave Helena pause. Tom was not denying their love to anyone, it appeared. Neither would she, although her natural reticence made the task more difficult. But she loved him truly and she would accustom herself to his words. She would not find the task too much to bear. "No, I do not."

She had no brush, nothing of her own, not even stockings, but she would make do with the ones she was wearing.

Getting ready for dinner had the makings of a dream, like nothing Helena had known before. For the most part, Tom used the adjoining powder room to prepare himself, leaving the wash stand in the main room for Helena, but he reappeared in shirtsleeves and a magnificent cream waistcoat with cut silver buttons to stand before the tall mirror that hung between the windows and allow his valet to comb his hair back and secure it with a wide black velvet ribbon. After shrugging into a dark green corded coat braided with dull gold, he was ready.

Helena tried to follow suit, but she was not accustomed to a man watching her dress, particularly one who meant so much to her. Unaccustomed nerves attacked her when she tried to supervise the maid dressing her hair, until Tom took over.

"I confess I have always wanted to do this." Pushing the wide cuffs of his coat back so the buttons would not catch in her hair, he took the brush and stroked it through her tousled locks.

Helena closed her eyes in bliss until she heard his low chuckle.

"You sound just like a contented cat," he said. He pulled the brush through her hair in long, luxurious strokes, the bristles merely contacting her scalp, as he tamed the waves. "What happened to the cat you used to have in your room?"

"You remember that?"

"I remember everything about you."

"Goodness." But of course, so had she. She'd gone over and over every meeting in her mind until she was ready to run back to him barefoot. "The cat died in his sleep one night. He was a good age, for a cat, but I missed him."

He put down the brush. "Are you sure you want to go down to dinner?"

"Yes." Although she had not realized until he asked, she was beginning to feel quite hungry. A novel feeling, as she had not had hunger pangs for some time now. Ever since the day of her abduction. Leaning her head back, she breathed deeply, savoring the moment, an activity she rarely engaged in. She would ensure more times such as these, even if she did not have the luxury of having Tom perform the task.

"There. I would have you go down like that, but I fear my grandmother would have an apoplexy. As far as I know, we are not expecting company tonight. Emilia and Chloe wanted me to take them to a musicale later, but I will fob them off with William."

"You should not. I will be perfectly fine here."

"I wouldn't dream of it. I need to take care of you, sweetheart." With a light kiss to her shoulder, he moved away, allowing the maid to move in behind her and dress her hair.

She used the same cap she had arrived with, a tiny circle of linen edged with lace, and she kept her own ruffles, but her gown and petticoat were borrowed. Since she had no jewelry save Tom's ring, the maid tied a ruffle of lace around her neck, and she was done, except for a pair of shoes which Emilia had also lent her. Helena's own shoes, delicate silk affairs, had been ruined in her mad dash through the streets.

Dressing well was second nature to her.

Although the Dankworths did not live too far from Brook Street, Helena would have run twice that distance if she'd had to. Anything to get away from her mother. Something inside her had broken when her mother had declared her intention of taking her daughter away, and she'd taken off like a bird in flight, hastening to the one place where she knew she would find sanctuary. Even her mother would not dare to come here.

When she was dressed, Tom took her hand and led her down to the drawing room. Candles were lit in the sconces either side of the fireplace, lending a golden glow to the formally arranged sofas and tables, not at all like the casual arrangement Julius preferred. But a lady of an older generation held sway here, one more accustomed to formality, and the style and setting harked back to an earlier time.

The family was gathered there, waiting for her. Helena had faced worse. Her presentation had been fraught with anxiety, but she had mastered walking backward in a gown with a train, so she could do this. Pleased to note her fingers held not a trace of trembling, she held her hand out to Lord William, who was forced to bend over it and murmur that she was a welcome addition to the household, when both he and Helena knew he hated her. But not because of who she was, but because of the family she belonged to.

"I trust you will leave your old habits behind," he said with a smile. "You will become a supporter of the Stuarts now?"

Helena withdrew her hand gradually and bestowed Lord William with a smile. "I am, when all is said and done, an Englishwoman, and as such, I will support the strongest and best alternative for the country. I can do no less."

"But is the country not personified in the monarch?"

"A quaintly old-fashioned notion." She spread the fan Lady Emilia had sent her. A lady without a fan would find herself with nothing to do with her hands, and she had neglected to bring her own. This, she was relieved to see, did not hold any slyly political statements, but was a simple arrangement of flowers and greenery. "I thought we no longer believed in the divine right of kings? I do like the medieval concept of a monarch for the spiritual world and one for the temporal, but alas, the Holy Roman Emperor is but an empty title these days. Perhaps you were born in the wrong time, Lord William, and you would have preferred the Tudor era."

The duke let out a guffaw. "He'd have lost his head in a week!"

The ladies Emilia and Chloe entered the room on their father's jest. Emilia, a stately young woman with gleaming dark brown hair and a spare figure, granted Helena a gracious smile. Chloe, shorter and rounder, altogether more fashionable, her hair more red than brown, dropped a curtsey and, after a glance at Lord William, gave Helena a sideways smile and a casual, "I am not sure I will ever recover from the shock."

"Of what, pray?" The duke, standing by the fireplace, asked. He sounded cold, and he did not wait for an answer from his daughter. "Helena is part of the family. Whatever she was before, she is now a Dankworth."

"I beg your pardon, sir," Helena said. "While I appreciate that is the truth, I am also a Vernon. I know this situation will be difficult, but I cannot cast off my family. Even if they abandon me," she added, her voice smaller than before at the prospect of the people she knew and loved most in the world—one other person excepted—never speaking to her again.

"We are a civilized family," the duke said, his deep voice filling the room. "We can allow cordiality, even if we will never be as close as others might wish. We have much to discuss, but perhaps tonight is not the right time. We have a marriage to celebrate." He paused, his hand curling around the curved edge of the piece of marble. "We may discuss whatever we wish within the confines of family. However, as always, I will not tolerate any disagreements outside the front door. Our future depends upon our continued unity."

That must be the way he had held the family together in the hard times they'd had recently. However, Helena could not help remarking the way the duke's normally harsh expression softened when his attention strayed to his second son. His first son in actuality, because whoever had fathered Tom, it was not him.

Helena marveled that she had not noticed the differences between the duke and Tom before. Maybe assuming they were related when a long way toward noting similarities rather than differences. The duke's eyes were a clear gray, a little small, and he had a great hooked nose, terrifyingly aquiline, and thin lips. Tom's mouth was full, his lower lip rather more than the upper, and his eyes large and brown, while his face had a lean quality, his cheekbones more prominent than his father's and set at a higher angle. Even the shapes of their ears were different.

However, father and heir had the same style of dress—good quality, but relatively plain—and they both favored darker colors. The duke wore a fashionable wig, which served to make many men appear similar, and until relatively recently, Tom had done the same.

But who was his father, since her father could not claim to have done the deed?

When the doorbell jangled, Helena started, not as steady as she had thought herself. She barely restrained herself from taking Tom's arm in a death grip and refusing to let go.

He must have seen something, the dear man, because he said firmly, "Nobody can take you away from me now."

And nobody would, his tone proclaimed.

Male voices were raised, the butler shouting, "You cannot enter, sir!" before the drawing room door burst open and Julius strode inside.

One wild look around the room located his sister. "I had to ensure you were safe." He crossed the room to her, heedless of anyone else. Taking her free hand, he pressed it, more emotion than she could ever recall seeing on him in public filling her heart. He cared. "If you wish to come home, you are welcome."

Shaking her head, Helena gently withdrew her hand. "It is not my home now. This is."

Julius flicked a glance at Tom. "You will make her the happiest woman alive, or you will answer to me." He shook his head slightly. "The second happiest woman."

Although obviously agitated, Julius was his usual magnificent self, dressed for dinner in shades of lavender and ivory. The clothes were part of who he was, and when Eve had described the plain ill-fitting coat and bob wig Julius had been wearing when she first met him, Helena had refused to believe it. For as long as she could remember her glorious oldest brother had been an arbiter of fashion, unafraid of even the most extravagant trend. Today he had taken care to change before he set out in search of her. She'd have rather he appeared in sackcloth and ashes, tearing out his hair in lumps, but she was glad he had come at all.

"I heard you were attending Lady Jermyn's tonight," he said. "I was going in search of you when Wilkins returned and told me where you were. I should have realized you would come here."

That statement of brotherly love did much to assuage Helena's agitated spirit. "You may call off the hounds. I am where I should be."

"Yes, you probably are." He glanced around the room and belatedly made his bows, first to the dowager, and then to the duke, and then to everyone else. Julius's obeisances were the stuff of legend. In his own way, he could make the person he bowed to appear his inferior merely by the depth and elaborations he employed. He sighed. "Then I will take my leave."

The expression in his forget-me-not blue eyes was so forlorn, Helena could have wept for him.

But the dowager took a hand in the conversation. "Nonsense! You will stay to dinner, Winterton. You may take Emilia in."

Julius bowed and said he was very gratified. He apologized for his unexpected arrival, and the duchess declared that he would even out the numbers nicely. They processed to the dining room. Processed was exactly the right word. Even though they were *en famille*, with the exception of Julius, they went into the dining room according to rank. At least they did not sit the same way, and Helena could sit between her husband and her brother and feel somewhat protected from Lady Emilia's coldness, Lord William's antipathy, and Lady Chloe's disdain.

The meal progressed in perfect amity. They limited discussion to society doings and books they'd read, since politics and family were more or less controversial topics from which people might not survive intact. The careful observance of civilized behavior was both a blessing and a curse. Polite conversation gave the diners time to digest a meal.

After they had eaten, Helena rose with the other ladies, but Tom touched her arm.

"Please stay. We have much to discuss, and since your brother is here, it should be now."

Julius shook his head. "I had no intention of causing Helena further distress. I merely wanted to assure myself she was well and cared for. She is. If you will excuse me, I'll return home to care for my wife."

"Is she ill?" For Eve to go upstairs for a rest, something she had taken to doing recently, surprised Helena, but illness would explain the new habit.

"No." A gentle smile curved Julius's lips. "Not precisely. The nasty taste she complained of in the tea has been explained. Eve is expecting our first baby. We would prefer the news to remain in the family for at least another month, but it appears we are family—although not as close as we had supposed."

Heedless of politeness or proper behavior, Helena sprang to her feet and flung her arms around her brother's neck, smiling up at him, her heart bursting with delight. "I can't tell you how pleased I am! Will you tell Eve, please, that I am well and happy, and she should be too?"

Julius unwound her arms, but not before giving her a hug in response to her impulsive action. "I will indeed. She has a queasy stomach these days, so I am anxious to see that she takes enough nourishment."

"Tell the cook to bake some plain flat biscuits," the dowager said abruptly. "Give her one or two when she wakes, before she even raises her head, and then before each meal. They worked wonders for me the last time I was increasing."

Julius gave her a little bow. "I'm much obliged to you, ma'am."

Pregnancy had increased Caroline's ill tempers, but Eve was not of the same temperament. Still, Julius must be worried about her. As well as very deeply in love. As Helena was with her husband. That above all was paramount in her mind and her heart.

Julius promised to return in the morning with what papers he considered relevant. When Helena reminded him that she would not be shut out and he would have to expect her there, he grinned and told her he was perfectly aware of that.

"And the annuity—I'll bring the details."

"There's no need for that," Tom said.

Julius gave him a direct stare. "There is every need. I'll also bring a marriage settlement. My father will sign it, of course, but he won't object if I conduct the negotiations."

"Is Papa speaking to me?" Helena tried to keep her smile bright, but the thought of her father, a distant but beloved figure, abandoning her brought a lump to her throat.

"Yes, of course." He drew out his watch. "You were planning a visit to the theater, you said?"

Helena exchanged a look with Tom. "I was not planning to do so."

"If you can bear it, do it," Julius said. "I will return home, assure myself that Eve is resting, and join you there." He took in the rest of the dining room. "I am convinced of the validity of the marriage, and I have no intention of cutting my sister. Tonight seems like a good time to appear in public. Let the gossips and the journals do the rest."

Helena glanced down at her gown.

Julius grimaced. "I would not have put you in that shade of green, but it will serve to make you noticed. I'll have your belongings sent around tomorrow, but you are not to think that I will shut up your room. It is always yours."

"Perhaps we should stay with you for a night or two." Helena did not miss Julius's wince, instantly suppressed.

He kept his smooth smile. "Indeed you could."

Although Tom was concerned for Helena, due to her distress earlier that day, she proved she could wind him around her finger by lowering her chin and gazing up into his eyes. Once he saw the winsome smile, he burst into laughter. "Only the main play, then, you minx."

"I see the honeymoon is over," she said, treating him to a mock pout.

"It has not yet started." His voice was so low, throbbed with such intensity that heat rose to her cheeks and she was forced to look away. "There is an alternative to the theater, if you wish it."

She lowered her voice, but feared everyone was listening. "Tom, it is barely seven!"

"You've had a busy day." If she accepted his offer, she'd have a busy night, too. But she was not so shameless. Everyone would know why they were in bed so early, and it would not be to rest. Not initially, at any rate.

Trying to case his suggestion off with a merry laugh, she failed miserably, and caught a gleam in Julius's eyes as he took his leave.

At this time of year, the theater was not full. They took two carriages, Tom and Helena in one, and the duke, the dowager, Lord William, Emilia and Chloe crammed inside the other.

Tom took the opportunity of the darkness outside by ordering the coachman not to light the lamps inside the coach and taking Helena in his arms as soon as the vehicle jolted into motion. Before she could voice a protest— not that she was about to— he brought his mouth down on hers and kissed her. As her mouth opened she groaned, sucking gently on his tongue. He thrust, withdrew and caressed her, tickling the roof of her mouth as he stroked along it with the tip of his tongue. Spreading his hand over her back, he urged her closer, pressing her body against his, silk and lace meeting brocade. He withdrew and then kissed her again. She rested her head on his shoulder as he dropped kisses down her neck and along the bare part of her shoulder. She tipped her head back, sighing at the shivering sensations rippling through her.

They had reached the theater almost without her noticing. Pulling away, he twitched the lace ruffle at her neck back into place and straightened the shoulders of her gown. "You see, you could have had all that if you were not so keen to see the play."

When she opened her mouth to protest indignantly, he laughed. "I love to tease you. You rise to the bait so easily."

"And I thought you a stern man."

He had appeared intimidating in public, with his severe way of dressing and his aloof bearing, the impression increased by his height. But now, sitting next to her, he had the look of a naughty schoolboy, caught in mischief and delighted by his own wickedness. His dark eyes gleamed with promise. "I shall enjoy this. Do you know what the play might be?"

She shook her head. "I have no idea. May we leave early?"

"Do you think that's wise? We should plan a campaign of appearing in public, don't you think?"

Only the innocent tone told her he was teasing her. His kisses had aroused her, reminded her that what they did was real and allowed. How strange to have their loving condoned, or at least considered respectable.

"We will leave after the play. I think we're capable of providing our own farce. Or maybe we should leave at the first interval. Would that be remarked upon, I wonder?"

Yes, it would. Helena lowered her head, trying desperately to regain her composure.

Chapter 16

Tom handed her down from the carriage, moving closer and waiting for his father and grandmother to enter the theater first. People were thronging around the place, a glowing palace of entertainment, its relatively plain front lit and busy. At the height of the season, they would need a footman to forge a path to the door for them. As it was, people fell back and not a few recognized them. They kept going.

Automatically, Helena turned left, since their family had a box on that side, but of course she was to turn right now.

Tom led her upstairs, nodding to acquaintances but not stopping. "The second interval at the latest," he murmured to her.

The murmurs grew, but Helena knew how to ignore gossip. "Best to let them get it all out there," she said.

"You have done this before," Tom said.

"Indeed I have." Flicking her fan open, she allowed him to take her upstairs.

After the duke and his mother had taken their seats, Tom ushered Helena into hers, and she took in the view from this side of the theater.

The play appeared much the same as ever. They were presenting a new piece tonight. Either it was not ready for an audience yet, or the actors were new ones, but they did not hold the interest of the audience.

Quizzing glasses flashed in the light from the chandelier poised overhead, and fans wafted as women gossiped behind them. They were giving London a new topic of conversation. Nobody cared about the play, but it appeared the actors were not too enamored, either. They kept glancing up to the box where Helena sat with Tom. He paid her flattering attention, procuring wine and tidbits for her that she did not in the least want. Not until he bade her open her mouth and popped a sugared almond there. Love play.

"I'm not used to this," she told him, after crunching what was admittedly a delicious treat.

"Neither am I. But we must do our best, must we not? We are garnering more attention than the performers down there, so we will just have to bear it. But not for long, my love."

"Promise me one thing."

Stilled by her serious tone, he stopped in his selection of another sweetmeat for her, his long fingers curled around another almond, a pink one this time. "What is it?"

She liked that he did not instantly promise her the world. "You will only call me that if you mean it." She glanced away, at the stage, at the eyes relentlessly trained on her. "My father calls my mother by that name, but he only does it to keep the peace."

"I promise."

The simple words meant so much to her. "And I will promise the same."

"Indeed. Now I think this almond is particularly fine, my love, so open and tell me if I'm telling the truth."

The gentle, frivolous play amused Helena and lightened her spirits. She ate the treat and considered it carefully, eventually deciding that he could continue to select them for her, but for now she had eaten sufficient. Putting the crystal dish aside, he beckoned to the footman and handed her a glass of Madeira wine.

A flash of brilliance caught her attention, and she knew without looking properly that Julius had arrived. He had taken so long, she had wondered if Eve had prevailed on him to remain, but the reason for his tardiness was evident now.

Julius, Lord Winterton, was resplendent. His coat was a gleaming ice blue, and the buttons on his pure white waistcoat diamonds. A large solitaire winked and flashed in the folds of his beautifully tied neckcloth, and the best lace money could buy cascaded over his wrists and frothed at his throat. He wore the merest suspicion of powder, but when he walked, the beautifully jeweled hilt of a sword glittered with menacing promise. If anyone accused him of unmanliness, he would take his accusations and shove them down his throat.

Smiling, sardonic and amused at once, he made his bow to the dowager, and then to Helena, and after that, Chloe and Emilia. He exchanged a chilly nod with Lord William. A seat was made available to him next to his sister, and he took it, leaning over to snag a handful of the almonds.

"You had time for a manicure?"

"A mere pass with the buffer," he murmured. "One does not like to be underdressed."

Helena snorted. "There's little chance of that happening. They're agog!"

"Even more so because I could not for the life of me remember which box belonged to the Dankworth family." A blatant lie, because they had been sitting opposite to each other for as long as anyone could remember. "I was forced to inquire in rather louder tones than I prefer to employ of the whereabouts of Lord and Lady Alconbury. Helena, I have told you before about your tendency to gurgle. A lady does not chortle, especially in company."

"This one does." Helena scanned the sea of faces below them. Even the actors on stage had lost interest in the play. "I'll wager ice blue will be the color of the moment this season."

"I bought the fabric years ago," he said. "I had meant it for you, and then you bought the rest of the bolt, so I was forced to put it by. But I believe you ruined that gown last season, so I felt safe in finally having the cloth made up."

Helena sighed and fanned herself. "Red wine does not go well with pale blue silk. I could have had it pieced, but I would always know the mark had been there. I prefer a symmetrical gown. I believe I have it somewhere. I'll have it sent to you, so that you have the spare fabric, in case you have a similar accident."

Tom did not gurgle. He snorted. "You truly do follow fashion slavishly. I had thought it a hum, especially after I saw you last year in Appleton." That was the village where Julius had met Eve.

"I was not aware that I had to meet with your approval before I decided to devote my time to fashion." Julius pulled a quizzing glass out of his pocket and leveled it at Tom, but then lowered it with the hint of a smile. "It amused me. Moreover, it proves a useful disguise. Very few ruffians believe a namby-pamby gentleman like me can give them any trouble at all. Believe me, there is great sport in proving them otherwise. However, since I married, I have found the pastime less interesting."

Helena remembered a time when Julius had been at outs with the whole world. Convinced the fashionable had done more than its share to drive Caroline to her early death, he had done his small part to get his revenge. The clothes and elaborate appearances had also hidden him from scrutiny. People who knew him did not make the mistake of taking him for a fashionable fribble with a head full of wool, but sometimes others did.

"You have found most things less interesting, since you met Eve," Helena remarked.

"And you went for five years without that felicity." Julius lowered his voice, but since the population of the theater had long since given up any pretense of watching the play and was now conversing loudly, his precautions hardly seemed necessary. "I would not have waited so long. In fact, I would probably have confronted the woman I had deceived years ago."

Tom did not pretend to misunderstand him. "I did. But I did not understand her persistent nature."

"Stubborn, I call it," Julius said mildly, crunching into a nut.

"A brother's privilege," Helena said in a warning tone.

"I prefer persistent," Tom insisted.

Even in the choice of words, the men could not agree. Helena could not imagine them ever becoming the best of friends. Even with all other considerations eliminated, these two men had too much in common to agree over many matters. They were both leaders, both concerned with living up to their responsibilities, too independent-minded to ever agree on much.

Nothing could keep her bubble of euphoria from rising now. By coming here, she had publicly claimed her husband. By coming here, her brother had acknowledged the marriage.

What would society make of the connection? She dreaded to think.

Julius got to his feet. "I fear there is little amusement to be found here. On the stage, at least. I shall probably call in at White's. Do you care to accompany me, Alconbury?"

Tom rose too and helped Helena up. Startled, she stared between the two men.

"You surely do not wish my husband to accompany you to a gentleman's club!"

"I have no intention of going anywhere near St. James's Street tonight," Tom said gently. "But you are tired, my dear." He smiled gently at Julius. "You, as an old married man, may do as you please, but I am taking my wife home and ensuring she has her rest."

He did not have to say "eventually." Helena heard the word in her mind.

Julius smiled as if he could hear it, too. "I will merely collect my winnings. I took a notion to stop off here on the way and see if I had any takers for a particular bet. I got six, probably because I laid excellent odds."

"The bet being?"

"That Lord Alconbury would be wed before the month was out. As is only proper, I did not mention the lady." He glanced at Helena, brimful of amusement, the corners of his eyes slightly creased as if he was about to break out into laughter. "They did not ask. They were a trifle bosky, but I chose not to ruin them. However, even the modest sums I laid out will have their effect. I daresay the whole of the country will hear of the marriage soon enough."

They moved out to the hallway behind the boxes. A footman followed them out, holding their outer wear. He stood outside the box, waiting for his summons.

"Indeed the notion to marry now is a good one. The news will race around the country, and then they will forget it in favor of something else. There's a highwayman due for hanging, and he looks as if he will put on a brave show. Not that I will be present to witness it. I might have been instrumental in his arrest, but I do not have to see the matter through to the bitter end. The ruffian who accosted you will also find justice soon enough. With your permission, I will call on you in the next day or two." For a bare instant, his mask of smiling moderation slipped, revealing the ruthless man beneath. "He will not escape me. I am determined on that."

"I should like to be in at the kill," Tom said mildly, but for all that, steel underlaid his voice. The muscles of his forearm flexed under Helena's hand.

"If I find sport, I will let you know. I daresay the matter will be tedious in the extreme, though." Julius stifled a yawn. "Dear me. I'd better be off before I fall asleep where I stand. It's been a tiring day." After bowing to them, he left.

"We should follow his example," Tom said mildly. His smile broadened. "And we will. You've had a hard day, my love."

Weariness swept over her, but it was more remembered than felt. That morning, when she'd run through the streets, seemed so far away now. They were swiftly moving toward normality—a new normality, but it remained in the background, seductively promising them delights to come.

Tom helped her into the carriage himself, as if she were some kind of invalid, and out after the short journey back to the house.

At the front door, he paused. "I was planning to hire a house for us, but I've been thinking of alternatives. Shall we go into the country instead? Tomorrow we may get the tedious business of settlements out of the way. We've done the needful this evening, and we may safely leave society to gossip. I can think of no reason for us to remain in town, unless you should wish it. I know your brother prefers the town to the country. Maybe you are of the same mind?"

She shook her head slightly. "Julius prefers anywhere to Edensor Abbey, because it has my mother in it. I cannot remember a time when they have not been at odds with each other. He has a small house of his own, but nobody goes there unless he invites them. I would love to go away with you."

"Then that is settled." He dropped a kiss on her lips, ignoring the sniff from the butler, who had opened the door to them, and then he led her inside.

This house would never be home, but it contained a plethora of servants, enough to keep her safe, since Julius still fretted about her and would until he had located the false Lord Everslade. Helena knew better than to argue. In many ways, Tom was cut from the same cloth. She just prayed they would be done with the search soon. If she were Everslade, she'd have headed straight for the port and caught the next ship with passenger space, heedless of where it was going.

Tom did not bother to stop at any of the other rooms but took her straight upstairs. Closing the door, he lifted his brow at his valet, standing there evidently waiting for his master's return. The man said nothing, but left.

"I want to do this. Is this our wedding night?" Tugging the robings of her gown, he brought her closer.

"No. We had one of those. This is our marriage night." Unaccustomed to feeling shy, she did not recognize the emotion for a minute, and then almost laughed with relief when she did. "I have believed myself married to you for five years. Yet I feel like a new bride."

"Because you are." He smiled down at her and slid his fingers under the gown to discover the fastenings. "Now I unwrap you. Will you show maidenly modesty?"

"Probably not." She was too eager to be naked with him and feel his body next to hers. This and more. "I want everything I missed all that time."

He arched a brow. "Now?"

"All of it." He would not deter her, and if he did not hurry, she'd strip herself.

When she tried to help him with the hooks at the front, he brushed her hands away and undid every single one with deliberation. Enough to drive her mad, but he only chuckled when she told him so.

"Patience is a virtue," he murmured.

"Also a waste of time."

Opening her gown, he pushed it off her shoulders and touched the slender chain that held his signet ring around her neck. Usually she wore it concealed, pinned to the inside of her gown. It rarely left her, and she preferred to have it touching her skin, which was why it had not been in her pocket that fateful night with Everslade.

Not even recalling his name dampened her mood. Nothing could, now, unless Tom turned his back and walked away from her, which did not seem in the least likely.

He stroked the pad of his thumb against the carved surface of the ring. "I think the figure is a Roman emperor," he said, "which is appropriate, since I married one."

"The Empress Helena was from the Byzantine Empire, really, but they considered it a continuation of the Roman one."

"Hmm." He let the ring drop and continued with his self-imposed task.

Her gown fell to the floor. She should really pick it up, since it did not belong to her, but she let it be. Perhaps she'd do it later. The color might not suit her, but she would recall it with pleasure, because in it she had become the publicly acknowledged Countess of Alconbury. Mrs. Dankworth. Mrs. Fisher. Tom's wife.

He loosened her stays and then drew her shift down. The lace at the edge tickled her sensitive nipples, and she moaned when he bent to fasten his lips to them. Sucking and licking, he coaxed first one and then the other to glistening, hard peaks.

Pausing, he shed his coat, and then he was back, loosening the drawstrings at her waist. Her petticoats, hoops and pocket fell to the floor.

After sparing a thought for her watch, she sent the rest to perdition. With a low laugh, she said, "I had no idea I could get naked so quickly." She tugged his waistcoat. "You, on the other hand, have some catching up to do."

"Now," he muttered next to her skin and pushed her shift down. Shoes, stockings, and garters did not afford her much cover.

Tom groaned, stroked her skin, and pressed the small of her back as he kissed and sucked his way down her body. When he licked the inside of her hip, she shivered, and he covered her backside with his other hand, urging her even closer.

"Open your legs, my love."

She did not question him. When she widened her stance, he went down on his knees and leaned back, looking at her.

"So pretty. All that pink inside the gold." He blew, parting the curls and hitting her sensitive flesh.

Gasping, she jolted in shock. How could he do that without even touching her?

He lifted his head, gazing up at her with a wicked grin. "We have all the time we need now, and I intend to make the most of it. And of you."

He traced a line down from her left hip to where her legs met and then between. Just as if he were drawing. The pressure of his fingernail was steady, the warmth of his finger a foreign intrusion, but never so welcome as this.

She had nothing to hold on to. She would have to bend to touch his shoulder, and that might force him away from her. Whatever else he did, she needed him not to stop. The bed was a modern canopy kind without the pillars of a four-poster, the top suspended from the ceiling. She gazed at it, memorizing the way the gold fringe was slightly uneven in places, a strand of thread hanging down from the part by the corner. The rich green velvet was soft, gleaming where the candlelight caught it.

Tom licked her.

Caught in her own dream, she gasped and cried out when a bolt of lightning shot through her. Tom traced the line at the center of her body with the tip of his tongue and dipped briefly inside her before returning and taking the hard knot of flesh at the front into his mouth. He sucked and Helena went wild.

"Ah, Tom, no, Tom, stop, don't stop, ah, God!"

Such babble was worthy of a madwoman, but she could not stop, until she clamped her mouth shut and let him take her. He steadied her by anchoring her to him with one hand on her buttocks, pressing her close. He gave her no surcease from the blissful torture he was delivering, increasing it by pushing first one finger inside her and then another, only the hand behind her securing her now.

Her peak came fast and hard—no gentle rise from the state of blissful euphoria he had put her in, but a sharp, violent edge of joy spiking up. If he did not have her safe, she would have melted bonelessly to the floor.

Tom gave her no respite, but continued until she had no more to give. When, finally, he got to his feet and circled her in his arms, she could do nothing but subside into them. His waistcoat buttons were cool and hard, the metallic braid edging his pockets harsh and scratchy. Every sensation was magnified, echoing and impressing itself inside her. She drifted— oh, wait, he was carrying her. That felt blissful.

She was coming around as he laid her on the bed and stepped back. She lay on the crisp linen sheets and watched, lifting up on one elbow when he set to undressing himself. He provided her with a delicious display. First he took out the discreet pearl pin from his snowy neckcloth and laid it aside. She didn't know or care where, because she was too busy watching him. He threw her a smile and unwound the folds, revealing his strong throat. Wrapping the cloth around his hands, he pulled it taut. She shivered and his smile turned wicked.

"Another time," he said softly, and dropped the cloth, his hands going instead to the long line of buttons on his waistcoat. He made short work of it.

His fine shirt revealed shades of his olive-toned skin, brushing against the taut flesh when he turned and leaned over to unfasten the fall on his breeches. He loosened his cuff buttons with two swift flicks and dealt with the buckles at his knee in a similar cavalier manner. Without looking behind him, he sat on the chair, which spoke wonders for his familiarity with this room. Kicking off his shoes, he rid himself of the clothes on the lower half of his body and dragged his shirt off over his head.

At last, there he was, powerfully, wonderfully, naked. His cock stood up proudly, its tip swollen and red, damp with the teardrops of clear liquid. Blatantly he took hold of it, swiped his thumb around the top, and gripped it. "Do you want this?"

"Yes." She licked her lips.

He groaned. "Soon, my love. But you remember what I said about us having all night? I meant it." He took a step nearer to the bed, kicking his clothes out of the way.

She glanced down, but she could not see his feet. She loved his feet, but then, she loved the rest of him, too. Lying back, she stretched out her arms.

He stood by the bed, still holding his erection, as if showing it to her, and grinned. "You want me to do all the work? Oh, no, my lady. Turn around. Get on all fours. I want this first time to be deep and hard. We both need this, something visceral and basic."

Then he used a word that shocked her and thrilled her to the bone, one she'd only heard her brothers utter when they didn't know she was around.

"We'll fuck first, and then we'll make love. Then we'll probably sleep for a while. Or not, as we please. This is our wedding night."

She shook her head. "As I said to Julius earlier, I've had one of those. This is a consummation, my love."

He laughed sharply. "Indeed, you are perfectly right. Then do as I say. Do you not take orders from your husband?"

"Only if they suit me." And oh, yes, they suited her right now. Her hair prickled, as she slowly moved, rolled on to her stomach, and then pushed up with her hands and knees.

The bed dipped as he climbed up behind her. A hot streak of dampness trailed along her right buttock as he dragged his erection over her flesh and down between her legs.

Briefly, he dipped his fingers into her wet heat and sucked in a breath. "You're soaking. All for me. Maybe I should take it and leave. How would you feel if I did that? Used? You would have been. But what if I have you exactly as I want and then hold you and love you afterward?"

She growled.

"I'm sorry, what did you say?"

His shaft rested at her entrance now. He was driving her crazy. "Shut up and do it. Just do it, damn you!"

He entered her to the echo of laughter.

The laughter faded. He drove in and in until he reached the heart of her. Finally, she understood the meaning of the word "filled," because she was surely filled by him. To the hilt. His groin rested against her rear. He pressed in and finally groaned.

"Beautiful inside and out," he murmured.

Before she had time to catch her breath, he withdrew and hammered back inside.

Her cry came from the same place, somewhere deep inside her, torn out of her by the thrill coursing through her, one he only built as he repeated his action, again and again. His flesh slapped against hers, and he dug his fingers into her hips, holding her steady, dragging her back when the impact of his thrusts impelled her forward. She lost control of her body, of her voice, and very nearly her mind. Her voice increased in volume, and he thrust harder, his groans adding to her sharper cries. She held firm and thrust back, hollowing her back and thrusting her rear at him.

He ground his body against hers, his power forcing her down onto her forearms, her face pressed against the pillow.

"Come, damn you!"

The lover-like words had their effect. The currents coursing through her coalesced, built to a peak and then stilled, that wonderful moment when she flew.

The plunge into mindless orgasm sent her soaring again, and then he joined her, his groin pulsing, his cock throbbing deep inside her.

Tom collapsed on to her, his body sheened with sweat, his heat burning through her, taking all the breath from her body. Almost immediately, he rolled aside and lay on his back.

Helena turned to him and curled into his arms, purring her delight. "Was that fast and hard?"

"It was certainly hard."

As if on cue, the mantel clock chimed, but neither of them bothered to count the hours. Already half asleep, Helena moved against him and felt him touch his lips to her hair.

Chapter 17

Tom woke to the delicious felicity of having his wife in his arms, in his bed. Exactly where she belonged. They would never spend a night apart again, he vowed. Tom didn't make many vows. He'd seen the results of too many foolish ones, but this one he meant to keep.

Helena stirred against him, murmuring his name. Ridiculously pleased that she knew who he was, even in her sleep, he smiled at her and adjusted the covers to a more sensible arrangement. They had lost the sheet somewhere, but they would make do with blankets.

"What time is it?"

Dawn was beginning to seep in, the gap under his bedroom door lighter than it was. Even as a boy, he'd marked the nights that way. He had never slept well, but with Helena in his arms, he found he could slide into the deepest slumber. He felt safe with her, and he had a reason to rest.

The scent of their activities wound around him, faint but persistent. Would she fall pregnant? She had not before, but maybe they had been fortunate. Or not. If she had, he'd have forced the issue. He'd have had to talk to her, despite his agony.

"Time we made love," he said firmly. Easing her on to her back, he came on top of her, but this time he took care to bear his own weight. Already he was aching to have her again, but this time he wanted to watch her and make sure he pleased her to the utmost of his ability. "I was a coward," he said, although he had not planned to say anything of the kind. "I stayed away from you because I could not bear to be near you and not know you were mine. If we had talked, we wouldn't have lost those five years."

"A lot happened in that time." She gazed up at him.

There was just enough light for him to see her lovely shape, and her eyes, holding everything he had ever dreamed of.

"Not least that I grew up. I learned that the world did not revolve around me, and I learned that I could be something and be of importance to someone merely by being myself."

To her brother Julius. He had always assured her that he valued her, where her mother had not. "Do you regret your mother's actions?"

"You mean yesterday? No. She was not a kind mother. Perhaps she knew my father did not love her, but I suspect that was the least of her concerns. She was determined we should be Vernons first, especially Julius. She took him away from the schoolroom and gave him a tutor of his own, but we contrived to share in many of the lessons. When she discovered that, she punished us all, but Julius the worst."

"I see." Tom was beginning to understand many things he had not been aware of before. For one, he'd had a happy childhood. Even though his family had been embroiled in near-treason, his parents, and then his father and grandmother, had taken care to keep the children away from the turmoil. They had never been forcibly separated or made to feel less than they were.

She would never feel that way again. She was his beloved wife and a precious member of his family.

Smiling down at her, he bent his head and kissed her, nudging her lips apart and stroking her body back into awareness. Her nipples, so sensitive, hardened into tiny delicious peaks, and she let her thighs fall open.

Watching her all the while, he slid his shaft down her crease, gathering her juices as he went, and slid into her, the movement as natural as breathing.

This time he took care to bring her to slow and profound ecstasy. Driving into her with firm insistence, watching her, he pressed his forehead against hers. She met his every stroke, arching her back to take her part in their dance, one neither needed to learn the steps for because it came as naturally as breathing.

He marked his slow progression toward his peak and watched her, saw how her eyes dilated and her mouth plumped and reddened. Her nipples pressed into his chest, evidence of her arousal, adding to his pleasure.

Her channel tightened around him in the first of the contractions that heralded her orgasm. Catching her lower lip in her teeth, she let it go with a gasp, and he kissed her, sharing their loving and the emotions he'd never looked for nor expected in his life.

When he came, it was with a profundity beyond speech. Deep inside her, he gave her all himself.

He always would.

* * * *

Although Tom intended to keep Helena in bed all the next day, she would have none of it. When the maid came in with a repast on a tray for them, she shrieked and burrowed against him.

Laughing, he lashed an arm around her. "Surely you have had a maid come into your room before?"

"Not when I have company," came the muffled reply.

"You don't. Your husband is a permanent fixture here." He drew her up, scooping his hands under her arms and hauling her into his arms. The tantalizing scent of fresh coffee and hot toast filtered through to him. His stomach rumbled.

She screwed up her nose. "You're such a man!"

"You were glad of that in the night. Four times, as I recall."

Laughing, he delivered a smacking morning kiss to her mouth, threw back the covers, and climbed out. Her small groan of appreciation fed his sense of well-being, and he waggled his backside at her, just to hear her joyful laugh.

After pouring the coffee, he brought the cups back to bed. "I shall be your maid this morning. And later."

"Can you lace stays?" Sitting up in bed, she plumped the pillows and leaned against them, taking the coffee with a happy sigh. "Is there any tea?"

"Ah, no. I will be sure to have some served tomorrow. Should I send for some now?"

"No. The coffee is fine."

He glanced at her. She was sitting in his bed, the sheet tucked under her arms, a steaming cup of coffee in her hands. As he watched, she blew on it and took a sip. She brought him to his knees right there. Oh, no, they would not be going far today.

A knock sounded softly on the door. More to assuage his wife than because the intrusion would have concerned him, he plucked his banyan from the daybed, where it had rested undisturbed all night, and thrust his arms through the sleeves. "Come!"

His valet entered. Lamaire did not glance at the bed once, but he bowed to his master. "Lord Winterton is below with a sheaf of papers. I have ventured to order food served to him in the morning parlor. He says he has the settlement, and her ladyship's luggage will be arriving within the hour."

Tom groaned. "Then I suppose I must dress and go down."

"*We* must," Helena corrected him.

He did not bother to contradict her, because she was right. Besides, the tedium of arranging the contracts would have much more interest if Helena shared the process with him. She would have to sign the contract, but he knew her too well to suppose for one minute that she would consent to have a pen thrust in her hand with a terse instruction of "Sign here, and here."

"Send a maid up for her ladyship." He paused by the tray to pluck a piece of buttered toast from it. "We need to engage someone for her."

"His lordship informs me that he will send her ladyship's maid with the luggage. Where shall I tell them to take it?"

"The room next to this one," he said.

"The duke has declared it too modest for his daughter-in-law," the man said smoothly.

"We will not be staying long. We have decided to repair to the country."

An expression of mild alarm widened the valet's eyes, and Tom suppressed a malicious grin. Lamaire went to the country under protest. When he had ordered the man to get himself engaged by Lord Winterton and keep an eye on him, Lamaire had not realized that Julius was shortly repairing to the countryside to look for one of Maria Rubio's children. He had berated Tom, in a fashion, by threatening to remain with Winterton. Tom had been duly punished and had promised to give Lamaire notice next time. Well, he just had.

"I do have some business to conduct before we go, and your help would be greatly appreciated." He needed to find that bastard Everslade, or rather, the impostor, before he left. He would not leave Helena open to such danger, and he wanted to reassure her that she was completely safe from the man who had tried to abduct her.

Lamaire bowed, but said nothing.

Half an hour served to see both Tom and Helena downstairs. He had used his powder room, as he had the night before, listening to the bumps and thumps from next door, accompanied by feminine shouts of "No, not there! In the clothes press!" Other comments had not been as patient. It enlivened Tom's ablutions remarkably.

He stood on the towel while Lamaire swabbed him down, and while the man went about his duties, he gave terse instructions about Everslade.

"I have been working on the problem," Lamaire said calmly, handing Tom a fresh pair of drawers. "I assumed you would wish the man ah…dealt with."

The pause was not for the Frenchman to work out the words. Lamaire had excellent, if heavily accented, English. Lamaire's delicate suggestion covered a far more sinister solution. Tom was not entirely out of sympathy with the man. A slice across the throat at midnight, followed by a splash as the body was disposed of in the Thames seemed like a suitable end, but he would not order such a thing. Lamaire knew this. He would merely report to Tom that the matter was "at an end."

Once he'd learned that, Tom had taken more care with his instructions. "I want to speak to him first. And I want him capable of answering questions."

"Very well, my lord."

"I want to know who he came from and what his instructions were. Why he wanted to abduct Lady Helena. Was it just because he wanted a rich wife, or was something else involved? And why was he masquerading as Lord Everslade? Most of all, what has happened to the true earl?"

"Yes, my lord." No expression marred Lamaire's tone.

Tom sat before the mirror so the man could comb his hair back and secure it. He had grown it on a whim. That, and the scratchy wigs he'd always detested. But washing, combing, and dressing it for balls was mildly tedious sometimes.

He would ask Helena which she preferred and let her guide him.

He startled his reflection by smiling. Tom very rarely smiled in the morning. This time he had a very good reason—the best reason in the world.

* * * *

Downstairs, Lord Winterton waited. The duke and duchess were with him, and Tom's father had summoned his man of business. The round tilt-table had been brought into the middle of the room, and now its surface was covered in neat piles of paper. Tom helped Helena to sit and greeted Winterton cautiously before he took his own chair. Not that he had any particular reason to treat the earl cautiously, merely that old habits died hard.

The crystal ink well and the matching stand lay in the center of the table, the stand bristling with quills.

Although the room was not particularly small, it seemed crowded with everyone sitting around the table. The sun streamed in, a valiant effort for this time of year, and the fire crackled. This was his grandmother's favorite room. A workbasket stood by the chair drawn up to the fire, and a shelf of obviously well-read tomes was fastened to the wall by the fireplace. Not to mention the china figures his grandmother loved sprinkled around the place.

Helena smiled. "This is a lovely room."

Tom had not realized how starkly masculine the rest of the house was until she said that. He could probably expect more rooms like this in his future. He exchanged a glance with Winterton, who gave him a wry grin.

"When you have a house full of females, you learn to take care where you put your hand. You could hit a china shepherdess or worse, a lapdog, if you don't take care."

"Helena has a lapdog?" The notion startled him. He could not recall seeing her with one.

"My daughter has one. A pug, to be precise. She got it earlier this year, and she's inseparable from the beast."

"She called it Lapin," Helena said with a chuckle.

"Why would she call a pug Rabbit?" Tom looked to Winterton for an explanation, but he only shrugged.

The duke dragged the nearest pile of paper toward him and dealt his son a glare. "Let's get on, shall we?"

The business of arranging the contract was not quite as tedious as Tom had imagined. Helena had a generous dowry, and as it turned out, Winterton had quietly had a contract drawn up, in case, he said, Helena took a notion to marry. "I did not wish my mother to become embroiled in long negotiations," he said.

Ah, yes, the duchess might well do that. Another delaying tactic.

Tom wanted to leave them to it. He hated paperwork. But because the matter concerned his wife and because he wanted her as happy as he could make her, he reined in his impatience and discussed all the details, even to the percentages and yields. He became more interested in the portfolio, because, unexpectedly, Helena had a ship.

The news startled Helena too. "A small vessel," Winterton explained. "But every member of the family has one in our enterprise. My cousin, the Marquess of Devereaux, is particularly interested in insuring ships, so we had to give him something to keep him busy."

A way to help the marquess when he'd been struggling, Tom guessed. Devereaux's father had been a wastrel, leaving his son very little in the way of inheritance. That the marquess was now a wealthy man was entirely due to his own efforts, plus a judicial marriage to a woman who, by all accounts, he adored. His relatives had kept his business afloat—pun intended—and Helena now had a ship.

"I have interests of my own in that direction," he said. "We should discuss the best way to deploy them. But not now," he said hastily, as Winterton showed every indication of doing so.

"Not many people are aware of the investment," Winterton said. "We decided to set up a corporation to amalgamate the ships into a small fleet. It has worked well for us."

They kept at it and in a remarkably short length of time, when the clock had just chimed mid-day, they had finished. Winterton had done a good job, better than his father, who was adept at financial settlements. But when he wanted to add the annuity he was setting up for Helena, Tom refused.

"I will provide the equivalent." He met Winterton's eyes, and the room fell silent. This was the test. For years, Winterton had cared for Helena's needs, when her family had proved deficient. Now it was his turn. He would care for her as ruthlessly as she needed.

Eventually Winterton nodded. "Then I will put the annuity toward my unborn child. Caroline is already provided for. I will not have the females of my family put under an undue obligation." That would be because of the way his parents had treated his sister and the way society had treated his first wife, provoking her to further excesses instead of helping her.

Instead of an enemy, a flat figure they could take aim at, Lord Winterton had become a fully rounded person. The transformation had happened so slowly that Tom was not aware where it had started. Perhaps in that fateful year when Winterton had married for the first time. The issue of the Old Pretender's children had emerged at the same time.

They must move on or atrophy.

The meeting broke up shortly after, and Winterton confessed that he was anxious to get back to his wife. "She says my fussing annoys her and sends me away on errands," he said in a rare moment of frankness.

The undercurrent remained unsaid. Caroline had died shortly after giving birth. The pregnancy had increased her volatility, affected her moods, and after the birth of her baby, she had plunged into a cycle of abject despair followed by frantic, joyless activity. Tom had seen it but at the time taken little notice of it.

Eve was entirely different, but perhaps her husband was having understandable concerns.

As Tom rose and helped Helena to stand, he had a moment of realization. Nothing would ever be the same now he had acknowledged the marriage. The families would be forced into closer contact, and he would have no windmills to tilt at any longer. His father, idealist and staunch supporter of the Stuarts, was wavering, slowly drawing away his more evident allegiance, driven to it by changing allegiances and the almost criminally stupid behavior of the Prince. He had even allowed that heretofore forbidden word "Pretender" to be voiced in his hearing.

At the moment, none of that mattered because he was with Helena, and they could love again.

A wave of blissful happiness swamped his misgivings.

While his father remained to discuss other business with the lawyer, Tom and Helena saw Winterton out. The butler opened the door and stood rigidly at attention as Winterton smoothed his gloves over his wrists and strapped his sword firmly into place. As a gesture of respect, or trust, he had removed it with his outer clothing, something that had gone unmentioned, but not unnoticed.

Helena laid her hand on her brother's arm. "She will be fine," she said.

Julius smiled wryly. "I know. Eve sends her best wishes. I will be taking her to Oxfordshire in a day or two, and then we will be calmer. I will be calmer. Perhaps she will regain her taste for tea, too, which she says is the only cloud in her sky."

He turned to leave.

A loud retort from outside was followed by an object zinging past him, stinging as it went. A bee?

But bees did not sound like that.

Bullets did.

Chapter 18

Julius flung his body in front of Tom's as Helena's husband plummeted to the floor, blood pouring from his head.

Bewildered, confused, she followed him down, frantically lying over him, as Julius barked instructions and people erupted from the rooms on the first floor, shouting.

Until a cry of "Tom!" had her wondering who had such a high-toned voice.

That would be her. Helena pressed her handkerchief to Tom's head, but it was almost immediately soaked with sickening gore.

His eyes were closed, and he was breathing in stentorian gasps. Panic tightened her throat. Just last night, just yesterday they had begun. She would not lose him so soon. Oh, God in heaven, no!

Julius rolled to the still open doorway while Lamaire rushed up from below stairs in his shirtsleeves.

Her vision blurred with tears, Helena looked up. "Help him!"

Lamaire dropped to the floor by the side of his master. Blood poured from Tom's head, and Helena felt sick. Her shocked mind stilled, unable to process the events.

Unlike the valet, who immediately set to work. "Cloths!" he snapped. "And hot water. Now!"

A footman scurried away to do his bidding, his feet clattering on the stairs.

Helena moved back to allow Lamaire to do whatever he had to, her new position giving her a better view of the street outside. A few people stood and gaped, but Julius got to his feet and raced outside.

After five minutes he returned, disconsolate. "He's gone."

The duke was standing next to Helena, his hand on her shoulder. "Pray," he said softly. Tears stood in his eyes.

Tom's hand moved. Thank God, he was alive, but for how long she had no clue. Forcing her mind back into action, she watched and waited to help. Lamaire knew what he was about. He'd taken a knife and cut Tom's coat away, baring his shoulder, and now held a cloth to his neck and ear.

Who would do such a thing?

Lamaire glanced up. "I want two footmen, if you please. Carry him to his bedroom and lay him there."

"But the jolting…" The duke seemed as bemused as Helena.

"It matters not. Carry him up. He'll be better in bed."

Why? Was he about to die? Did the loss of blood not matter because she was about to become a widow?

Before the men took him upstairs, Lamaire bound a cloth around Tom's throat. The seepage had lessened now, but a puddle of bright blood on the black-and-white tiled floor left the evidence of his injury. Lifting her skirts, Helena trailed after the cortege.

The duchess joined them on the first floor and gripped her hand tightly. The older lady's face was stern, but not for Helena. Now Helena's mind had begun to work again, it raced. She could be a pregnant widow. That would perpetuate the line that the duke would probably rather died with his son, since Tom was not his. William could become duke in his turn. Nice and tidy, eliminating the late duchess's error. Unless she was pregnant. Perhaps she should go home, back to the Abbey, or ask Julius to give her the annuity and go to live quietly somewhere, where she could mourn in peace.

To live without Tom? To know he was not in the world anymore? Impossible.

As the footmen gently turned their burden, Tom's chest moved in a convulsive gasp for breath. He wasn't dead yet. She wouldn't wear black until she absolutely had to.

She'd worn a lavender gown the first night they'd met, a small rebellion against her mother, since lavender was a color of half mourning. She might have to wear that color in earnest now. If he died, she would wear that color for the rest of her life. She swore it, made an oath that was as sacred as any she had ever committed to. She'd be that odd lady in lavender, the one sitting in the corner, waiting for death.

How could she do anything else?

Her mind would not accept what had just happened. It was as if she'd dreamed it all, and the next moment Tom would wake her, laughing at the fine joke.

The room she had shared with him last night was now neat and tidy, as if nobody had ever slept in the bed or scattered their clothes all over the floor. Her maid stood in one corner, hands folded demurely before her.

She had several clean cloths draped over her arm. For laying out? How often did a man shot in the head survive?

Lamaire followed the footmen as they laid Tom on the bed. Without compunction, he climbed on to the covers and tucked a wadded cloth under his head.

Then a miracle happened. Tom opened his eyes.

* * * *

Helena rushed to the bed, and climbed up on the other side, leaning over him. Lamaire tutted, but she took no notice. Blinking the tears from her eyes, she forced a smile to her face. "My love, I'm here."

He lifted his hand and gripped hers firmly. "So am I."

"Tom?" He sounded lucid, even amused.

Lamaire glanced at her. "If you could bid him remain still for a moment, I will patch him up. My lord, you will have a magnificent scar, and I fear you may lose the extreme top part of your ear." He had piled some fresh towels under Tom's injury.

"Pray that I never need spectacles, then."

God help her, he smiled.

"What, love, did a little blood disconcert you?"

Had he seen how much she was worried? Blood had always sent her into a spin of panic. Was that all?

"A lot of blood," she managed to reply.

His smile faded, and he reached for her hand. "You're not fond of blood," he said.

"Not when it's yours."

"Who would have known that someone would try to shoot my ear off?"

"My lord, hold still," the valet muttered.

Tom sucked in a breath as the valet applied something to the wound. "That will staunch the blood. Lie still for ten minutes and you may move. My lord, look at me."

Lamaire straddled his master, sitting astride his thighs.

Blinking, Tom looked up. "I don't allow many people to take that position."

Lamaire gave an essentially Gallic shrug. "I am aware of that, my lord. But I need to test you. You fainted."

"Was knocked sideways. Fainting is not something that I do."

Another shrug. "As you will have it, my lord."

The duchess's voice rang around the room. "So he will recover?"

"Undoubtedly, your grace." Lamaire did not look around. "He will be sore for a time. My lord, if you will keep your head still and follow my finger with your eyes only."

Lifting one finger, he trailed it to the right, up and swiftly down, before moving it to the left. Helena found herself watching, as if the valet were about to reveal a profound truth.

Lamaire put Tom through a series of interesting visual tests. By the time he'd done, Julius had come in, but he held up his hand, preventing speech until Lamaire had finished. "You doubtless have a sore head, my lord." He climbed off Tom and then the bed.

When Helena tried to do the same, Tom gripped her hand, forcing her to remain where she was. Her head still spinning with the turn of events and her giddiness at the sight of so much blood, she straightened her skirts as best she could and sat back against the bed head.

Taking the soiled towels with him, Lamaire left the room, returning in a few moments with a great pile of pillows which he must have collected from the next room. He laid them at the top of the bed and helped Tom sit up.

Tom closed his eyes briefly. He was pale but composed, and Helena wanted nothing so much as to fling her arms around him and hold him tightly.

Julius gave her a perceptive look. "Are you feeling ill, Helena?"

"I'm fine, Julius. I will, I promise you, not faint."

Julius spared Tom a grimace. "She always used to faint at the sight of blood. My sister is an intrepid woman, but for some reason gore sends her into a spin."

"I was not aware." Tom winced as he turned his head, but what pain he was feeling did not prevent him from touching the pulse in her neck and narrowing his eyes. "You should rest."

"That is what you should be doing."

"Then we both will." Before his father, his grandmother, and her brother, he kissed her.

Although heat rose to her skin, Helena did not do him the disservice of rejecting him. Not when she had feared she would never feel his lips on hers again. Acknowledging that much of her terror had been engendered by the blood and her deepest fears, she let his warmth flow through her. She would not lose him just yet.

He studied her. "I should stay away, perhaps, since this will not heal for a while yet. The man creased me. I take it the perpetrator of this outrage was a man?" He turned his head to meet Julius's gaze.

In the process of shaking his coat into some semblance of order, Julius nodded. Lamaire appeared with a clothes brush and began to attend to Julius's magnificence.

"Four times your salary," Julius murmured.

"Non, m'sieur."

Julius gave a crack of laughter, although Helena had not the least idea why Lamaire's reply would amuse him so much.

He spoke to the valet in French. "Since you are fluent in English, unlike the image you preferred to present to me when we first met, your price has gone up."

"I am flattered, monseigneur," Lamaire replied in the same language, "but I have sufficient where I am."

Julius allowed Lamaire to continue to work his magic but spoke to the company. "I did not catch him, but the man who attacked Alconbury was undoubtedly the man known to us until recently as Lord Everslade. I saw him clearly."

* * * *

Tom closed his eyes and groaned. Not only did his head hurt like the devil, now he had more problems to cope with. He could hardly laze his time away in bed while his wife was in danger. "Everslade wants Helena so badly he would kill me to get to her." He tightened his grip on her hand when she flinched.

Winterton frowned. "I'm not sure about that. However, I did get a runner to follow the man." He twitched his coat. "I could hardly chase him inconspicuously dressed like this, so I gave a boy half a guinea and told him if he could bring back the address of Everslade, I would give him double that amount."

"The boy is likely to abscond, and you'll be half a guinea worse off," the duchess said. She crossed to the window and glanced out. "You've caused quite a stir, Alconbury."

Julius nodded. "I saw that. We could turn that to our advantage, if we wished."

His grace of Northwich grunted. "Now we know who, we have to discover his identity."

Winterton studied the duke, as if trying to solve a particularly difficult puzzle. "I will not have my sister put in danger. If Everslade is mad enough to believe he loves her, and wishes to abduct her, he must be stopped."

"I feel the same way about my wife," Tom said calmly. Releasing Helena's hand with reluctance, he swung his legs down so he was sitting on the edge of the bed. Another wave of nausea overtook him, but he fought it down. He'd known worse. Resting his hands on the coverlet either side of him, he allowed himself a moment to accustom himself to the new position. "I want this matter settled. Today, if possible."

A maid carrying a full tray knocked and entered. "Downstairs," the duchess said. "The drawing room. And if anyone should call, we are not at home. Do not give out my grandson's condition to anyone who might ask." When the maid left, she dusted her hands, as if getting down to work. "We will decide how to manage this situation. I detest vulgar gossip."

"Sometimes it can work to our advantage." Winterton touched his chin, his habit when working out a problem. "We could always put out that Alconbury is at death's door. That would flush Everslade out. He'd come to collect his prize."

"That will not happen today," Tom said stubbornly. He was tired of the subtle subterfuges and elaborate games his father played. He would not start a long game now. "I said I wanted the matter cleared up today, and I meant it. If that boy comes back with an address, we will use it."

A plan began to form in his mind. Simple, true, but he would carry it out properly. "I have a house, a private house I bought years ago." The small intake of breath told him Helena knew which house he meant. "If we can capture Everslade, or whatever his name is, we may take him there. The house is maintained, but empty."

Julius grunted. "I have one or two such places myself, but I rarely keep them empty. What if the boy does not return?"

"Then we'll think of something else. Everslade has been preening around society. Somebody must know more than they think."

"If you're in any state to do so," the duchess said, "come downstairs and drink some tea. I'll have refreshments served."

Only when she said that did Tom realize how thirsty he was.

* * * *

Helena protested, Winterton declared he could find out more if he was given the chance, but Tom remained firm, especially when the boy returned with an address. Tom added his fee to the one Winterton gave the lad, so he was four times better off when he left the house.

Everslade had run to a room in a lodging house, close to Red Lion Square. No wonder he had taken nobody home. He must have worked hard to conceal that address from the people he mixed with.

After drinking a gallon of tea and allowing Helena to ply him with patties and soothe him with kisses, Tom declared his intention of, as he put it, being in for the kill. Not that, he added, he intended to kill Everslade.

Although he added a silent promise that if he found Helena was not safe with the scoundrel in the world, he would certainly attend to that small matter. Winterton did not even try to deter him, but he did send to two of his cousins who happened to be in town.

Tom remembered the twins Valentinian and Darius Shaw, sons of the Marquess of Strenshall, from an incident on the Heath. They were likely men in a fight, and he was glad to have them with him. When they arrived at the house, brows raised only slightly from the fact that their cousin had invited them here, they were dressed plainly and bristling with weaponry.

"Father wants us back in the country," Darius explained. "He wants to bring me up to scratch with Charlotte, and he has determined I should be married by Christmas. I had thought of joining your brother abroad. Do you think he has room?"

"I doubt it, with the number of books he has and the size of his lodging," Winterton said dryly. "Moreover, he does not live as if each day was his last."

Darius, a big dark-haired bruiser, snorted. "Neither do we."

Valentinian, just as big as his brother, but with a more sardonic air about him and certainly a greater refinement of dress, grinned. "Papa usually has his way."

The Shaw family obviously did not have the same kind of problems offered by the Kirkburton family. Notoriously close and welded together as only a loving family could be, they were a force to be reckoned with in their own right. Being Emperors of London merely made them a bit more formidable. Not that Tom would hesitate to take them all on should there prove a need.

The twins were in charity with Tom, after he had offered them aid before, and spoiling for a fight, so they readily agreed to join in the raid on the house.

"But in my opinion," Darius said, snagging a lone slice of bread and butter from the porcelain plate on the butler's tray, "we should do it soon, before the man makes a bolt for the continent."

"My opinion exactly," Tom said. He glanced at Helena, who was sitting bolt upright on a sofa. She looked adorable, and he would have liked nothing better than to plead a headache and retire to bed with her. The headache would not have been a lie. He glanced out of the window at the street outside, where several people stood in a bunch, staring up at the house. "Don't they ever grow tired of stretching their necks?"

"They're ghouls," Valentinian remarked. "They're waiting for you to die." He joined Tom at the side of the window. "Nothing they like better than a good funeral."

"Unless it's a good funeral and a scandal," Darius said sagely. He looked around the drawing room, as if expecting more bread and butter to appear from midair.

Tom returned his attention to the people outside. They were dressed in nondescript but respectable clothes, the kind of people he would pass in the street without a second glance. "Lamaire, bring me a plain town coat and waistcoat. And my pistols. A decent sword, too. Not a town short sword."

"Monseigneur."

He touched his ear and winced. At least the bleeding had stopped. "And a large hat."

When the valet returned with the necessary items, Tom lost no time getting into them. By that time, William had arrived, similarly attired and armed. William tended to the dandy, but today he had stripped the fancy trappings of society off and looked like the soldier he had always wanted to be. Tom felt for his dilemma, but little could be done about it. Either he joined the army and swore an oath of allegiance to the Hanoverian monarch, or he joined the rebels in what was increasingly a hopeless cause.

Events like this one gave his brother a chance to use some of the skills he'd practiced relentlessly but had little use for in everyday life. William nodded to the others, but kept his distance.

Darius eyed him doubtfully. "Do you wish to help your brother?"

William raised a brow. "Why would I not?"

The question was a challenge, a dare to anyone who would say, "Because if he were dead, you'd be the heir."

Tom had no idea if William knew of his dubious parentage, but he might see this as a way to even the score. But he trusted William. Whether he trusted him with his life was another matter, but he was about to find out. "We're rooting out the man who shot at me and abducted my wife. I want him alive if possible. For now."

Finally in control of his pain and his headache, he strolled across the room to take Helena's hand and kiss it. "Do me the honor, my lady, of remaining here. On this floor or the one below, out of sight of the windows. I will send a footman to guard you."

She met his eyes. "I nearly lost you today. Don't make the possibility a reality."

He was probably the only person who would see the fear lurking deep in her. Not with a twitch or a telltale movement did she betray her anxiety. Her lovely face remained clear of frowns or tightened muscles, and her hand lay quietly in his. But he knew. He needed no outward signs to tell him. "I swear I'll come back to you." He could do nothing else.

Turning, he surveyed his troops. Like him, all were dressed plainly, and also like him, wore substantial swords, not the fine jeweled dress swords most men his kind wore in town, more fancy hilt than blade. The bulges in their pockets suggested other weapons, too. All to take one man. No, to be certain of taking him.

"Come, then. We should travel separately, otherwise we will draw a crowd all by ourselves." Five heavily armed men marching through London? Oh, yes, they'd be followed well enough. He gave them all the address and outlined a brutal, effective plan. Two at the back of the house, three at the front.

Half an hour later they were all at the end of the street. Lace Street was a small thoroughfare at the edge of fashionable London. The house was like a miniature version of the ones many of them used in town, with shallow steps and a portico leading to the front door, but the portico would barely allow one person at a time, and the steps were token rather than a real distinction. The black-painted door was scuffed and muddied. This October had been a wet one, and the building showed every mark of it. No maid cleaned it down every day, as they would even in modest households. This was a lodging-house.

As he came to that conclusion, the door opened and a well-dressed man stepped out. "Oh, I say! Are you new residents?"

Tom glanced at Darius and Winterton, who had ordered him to call him Julius.

"We're thinking about it. Is it a pleasant house?" Darius spoke for them, since if they were within hearing distance, Everslade would recognize the other two.

The man shrugged. "The rooms are small, but they are in the right part of town, if you know what I mean." He winked.

Oh, yes, Tom knew. A card sharp, fortune hunter or some kind of trickster, he'd be bound. He grinned and nodded, since they were declining into male sign language.

"Wouldn't mind a look inside," Darius said in a casual tone. "I'm always looking for a reasonable place to stay."

"The landlord doesn't live here. If you come back at six, I daresay he'll be at home."

"Thanks."

Tom growled. "Enough." Pushing forward, he bundled the hapless tenant inside, blocking his cries by the effective if distressingly blunt method of putting his hand over the youth's mouth.

"Oh, wonderful," Julius rolled his eyes. "Now one of us has to look after him."

"No, we don't." Now they were inside, Tom clipped the man under the chin. Darius caught him and laid him gently aside, propping him against the wall. "Though we don't know which room he occupies." He kept his voice low.

"Could we set fire to the place?" Valentinian enquired.

Julius sent his cousin a disgusted glare.

The stink of old food and damp made Tom swallow the bile that rose to his throat. His head throbbed, but he pushed those concerns aside. "Tempting, but no." He frowned, and opened the door as shadows skimmed the glass in the door. As he'd expected, the others came in. He nodded to Val and William.

Val glanced at the man on the floor and grinned. "What now?"

Tom's knowledge of the layout of these houses helped. "One man each room, starting with this floor. If they don't answer, break it down. Let them shout, we'll stop them."

"How many rooms?"

"If they have not sublet, two on each floor and one below. Three or more in the attics. Ten minutes each floor."

Julius grunted, turned, and rapped on a door on the first floor. Leaving Julius and William downstairs, the others hurtled up the stairs to the first floor. They were fortunate, as someone opened the door at the front and cursed. Not their man.

Neither was the man in the back room. This appeared to be a gentleman's residence, but the heavy smell of coupling came from the room. Not the aroma that quickly dissipated but a full stink, as if the room were used for nothing else and nobody changed the sheets or opened the windows. The man was dressed in breeches that he'd obviously donned in a hurry. He was primped to the point of tipping over the edge into pure artistry.

At least Everslade could simulate respectability. Tom shook his head and moved on. The man shrugged and closed the door. Everyone had to make a living, but doing it by selling one's body, male or female, repulsed Tom. Not that he had ever admitted to that, but remaining celibate struck him as preferable to paying for the privilege.

Upstairs the rooms would be at the bedroom level if this was a private residence. He nodded to the back room.

Nobody answered either knock. Gently, Tom tried the door of the room at the front. It did not open, but he had the cure for that. The door showed a gap when he tried it, the lock a simple one and the door showing signs of rotting at the base.

He took a pace back, lifted his foot, and kicked. The door burst open and bounced off the wall. Expecting the rebound, Tom caught it with his hand as he strode in, taking a quick step to one side in case the occupant had a weapon.

The coat on the rickety chair by the tiny dressing table was one he recognized. Everslade had worn it at a ball earlier this season. That pattern of pansies was hard to forget.

The bed was rumpled, evidently used, but empty. Nobody was home. Tom strode to the table tucked under the window and rifled through the pile of papers that lay on it.

Downstairs a triumphant cry erupted. "We have him!"

Darius made a shooing motion with one hand. "I'll search this place. If there is anything to be found, I will find it."

Tom left the room long enough to call out, "Bring him up!"

He had thought of taking the villain to the house of Folgate Street, but this place was secure enough. Julius came up with Everslade slung over his shoulder. After glancing around, he dumped the man in a chair that William dragged to the middle of the floor.

Darius made himself busy up-ending every drawer, tearing the sheets off the bed, and wreaking general destruction. Julus took a position near the door, and Val stood by the window. Their prisoner might consider risking leaping out, if he could squeeze his way through the narrow casement. At the moment, he was blissfully unconscious. A reddened, swollen lump under his chin demonstrated the cause of his slumbers.

"You did not break his jaw?" Tom moved it roughly. No, the jaw was still attached, it did not grate and more significantly, the man did not wake up screaming. "I need to know several things first."

Julius plucked a well-worn flintlock out of his pocket and dropped it back. "That was all I found, together with a couple of blades."

Darius lifted his attention from Everslade to the room. "This is a poor place."

"A base for his more underhand activities," Julius said. "Everslade lives in a respectable house farther west."

No wonder Julius had proved a formidable opponent. His perceptiveness matched his strength. Would he prove an ally now they were in-laws? He would find out in the following years.

Tiring of waiting, and with the sounds of Darius's joyful destruction around them, Tom backhanded Everslade, taking care to hit the sore patch.

He woke up on a scream. Small compensation, but not nearly enough for what he had done to Helena.

Tom swept an exaggerated bow. "Lord Everslade, well met."

The man did not reply, but swallowed. Somehow, probably on the journey upstairs, he'd lost his hat and his wig.

Tom removed his hat now, bracing himself for the inevitable shot of pain when the newly formed scab on his ear tore off. "You left your mark, but I fear your pistol is an old one, and it may not have its sights properly aligned. Either that or you are a very poor shot."

Tom drew his own pistol out of his pocket, one of a pair he'd ordered last year. He leveled it at Everslade and drew back the hammer, the deadly sound easily audible above the joyful racket Darius was making.

Everslade tipped back his head and regarded Tom steadily.

"Who are you in truth?" Tom asked.

"I've been Lord Everslade long enough to be known by that title." Eyeing Tom doubtfully, he sighed. "I used to be Ian McKinley, a loyal servant of the true King. As you should be."

"As I am," Tom said. He tilted his head to one side, so the light from the window fell on his wound. "Who told you I was not?"

McKinley—how good to have another name for him—curled his lip. "The highest authority. The man you betrayed."

"What did you do with Everslade? The real Lord Everslade, that is."

"A lucky accident." McKinley lifted his hand and cradled his jaw. "It hurts to talk."

"Good. Then keep your answers brief." Flicking up the skirts of his coat, Tom half sat on the edge of the table, swinging his leg. "So it was me you were aiming for?"

McKinley's eyes widened. He shot a glance at Julius, standing with his arms folded and a gun hanging negligently from one hand. "For a loyalist, you keep very poor company."

"He's my brother-in-law. Why did you try to abduct Lady Helena?"

McKinley shrugged, and dared to smile. "She was not unappreciative of my attention. She's wealthy and a known traitor, so why should I not? I would have taken care of her. Married her."

"Under a name that is not your own?"

"By the time we reached Scotland, she'd have been ruined. She'd have married anyone." He smirked.

Tom refrained from knocking the smile off his face. "You really don't know my wife, do you?"

"Or my sister," Julius murmured.

"With her a widow, I might have taken another shot at her," McKinley said.

Tom exchanged a glance with Julius, marveling at the man's foolishness. Except for one thing. Either the Old Pretender or his son had labeled him a traitor. Why? Because he'd married Helena? No, because McKinley had courted Helena before anyone knew they were married or that he was even interested with her. His public demeanor toward her at the time would have told most people precisely the opposite, in fact. "Tell me exactly why your masters considered me a traitor."

"Your behavior in recent years has given his highness pause to concern himself with your loyalty."

"Ah, so it was Charles rather than James who set you to kill me." Together with Tom's undoubted personal dislike of the man. His mind went back to the last time he'd seen the prince in person. They had not liked each other, and Tom had clearly seen the seeds of what the man had since become. A sulking, broken drunk, to be precise. "Why would he do that?"

Julius closed his eyes. "I think I know why."

McKinley shrugged. "Let him tell you then."

Tom's mind was working now. This man was sent to kill him by the Young Pretender. He decided to abduct Helena. Was it coincidence that he chose the very woman bound to Tom for life? Tom did not believe in coincidences. "Why Helena?"

"She's beautiful and wealthy. And taking her would strike a blow to our enemies."

"I see."

"No you don't." Darius had been sifting through the papers he'd collected from their hiding places. "This was on the underside of the chair. I'm bracing myself to go under the bed, but I'm terrified of what I'll find there. Whoever cleans this place is not worth the money she's paid." He handed Tom a piece of paper.

Tom took a moment to absorb the information. "This is a copy of my marriage certificate. So you knew she was married when you courted her?"

Darius's chin jerked up sharply.

Julius shook his head slightly. "Later."

Val made a sound at the back of his throat, and tension filled the air. William stepped forward, the floor beneath him creaking ominously.

Tom shrugged as if the information meant nothing. "You knew that and what we were doing about it." He looked at nobody but McKinley, whose triumphant air revealed he'd gained a point.

Tom stilled. "How did you find out?" He got to his feet and turned around, his features working. "We were married by a man named Clegg. We had a Fleet marriage."

"I followed the trail. Actually I followed Lady Helena when she went to the Fleet and purchased a copy of her licence. I bought one, too." All amusement faded from McKinley's voice, and only venom remained. "With the knowledge the prince had vouchsafed to me, I knew I had my revenge in my hands. Besides, I had a score to settle with you."

Tom spun back, his face carefully composed. A cracked and tarnished mirror opposite told him he was not as successful as he'd wanted. "Why would you want revenge on me?"

"Why do you think?" He curled his lip. "You did not even notice me that night, did you?"

Tom shook his head. All he remembered was bliss. He hadn't looked at anyone except Helena.

"I arrived in London with the prince, but I stayed when he left. I had orders to serve his interests. I took the identity of Everslade when I arrived."

"Did you kill Lord Everslade?" Julius rapped out.

McKinley glanced around at the expectant faces. Everyone stilled. A corner of one of the papers Darius held flapped down, the only movement in the room until McKinley shrugged carelessly. "Yes. But you will never find him. You can't try a man for murder without a body."

"Oh, I think we can," Julius said softly.

Darius waved the papers. "I have not found everything yet, but these will serve to hang him. The man is a traitor. That's for sure. He plotted the death of a subject of his majesty, and he spied for a foreign power."

Tom nodded. "I would rather he died for murder. There is less honor in that."

"I believe we can discover when and where," Julius reiterated.

"Not from me." McKinley lifted his head, tilted his chin. "Do your worst. Kill me now, if you will."

Tom sniggered. "So we can be hanged alongside you? I think not." He glanced at Julius. "We should call the authorities."

"You would do that?"

Tom kept his attention on McKinley. "For Helena, I would do anything. This man hoped to disgrace her."

"How long could you have expected to continue your masquerade?" Julius asked, his voice tight.

"Everslade was on his way to London. He told me that his mother had died, and now he intended to live a little. She had kept him in the country for years." McKinley clamped his mouth shut.

He didn't need to say any more. McKinley could have murdered the garrulous Everslade on the road, dismissed the servants who knew him, never returned to that part of the country, and lived as Lord Everslade. The man was not mad, as Tom had begun to believe. He was cunning and vindictive. He thought of nobody but himself. Well, he would have nobody but himself to think of now, for the short time he had left.

"I made it my business to discover everything I could about you," he said. "I was courting Lady Helena when you made your move. When I showed the evidence to the Prince, he agreed you had to die. So I got my dearest wish. I had the means to kill you and to make you suffer first."

Tom had no compunction in sending this disgusting man to the gallows. "How fortunate Bow Street is so close," he said, satisfaction filling his voice. "You won't find it as easy to escape Newgate. You will find the vails there onerous, but you won't have to pay them for long." Then he struck him and gave him a matching bruise on the other side of his face. Such a pity Tom had not held back, because this time he did break McKinley's jaw.

While the man was still squealing in pain, Darius handed him a piece of paper. Tom glanced at it.

When he was a child, he'd been given a picture of the world, but his tutor had cut it into small pieces. By putting it together again, Tom had discovered the way the world was built.

The last piece of his personal world fell neatly into place.

Chapter 19

"He says he will be up directly," Lamaire told Helena.

"Oh, does he, now?" With a rustle of silk Helena climbed off the bed. She'd been sitting reading the journals, waiting with increasing impatience for her husband's return. No secrets, he'd said. And where was her brother? Why had he not come back with Tom?

After shaking out her skirts briefly and glancing in the mirror to make sure her cap was on straight, she went downstairs and knocked on the study door, entering on her knock.

Tom stood before the desk, and his father was sitting behind it. Papers were scattered over the surface, grazing the crystal inkwell, some in a strange mixture of numbers and symbols that could only be code.

"He was an agent for Charles Stuart," Tom was saying. He turned his head and met her curious gaze.

Nodding with a wry smile, he held out his arm, and without hesitation she walked under it, nestling close to him so he could close his arm around her. She only felt complete in his embrace.

He kissed her forehead. "The man's name was McKinley. He was an agent of Prince Charles. He is currently locked up in Newgate."

She sighed in relief. She hadn't wanted the man she'd known as Lord Everslade to die at Tom's hands. He should not have that stain on his soul.

The duke took up a paper and read it again. The wrinkled document trembled. What was wrong?

"Are we married in truth?" Perhaps that was it. Then her fears in those years they had spent apart were real. And they were not married now. She did not move away. Even if their marriage wasn't real, their love was.

"We are." He pressed a kiss to her forehead. "But another difficulty has emerged. Or another complication."

"Tell me," she demanded impatiently. "What are you talking about?"

"McKinley was a member of the court. Prince Charles's court, one of the people who owed his loyalty to the prince rather than his father. There he discovered the quest to find the children of his father, the legitimate ones. He came to London five years ago to continue the quest and to work for the prince."

"So he worked as an agent?"

"When he discovered that I was one of those children, he kept the information to himself. Until this year."

"Why would he do that?" The truth hit her with the force of a hammer. Helena's legs gave way. "What did you say?"

He turned her to face him, holding her firmly, his eyes dark and fathomless. "I am the son of the Old Pretender and Maria Rubio. As far as we know, the oldest legitimate son."

The duke looked up at them, "And he tried to kill you. The man I have followed for all these years—the one I nearly lost my fortune and title to, the man I have supported with money and loyalty—tried to kill my son." His mouth flattened. The lines on his face deepened. He looked less like his usual vigorous self, his strength leaving him. "Whoever fathered you, you are my son. The king made my wife, my bride, tell me that she had betrayed me, that she bore another man's child. He cared nothing that the knowledge might make me cast her off. Instead, she gave me the child, the one he wanted hidden. The perfect disguise. He may have intended my wife to tell me, but she never did. She sacrificed herself for him." He clamped his mouth closed, gritted his teeth before he crumpled the paper in his hand. "I will never refer to the Stuart as the king again. I owe his son nothing. He owes me. My loyalty is first to my family and then to my country, whoever represents it."

Scraping his chair back, he got to his feet. "Never allow anything to come between you two. Family is always paramount."

Tears misted her eyes, so Helena did not see him leave. "He's right. I love you, Tom."

"And I love you."

They kissed, and as always, everything else went away.

Epilogue

"He died hard, they say." Tom dropped the journal on the breakfast table, among the debris of a good breakfast heartily taken. "Shall I read you the rest?"

Helena shook her head, surprised at how empty she felt about the situation. McKinley had been hanged for the murder of Lord Everslade. Julius was as good as his word and had discovered the body. The remains had enough evidence to prove he was his lordship. Letters wrapped in a wax pouch, the remains of his clothes, and a signet ring. Julius had also proved that Lord Everslade and McKinley had shared a room that night, the inn they were staying at being full. Everslade had offered McKinley a ride in his chaise the next day instead of having to suffer the depredations of the stagecoach, and they'd left together.

Helena recalled how charming McKinley could be when he set his mind to it. She shivered, despite the fire burning merrily in the grate and the snug fit of the sash windows. Outside, the sun shone down, the rains of October having given way to a chilly but fine November.

McKinley had murdered Lord Everslade the following day, thrown the body from the coach, and when the vehicle stopped to change horses, claimed his lordship had changed his mind about traveling to London.

He had hired a fresh chaise, together with ostlers and outriders, and traveled on, becoming Lord Everslade somewhere along the road. At the next inn, he wrote a letter to the house the Everslades had hired for their stay and dismissed the servants, claiming they had changed their minds and were returning home to Cumbria. When he arrived at the house, he hired fresh servants. With the knowledge that he was breaking free after years of domination from his mother, few people who knew the real Everslade thought much about it.

If he'd married Helena, he might have escaped detection. Years of subterfuge and harboring resentment had driven him from that moment, but the court had not questioned him about that matter. The murder was enough. Julius had made it his business to discover the ostlers who'd been paid off and traced the fateful journey.

"Justice is swift sometimes." She tried to feel something for the man, but she could not. He'd been the son of a country squire, from Lanarkshire and had taken the Cause as his own at university. He could have lived in moderate comfort for the rest of his days, but he had chosen the darker more lucrative path and had worked as an agent for the Jacobites ever since.

Now he was dead.

Glancing out of the window, she got to her feet. "I will visit the new kittens in the stable and then perhaps read for an hour."

"Very commendable, my love." Pushing his correspondence aside, Tom rose from the table and joined her. "How would you feel about visiting my father's house for Christmas? If we do so, we will have to do it soon, before the frosts set in." He nodded to the letter he had just discarded. "My father mentions that Lady Abercrombie will be visiting. He has long admired her, you know, but he always said he would remain faithful to the memory of my mother."

"Ah." She went into his arms as naturally as breathing and smiled up into his dear face. "We should go. Do you think your father would marry again?"

"The scales have fallen from his eyes. He adored my mother, but she adored her king more. That was a shock to him. He has reassessed his priorities, I believe. Will is still a complete supporter, though, and my father will never be a loyal Whig."

"He could be a loyal Tory," she pointed out.

"We shall see." He smiled down at her. "I care not."

"Could we visit Edensor on the way?" Her father's house was in North Derbyshire, in the area sometimes known as the dukeries from the plethora of great houses that were situated there. "Then we will have done our duty to both families."

A crease appeared between his brows.

She pressed her finger against it to smooth it out. "My parents will welcome you, or at least my father will. He dislikes talking politics in any case. You can see him in his true setting. He lives for the land and the estate, where my mother—" She grimaced. "She lives for power and influence. To quote someone not too far from here, I care not."

"What about your brothers?"

"Augustus likes to keep to Rome. He says life is quieter there. Julius is too busy caring for Eve and his family to give much thought to our parents, but he'll be there for Christmas. We do not have to stay long. I like it here. I loved this house the moment I saw it," she said.

"Much as I fell in love with you the instant I saw you. I tried to tell myself it was lust or mere liking, but it was not. I could not reason the love out of me."

She gazed into his dear face. "And I you. I believe love can last a lifetime. I believe ours will."

He touched her cheek and bent to kiss the place, before moving to her mouth and delivering one of the luscious kisses she adored. "Do you really have to visit the kittens? They're snug in the stables with their mama and perfectly safe. You must be tired, my love. After all, you had little rest last night."

"You want me to go upstairs and rest?"

"Eventually."

As she curved her hand around his neck and went on tiptoe to kiss him back, Helena reflected on her luck. The best in the world. Five years? She'd have waited a lifetime for this.

Historical Note

Charles Edward Stuart, known during his lifetime as the Young Pretender and later as Bonnie Prince Charlie, did indeed visit London in 1750 and was converted to Protestantism. If he'd hoped it would endear him to the people, the attempt was doomed to failure, and Charles soon returned to his Catholic upbringing.

The visit was known to the authorities and was carefully watched, but they elected to leave him alone, as to arrest him would be to create a Stuart martyr.

Another reason was to court and perhaps marry a British noblewoman. At this stage in the campaign, that would have given Charles a foothold at the heart of power, a strong negotiating counter and access to the money he desperately needed.

The next year, 1751, the popular Prince of Wales, Prince Frederick, died, leaving only a young boy to succeed him, so the Stuart cause looked hopeful again. However, this time they didn't have a great army at their beck and call, so they had to rely on negotiation and intrigue.

Another Stuart, Lord Bute, helped to thwart the cause by befriending the widowed Princess of Wales and taking over the education of the heir, young Prince George. The Whigs hated him, but after Prince George became King George III, Bute became Prime Minister for a short period.

That story is for another time.

Due to the constant complaints about fortune hunters eloping with heiresses, sometimes abducting them, raping them, and ruining their reputations, the law was changed in 1753, coming into force in 1754. Now marriage was strictly regulated and only valid under the circumstances detailed in the law. Any marriages conducted before that date were valid, if they could be proved.

Meet the Author

Lynne Connolly was born in Leicester, England, and lived in her family's cobbler's shop with her parents and sister. She loves all periods of history, but her favorites are the Tudor and Georgian eras. She loves doing research and creating a credible story with people who lived in past ages. In addition to her Emperors of London series she writes several historical, contemporary and paranormal romance series. Visit her on the web at lynneconnolly.com, read her blog at lynneconnolly.blogspot.co.uk, find her on Facebook, and follow her on Twitter @lynneconnolly.